The Abandoned Realm

Brittany Hansen

BETWEEN THE LINES
BOOKSHOP & CAFE

Book Cover by Jeff Brown
Interior Design by Stephy's Bindery
Illustrations by Elivrayn and Sosnovska Anastasiia
Logo by Desiree and Erick Rangel

First Edition : June 2023
Printed in the United States of America.

ISBN Paperback : 979-8-2181-4206-3 Hardback: 979-8-2181-9072-9
ISBN E-Book : 979-8-2181-4209-4

To anyone who has used stories to combat the dark.

Playlist

Daydream - Lily Meola
Anti-Hero - Taylor Swift
War of Hearts - Ruelle
Bury a Friend - Billie Eilish
Everybody Wants to Rule the World - Lorde
Arsonist's Lullabye - Hozier
I Found - Amber Run
Make me believe - the EverLove
I'll Be Good - Jaymes Young
Silhouette - Aquilo
Villain of my own Story - Unlike Pluto
Man or a Monster - Sam Tinnesz / Zayde Wølf
Sirens - Fleuries
Madness - Ruelle
River - Bishop Briggs
Scars - boy epic
Going Under - evanescence
Holding out for a hero - nothing but thieves
How Villains are Made - Madalen Duke
Trouble - Valerie Broussard
Until we go down - ruelle
Running With the Wolves - aurora
Believer - Imagine Dragons
Legions (war) - Zoë keating
Bleeding Out - Imagine dragons
Keep on - Sasha Alex Sloan
Blame's on me - Alexander Stewart
Radioactive - imagine dragons
The author - luz

Pronunciation Guide

Characters

Adaira:	a-DIE-ra • A-dī-ra
Aldar:	ALL-daar • ALL-därr
Faelyn:	FAY-lin
Gaelira:	gay-LEER-uh
Sekzelt:	SEC-zelt
Talera:	tuh-LAIR-uh
Rehnir:	rah-NEAR

Places

Raebourn:	RAY-born

CONTENT WARNINGS:

DEADLY DISEASE, GORE, BODILY FLUIDS, BLOOD, MURDER, EMOTIONAL ABUSE, MANIPULATION, NEGLECT, INTRUSIVE THOUGHTS, CORPSES, LOSS OF A PARENT, CHILD ABUSE, PHYSICAL ABUSE, ASSAULT METAPHOR, VIOLENCE AGAINST WOMEN, KIDNAPPING MENTION, RESTRAINT, MASS MURDER, SUICIDALITY MENTION, VOMIT MENTION, POLICE, DRUG MENTIONS, EUGENICS, PHYSICAL ABUSE, SELF HARM.

PART ONE

Between the Lines

CHAPTER ONE

BOOKSHELVES AND WINE CELLARS

BEX STOOD BEHIND THE checkout counter at Between the Lines Bookshop and Café and found herself once again contemplating killing Talera. A shiver ran under her skin, prickling and whispering against her bones—the unnerving sensation that if she didn't get Talera's story onto the page, it'd burst out of her and swallow her whole.

Which made her writer's block rather inconvenient.

Between the Lines didn't have employee uniforms, so Bex was wearing her usual high-waisted jeans and a boxy T-shirt. Comfort always won over fashion, and anyway, she liked how these clothes complemented her full hips, generous thighs, and soft stomach. Ignoring the mug of coffee from the café—it had gone cold several hours ago—she tapped her pen to the soft music playing over the speakers. Her black notebook lay open next to the display of assorted bookmarks, postcards, and chocolates. The usual stream of customers had abated, leaving a cozy stillness behind.

She couldn't seem to get the wording right for the fight sequence. Glancing around to make sure no one was looking, Bex shifted her weight and mimed swinging a sword.

The bookstore's bell rang. Bex straightened up, swiping her notebook aside as a few customers walked in. She pushed Talera out of her mind as she fiddled with the San Francisco postcards. The newcomers made their way through the vibrant stacks without looking at her, and Bex's shoulders relaxed. Even so, her mother's voice mentally chided her to *stop daydreaming.*

The irony that Between the Lines was Bex's definition of a dream, with its floor-to-ceiling shelves full of colors and tantalizing spines, wasn't lost on her. Overstuffed armchairs squatted in corners and alcoves. Round tables showcased varied special edition hardbacks. Notecards with staff recommendations were stuck to the front of the shelves below the book. The children's section always had a few rambunctious toddlers playing on the beanbags. A bulletin board announced an upcoming Sherlock Holmes–inspired cocktail night at the bar in the café where scones, coffee, and tea were available throughout the day.

Fondness tinged with guilt pressed against her skull.

Logically she knew leaving Between the Lines was the responsible thing to do—the adult thing. Working at the bookshop meant she barely had enough money to cover her living expenses, let alone make a dent in her student loans.

Still, Bex couldn't help but feel like she'd failed. She was already dreading the phone call she had to make later. *It doesn't matter if she says I told you so. I'm doing this because I want to, not because she wants me to.*

Pushing aside thoughts of her mother, Bex bent to retrieve a box of hardback books. She balanced the weight on her hip, ignoring the way the corner dug into her flesh, and grabbed the stack of autographed copy stickers. Arms burning, she hefted the box onto the counter and began the mindless task of slapping one on each cover. She tucked a loose lock of dark hair behind her ear. It slipped out almost immediately. Bex let out a sharp huff to blow it out of her eyes and tugged her ponytail tighter.

"Hey, keep it down over there, will you?" Owen sauntered over with a crooked smile, pushing his sleeves up past his forearms before untying the black apron from around his hips.

"Oh, I'm sorry, is my breathing annoying you?" Bex smoothed a sticker with her thumb.

Owen shrugged, coming around the counter and

reaching into the box. "I'm just saying, this is a sacred place, B. We can't have you scaring away customers with your heavy sighs."

Bex snorted, passing him a few sheets of stickers. "Har har."

Owen grinned, pushing a hand through his dark curls. Unlike her chaotic waves that had no rhyme or reason to them, Owen captured that effortless James Dean bedhead look. Standing about a head taller than her with a slim and strong frame, his skin had a warm sandy complexion. The summer sun had caused the smattering of freckles across his nose to darken, while Bex, who arguably spent just as much time outdoors, was still pale white.

Their conversation slipped into the steady ebb and flow that can only be honed through years of friendship, arguments, and awkward adolescence. When his parents' marriage had fallen apart toward the end of high school, Bex—a seasoned child of divorce by that point—had become Owen's closest confidant. She was the one who had ditched class to hide out in the library with him when he was upset. And after her last breakup, Owen had shown up with ice cream and an extensive list of terrible mystery movies and had very graciously not brought up the fact that he'd said her ex was bad news from the beginning.

"Incoming," Owen muttered with a slight nod. Bex looked up to see their boss, Peter, coming around the corner, his mouth set in a grim line.

Peter didn't waste time with pleasantries, just looked at Bex and said, "We need to redo the schedule for this month. They admitted Benny to the hospital with the Fading."

It felt like all the air had been sucked out of the bookshop. Bex blinked several times. "But I just saw him a few days ago. He seemed fine."

Anxiety snaked up her spine. The deadly sickness was characterized by the translucence of its victims' skin. The Fading typically started with flu-like symptoms before mutating. She'd spent her last shift with him—had she been exposed?

Her chest tightened as she tried to mentally catalog every odd sensation she'd felt for the past week before she realized Peter had responded and was now looking at her expectantly. "We should send some flowers or a card." Flowers seemed pointless, but they had to do *something*, didn't they?

Agreeing to find out where to have flowers sent, Peter retreated back into the stacks.

"Poor Benny." Owen gave his head a small shake, tension bracketing his mouth.

"I know," Bex said, worrying her bottom lip. "I hope he's okay." Mind spiraling, her eyes flicked over to the bar, where Carlos was wiping down the counter. She latched on to the normalcy of the motion. "Did your shift just end?"

Owen waited a beat before answering. "Yeah, Heidi's going to meet me here soon. We're going to go see that new superhero movie." He glanced sideways at her. "What time are you off? You should come."

Bex snorted. "And be the third wheel? No, thank you." She rubbed her neck, suddenly feeling a bit flushed.

"Oh, come on."

"That was the only thing Todd was good for."

Thankfully, Owen dropped the subject.

The peeling and smoothing of stickers was the only sound as Bex's thoughts wandered back to Benny. They'd worked together only a short time, but she liked his systems for setting up displays (by mood, tropes, and niche indie authors) and extensive knowledge of horror novels (she didn't have to agree with his taste in literature to recognize his expertise).

Selfishly, she'd been grateful when Peter had hired him. It would feel less like abandoning her post if her responsibilities fell on someone equally as devoted to the special magic of a local bookstore.

Peter didn't even know she was leaving yet; that conversation was also on her list of awful things she was avoiding. Her stomach knotted. *I can tell him after StoryCon. There's no need to tell him beforehand.*

"Earth to B." Owen pressed a sticker to her cheek, and her whole body jolted. He laughed as her hand flew out, knocking over her coffee mug.

"Owen!" Her voice was shrill with embarrassment, and she scrambled to rescue the hardbacks from the fast-moving river of coffee.

Owen deftly snatched up her black notebook, shoulders still shaking with mirth.

Bex grabbed a rag from underneath the counter. "So immature," she grumbled.

"Since when are you the jumpy type? Grab me one of those." Owen motioned to the rag while he lightly shook the notebook, sending drops of coffee onto the carpet.

Bex tossed him the towel, eyeing him as he dabbed the notebook.

Owen caught her look and grinned. "Don't worry, I won't peek. Although I don't see what the big deal would be. You've been telling me about your idea for months now. Why would it matter if I read it?"

Bex reached for the notebook. "Because reading it

would destroy your delusion that it's any good. And as your best friend, I reserve the right to keep that delusion intact." She wiggled her fingers. "Give it."

"Come on." Owen pouted but handed it back. "Just let me read something—*one* thing."

Bex tried to keep her face stern, but it was impossible when he was grinning at her like that. She settled for an eye roll. "No, because I'm probably not even going to finish this one. Maybe I'll just kill Talera off."

Owen jerked his head up. "What? You can't do that."

"At least then I'd be able to say I've finished a story."

Owen's eyes narrowed. "I thought Talera was supposed to be a badass warrior elf. What about all those jujitsu moves we're learning?"

"If I'd known you'd keep using that ridiculous class against me, I wouldn't have invited you."

"Liar," Owen shot back, then reached out to peel the sticker from her face, fingers ghosting across her cheek. Bex's stomach fluttered. "Anyway, you have to finish."

"Why? It doesn't matter, it's just a silly story."

Owen opened his mouth, no doubt to protest, when a few girls strolled up to the counter. The one whose arms were laden with books—Annika, Bex thought—was a regular.

Bex pushed aside the mixed emotions swirling in her chest, forcing a smile. "Find everything you were looking for?"

"Yes, and then some." Annika slid the stack across the once-again-dry counter.

"That's how it always goes." Bex grinned down at a familiar blue-and-gold cover. "This is one of my all-time favorites."

"Yeah? I've heard really good things about Arthur Huxby, but I haven't read any of his books yet." Annika bounced on the balls of her feet. Her friends giggled, one reddening as she averted her gaze from Owen, seeming suddenly fascinated by the postcards.

"It's so good. A portal in the city that opens to another world—it doesn't get any better." Bex tapped the cover as she accepted Annika's payment. "He's going to be at StoryCon, you know."

The other girl abandoned her ruse of looking at the postcards and began openly gawking at Owen again. Oblivious to his effect on her, Owen packed the now-stickered books back into the box. Bex commiserated with the girl.

As they chatted about the upcoming convention, Bex ripped Annika's receipt off the machine and stuck it between the pages of the top book before sliding the stack across the counter. As the girls made their way to the exit, Bex's gaze snagged on one postcard's dazzling photo of the Golden Gate Bridge. Heavy fog hung in the air, giving the scene a mysterious and magical quality. Another faint shiver fluttered through her blood, a siren call that promised belonging and destruction in the same breath.

"Well, the offer still stands." Owen leaned back against the counter.

"Hmm?" Bex adjusted the books in the box, ignoring his exasperated look.

"The movie."

"Oh, right. Can't." She shoved the box back toward Owen. "I've got a big night planned."

He rolled his eyes, setting the box on the ground. "Let me guess: make a London Fog and then read until an ungodly hour."

"Precisely." Bex waved a hand at the fluttering pages on the bulletin board. "Plus, I have to do some research on cocktails for the Sherlock Holmes night."

Just then, the shop bell rang and Heidi strode through the door. She waved at the two of them and sauntered over. Bex brushed the offending lock of hair out of her face again. She tried her best to look unfazed as Heidi kissed Owen hello, focusing on the bookmarks. Owen cleared his throat as Heidi greeted Bex.

"Oh, B, I almost forgot—did you put aside a copy of the new *Dresden Files* for me?"

Bex hummed affirmatively. She bent to snag the book from the holds shelf, adjusting the remaining books before handing it to Owen.

Heidi smiled in what Bex assumed was meant to be a conspiratorial way. "I swear, you've never met anyone with more unread books on their shelves."

Owen scoffed.

Bex shrugged. "Buying books and reading books are honestly two separate things."

"People have wine cellars filled with unopened bottles of wine. Why not have unread books on your bookshelves?" Owen said.

Heidi smiled fondly. "Whatever makes you happy, babe. But we've got to leave pretty soon or we'll miss the previews."

Owen pretended to be horrified at the mere suggestion, and they said their goodbyes. Heidi looped her arm around Owen's elbow, and he threw Bex one last smile and wave over his shoulder as they left.

Through the windows, Bex could see that the sun was

setting, purple muddling with red, painting the San Francisco skyline. The fog almost looked like it was burning.

The coffee on Bex's notebook had caused the ink to smear and bleed. With pursed lips, she mulled over the scene she'd written. The words looked lifeless on the page.

Something about the story still tugged at her, but icy anxiety pierced her between the ribs, severing the pull of the string. Failure hung over her like a shadow, waiting to plunge her into darkness, smothering her excitement. She tossed the notebook into her bag, ignoring the phantom ache the motion caused in her chest.

CHAPTER TWO

An Elf Named Talera

When her mother had first insisted on accompanying her on the journey to the Challenge, Talera had been less than enthused. She was well aware that her mother disagreed with her choice to compete, and she wasn't keen on being reminded of that fact every day for the fortnight it would take to reach the edge of the Irithel Sea.

But as Talera warmed herself by the fire while her mother prepped their Faelyn Fog for the evening, a warmth blossomed in her chest at her mother's presence.

"And what, pray tell, are you smirking at?" her mother, Gaelira, asked, snapping her out of her thoughts.

"I don't smirk." Talera reached her palms out to the fire's heat.

Her mother snorted. "Believe me, dear one, you've smirked since the day you came into this world." She stirred the small pot of water, adding in sticks of dried vanilla root as it heated.

"Just thinking that if you'd mentioned you'd make the Faelyn Fog every night, I would have asked you to come with me from the beginning."

Her mother shot her a look. "You really need to learn to brew it yourself, you know. I won't always be here."

Talera rolled her shoulders, trying to work out some of the tension from the day's travel. They sat a ways off from the rest of the caravan, preferring each other's company to that of the group of strangers, merchants, and bards. They'd stopped for the evening next to a cluster of stone ruins—former battlements, if Talera had to guess. The dense forest they were traveling alongside cast long shadows on the ground.

"Especially," her mother continued, "if you insist on foolishly relying only on sleep to restore your Faelyn."

Talera groaned. The argument was one they had frequently, and as her mother opened her mouth to continue, Talera rushed to cut her off. "Yes, yes, Mother. *Conscious breathing is the most efficient and powerful way to spiral down into your Faelyn, Talera.*" She mimicked her mother's tone and inflections. "You've only told me a thousand times."

"Well, evidently it hasn't been enough times, as you

still refuse to listen to reason." Her mother sprinkled lavender next to the concoction.

Talera grinned. In truth, she'd spent most of that day focusing on conscious breathing to slip into that twilight state somewhere between dreaming and wakefulness in order to replenish and strengthen her magical essence. "Don't be too hard on yourself, Mother. What else is to be expected of an elf who came out of the womb smirking?"

The burning wood popped and crackled, the dancing flames the same shade as Gaelira's hair. Talera had her mother's alabaster skin and lithe toned limbs, but the resemblance stopped there. Gaelira's red-orange mane and green eyes contrasted starkly with her ash-blond hair and violet eyes. Their physical appearances differed as much as their personalities.

A small human girl approached, expression timid. "E-excuse me, my lady." She gestured to Talera's mother's bag of herbs, poultices, bandages, and elixirs. "Are you a healer?"

Talera shifted, glancing at her own belongings: extra daggers, a kit to sew on new arrow fletchings, a quiver and bow, and the gleaming hilt of her long sword poking out from behind her bedroll.

"Yes, dear one. What is it you need?"

Gaelira's voice, soft and healing all on its own, seemed to work magic on the skittish girl, who visibly relaxed. "It's for my sister, lady, not me. She's been suffering all day, as she always does when…" The girl's face burned red even in the firelight. "It's that time, you see."

Gaelira waved her hand. "Say no more, child. Just remember that the monthly bleeding is natural and there's no need for shame around it." She plucked a few small pouches from her bag, including a few the girl had not asked for and gave instructions on the use of each. The red was to be smeared under the navel as long as the bleeding lasted to lessen cramping. It would also break a fever if placed under the tongue. Orange was to keep infection away. The blue was for burns from fire or the sun. The girl retreated, stammering out her gratitude, armed with the healing powders and clean strips of cloth.

Talera watched in silence, a nagging sensation of guilt ghosting across her neck. She cleared her throat. "I still can't believe humans are cursed to deal with that *every month.* And I thought four times a year was torture."

Her mother clicked her tongue in agreement.

"Do you always pack extra like that?" Talera dug the toe of her boot into the dirt.

"It's my responsibility as a healer to do what I can for

others, Talera."

The words hung heavily over them. Talera drew a knee up and rested her chin on it, shoulders inching toward her ears.

Her mother sighed, sounding more tired than she looked. "Talera."

There was a buzzing beneath Talera's skin, a shiver of a promise that she couldn't name. The beat of her heart punctuated the desire, the pull toward something beyond—a call to adventure that she couldn't ignore anymore.

"I have to do this, Mother." Talera stared unblinking into the fire, restlessness crawling up her neck. "I know you think I'm making a mistake by not becoming a healer, but that's not me."

"I never said—"

"You didn't have to." Her mother had never pretended to approve of Talera's desire to join the Challenge. As a healer, it was her sworn duty to save lives, not take them. She'd always been reluctant to let Talera learn to fight. But after surpassing the skills of the elder elven warriors who'd instructed her back home, Talera knew the only way to reach her full potential was to enter the Challenge and hope to win a coveted spot as a trainee of the last remaining Faelyn Warriors.

The blood elves were an ever-growing threat to her people, and Talera refused to sit back and do nothing to protect her home and family.

Her mother said nothing for several heartbeats. When she finally spoke, Talera felt stripped of all her walls, vulnerable and exposed. “Your worth already flows through your veins. Your magic is a part of you. It’s your essence. Sometimes…sometimes it’s easy to be tricked into believing that more power, more magic, more of something external will make you enough. But what you must discover, dear one, is that you already have all the magic you need inside of you.”

It was too close to the truth that she couldn’t—wouldn’t—examine. Talera huffed a laugh and leaned back on her palms. “Yes, Mother, let’s forget the Challenge and just go straight to the Faelyn Warriors. Surely they’ll accept me once I tell them that I already have everything I need inside me.”

A shrill scream pierced the air, shattering the calm of the caravan. On instinct, Talera sucked in a breath, quickly spiraling down inside herself to reach her Faelyn. Her muscles became taut with powerful energy, and her focus sharpened like a knife. The magic unspooled from her center, flowing out through her limbs. The touch of Faelyn tasted like moonlight and stars.

Another scream tore the air as Talera and her mother sprang to their feet. There was a commotion coming from the other end of their encampment near the ruins, frenzied cries and panicked movements.

Talera snatched up her quiver and unsheathed her sword, her eyes darting around the chaotic camp. “Mercenaries,” she whispered to her mother when she finally saw them. A dozen men armed to the teeth cut their way through the caravan. Several women fled past Talera, children clutched tight to their chests. Rage boiled inside her, spreading across her collarbones and up her throat.

Her mother was speaking, but Talera was focused on the attacker rushing toward her. The clash of metal rang in her ears, and her muscles burned as she parried the blow meant for her throat.

Talera shifted back a step, giving her attacker the illusion of retreat before a quick flick of her wrist whipped her sword in an upward arc. Her attacker’s eyes widened as he realized she was using his momentum against him, and then the edge of her sword sliced deep into his shoulder. The man stumbled back, and Talera planted one leg firmly and kicked him squarely in the chest with the other. She didn’t bother to watch him hit the ground before pivoting away, scanning the chaos, seething.

"Get them into the trees!" Talera yelled to her mother, who was already ushering the other women and children away from the fighting as quickly as possible. She knew that among the two dozen travelers, there were barely two decent fighters besides herself. Why in the Seven Hells were these people attacking a harmless caravan?

A hand gripped her elbow hard. Her mother's green eyes flashed as she said, "Come back to me in one piece."

Then she was gone.

Talera adjusted her grip on the hilt of her sword as she dove into the fray.

CHAPTER THREE

MOTHERS AND MEMORIES

THE NEXT HOUR PASSED quickly as Bex helped a stream of customers: a young boy looking for an obscure sci-fi novel, an elderly man picking out a series for his granddaughter's birthday gift, and a blushing woman who piled seven steamy romances on the counter. She chewed the inside of her lip absently as the printer whirred and spit out flyers for StoryCon.

The fantasy convention was still a month away, but the whole city seemed abuzz with anticipation. The printer beeped, signaling that it needed more ink, and Bex switched out the cartridge, moving on autopilot. The machine continued its job.

Maybe Peter would still let her be the event planner for the store even after she quit. The community's response to the ones she'd put together so far had been enthusiastic, and she loved the creative outlet. Even though Between the Lines had long hours because of the café and bar, Bex knew herself well enough to know that early-morning or late-night shifts wouldn't work when she had another full-time job.

After studying the employee schedule whiteboard for a few minutes, she made a few quick adjustments to make sure Benny's shifts were covered. Sighing, she plucked the warm stack of papers from the printer and headed for the front of the store. Peter thanked her as she deposited the fresh pile of flyers. He tapped his long slender fingers on the counter, and Bex propped her elbows on the desk. A small smile played around Peter's mouth, and he pulled something from his back pocket. "Would you mind passing this on to your dad?"

Bex blinked in confusion until he held up a ticket to StoryCon.

"Oh my god, Peter." Bex gaped at him. "Are you serious?"

"They gave each vendor two guest passes." He handed her the ticket. "I kept one for Drew, obviously."

Bex nodded—she'd always been fond of Peter's husband. "But why are you giving me this?"

"You're a big reason we got the booth in the first place. Seems fitting that you should get the other pass." He shrugged, tossing his black curls off his forehead. "Plus, I know how much your dad loves Huxby."

"Peter, thank you." Bex stared at the ticket, her mind spinning to conjure up a way to repay him. "He's going to be so excited. I can't wait to tell him."

Peter cocked his head thoughtfully. "I can't imagine what it'd be like to have that kind of relationship with my dad. I've talked to *your* dad more in the last three years than I have mine in my entire adult life."

Bex blushed. "Yeah, he's pretty great. Though I have to say, as an awkward teen, I did *not* appreciate him being so involved in my life. Owen swears to this day that it wasn't him, but I know he's the one who told my dad about my oral presentation for my writing class." She shook her head, still wincing at the memory. "He showed up wearing a T-shirt he'd made that said *metaphors be with you* across the front. I thought I was going to die of embarrassment."

"Wow. That is…that's pretty bad." Peter laughed. "Still, it must be nice to have parents who care that much."

Bex nodded, her smile faltering a bit as her mother's sardonic smile flashed in her mind. Somehow the stars had aligned—maybe Mars had been in retrograde or hell had momentarily frozen over—to allow her parents the short fling that had made Bex. She cleared her throat. "Yeah. My dad's great."

ᛞᚨᚦ

Bex pushed open the door to her one-bedroom apartment and dropped her bag on the floor. She tugged the curtain closed over the small window that looked straight into the building next to hers and flipped on a light. She had a tiny kitchen consisting of a few cupboards, dismal counter space, a fridge, a microwave, and an old stovetop. The small table and chairs she'd purchased from IKEA back in college were set up in the corner, leaving ample room for the more important furniture.

The old couch was perfectly broken in to fit the curves of her body and faced her two large bookshelves. Built of teak or mahogany—she could never remember which—they'd been a gift from her mother. Even though she'd never approved of Bex's "reading addiction," as she called it, Meredith Andrews didn't skimp on anything.

The intricate carvings of trees along the top and the natural knots in the wood made Bex think of secret doors to other worlds. Every inch of the shelves was full to bursting with books. Framed next to the shelves was a map of Middle Earth, the paper stained to look like authentic parchment.

Bex flopped onto the couch, muttering to herself as she

pulled out her phone, "Just do it and get it over with."

She stared at the contact on the screen for a solid minute.

Meredith Andrews

Bex ground her teeth. *Don't be such a baby.* She hit dial, waiting for an answer but hoping for voicemail.

There was a short click followed by an even shorter, "Hello?"

"Hey, Mom," Bex said.

"Hi, Bex." Her mother's tone was as cool and empty as the office she likely still sat in across town.

A tense and awkward silence followed. How long had it been since she and her mother had actually spoken rather than just exchanging clipped texts? Six months? Eight months? Bex cleared her throat. "Sorry to bother you. Are you working?"

"Yes, Bex." She didn't hear a sigh but could picture the exasperated look on her mother's face. "What is it you need?"

Bex bit down on her tongue. She shouldn't be irritated—theirs had never been a call-each-other-up-to-chat-and-say-I-love-you relationship. "Uh, yeah, well…see, the thing is…" There was the sound of a keyboard clacking on the other end. "I was calling because I have a…favor I need to ask you." Bex cringed at the words.

"I'm listening," her mother replied in a distracted voice.

"Well, as you know, I've been working at the bookshop for a few years." Bex picked at a loose string on the couch's armrest.

"Mmmm." Her mother's disapproval practically leaked through the phone.

"I know you don't approve, so you'll be happy to know that I'm…looking for a new job."

A pause. "What sort of new job?"

Bex worried her lip. "Well, I've actually got a lead on one at a publishing house." Bex rushed to explain, knowing she needed to present this correctly. "They're looking for someone for an editorial assistant." *Shit. Why did I think this was a good idea?* "Something that could be a stepping stone to an editorial assistant or—"

"You're not trying to be a writer yourself." It wasn't a question.

Bex's shoulders sagged, a tiny twist of anger in her chest at her mother's ability to read her so easily. She saw what Bex assumed she hid so well from the world, only to rip it from her heart and present it with scorn and contempt. Refusing to let her mother know how much that stung, Bex let out a scoff. "No. Of course not. Maybe I could be a literary agent—I'm still not sure."

"Bex," her mother cut in impatiently, "look. It's my responsibility to be honest and real with you. I'm not doing you any favors if I coddle you."

As if anyone in their right mind could accuse you of coddling. Bex dug her fingernails into her palms but said nothing.

"An editorial assistant? I can't imagine there's much money in that." Her mother snorted, and Bex bit the inside of her cheek.

I need her help. I need her help. Choking back the retort rising to her lips, Bex said, "It'll pay better than the bookshop, and there will always be a need for editors." There—matter-of-fact words to appeal to her mother's logic. She was a defendant offering up evidence to the judge, no foolish sentiment or dreams involved.

"Well, of course it pays better than the bookstore. Honestly, Bex, saying you want a career as a bookseller is as ridiculous as saying you want to be a lifelong Gap employee."

Bex's temper flared, and she lost sight of the point of the conversation for a moment. "Mom, you have no idea how much knowledge my job actually requires. No one is going into Gap and saying, 'Hi, I like this white shirt, but do you have anything like it in blue with ruffles on the cuffs and something with queer rep?' Not to mention that I'm a manager!"

"I'll never understand you, Bex," her mother said, completely ignoring her outburst. "I practically handed you a career path on a silver platter—"

"I'd hardly call suddenly deciding not to pay for my school after all a silver platter." Bex could feel the heat coming off her face.

"You broke the terms of our agreement, young lady—"

"What agreement?! There was no agreement!" Bex shrieked into the phone. "I never said I wanted to be a lawyer, Mom—"

A crinkling interrupted her as her mother spoke to someone on the other end, most likely holding the phone to her chest as she did.

Bex swallowed hard and pressed her thumb and forefinger into the space between her eyes, trying to squash down her rising anger. She wanted this conversation to be over. She wanted not to have picked up the phone in the first place.

Her mother's attention turned back to their conversation, and Bex hated herself for staying silent as her mother repeated the words she'd said a million times before. *You're an adult, Bex. You have to live with your decisions at this point. I shouldn't have agreed to your father having majority custody.*

Bex fixed her attention on her books as the words washed over her. A worn spine called to her, and she stood to retrieve it before sinking heavily back into the corner of the couch.

Finally, her mother said, "You said you have a favor to ask."

Bex fought the urge to hang up. "The position is at Lynx Publishing."

"Ah."

Bex hated the smug, knowing tone in her mother's voice. "Yes, so I just thought…maybe you could call and refer me." The words tasted bitter as they left her lips.

"Well, Stephanie does owe me for helping with her brother's deposition, so I suppose I could call in a favor."

Bex tucked her feet beneath her. "I just need help getting an interview."

"All right."

"Thank you." Bex grimaced, feeling small.

The clack of a keyboard began again in the background. They stumbled through their goodbyes, and when she hung up, Bex chucked the phone onto the other end of the couch with an exasperated groan.

Flipping open her book, she burrowed into the cushions. She read the same page three times, not absorbing any of it. She shoved off the couch, turned on her electric teakettle, and pulled out an Earl Grey tea bag. *At least I have Dad*, she thought as she pulled milk from the fridge and grabbed the small bottle of lavender syrup from the counter. When the water was ready, she poured it over the teabag and let it steep.

Bex heated the milk for a few seconds in the microwave before adding it and the lavender syrup. The swirling colors turned a lovely, misty, fog-like hue.

The ritual complete, Bex took a sip, letting the flavors dance across her tongue and the heat warm her chest. Smacking her lips together, she returned to the couch, tea in hand, and skipped to where the book's spine was cracked from repeated use. The familiar words washed over her as she escaped to another world.

A few hours later, after she'd nearly dropped the book on her face for the third time, Bex finally pulled herself off the couch and shuffled toward her bedroom. Her foot caught on the strap of her bag, and she threw a hand out to steady herself on the wall. Blinking slowly, Bex stared down at her notebook, which was now peeking out. Sighing, she picked it up and flipped to where she'd left off writing about Talera's battle.

She cringed. In comparison to what she'd just been reading, it was embarrassing and derivative. It was painfully obvious that the jujitsu workshop she'd gone to with Owen in Crissy Field had been a waste of time.

You're not trying to be a writer yourself.

Why do I always do this to myself? I've never followed through on any story. So why do I keep trying?

"Just stick to something you can actually do," Bex chided herself. She snatched up a pen from the floor and made a heavy slash through her writing, the motion like the stroke of an executioner's axe.

into her palms as she slammed to the ground, gasping.

The ruins and the men she'd been battling had vanished, along with the rest of the caravan.

She was alone at the base of a canyon.

The ground beneath her felt strange. The air didn't taste right. It was as if her lungs were being crushed by someone sitting on her chest. Cliffs with red, brown, and tan striations rose above her on either side.

Talera forced herself to her feet, sucking air through her teeth as pain lanced through her leg. Dark red blood soaked the top of her leather boot. The thrum of her heartbeat sounded *Mother*, *Mother*, *Mother* in her ears.

Talera whirled around.

What in the Seven Hells just happened?

She shook her head, trying to clear her mind, to wake up, to go back, to understand—

Her breath sawed in and out of her lungs. Spots flecked the edges of her vision.

Think, Talera. Think. Keep your wits about you.

She glanced down at the weapon still embedded in her leg. Could it have been laced with poison? Blood slipped through her trembling fingers as she bit down on a cry, wrenching the impaled metal free. Sharp, hot pain overwhelmed her, and she braced herself on a boulder to keep from collapsing. She ground her teeth at the burning sensation as she rubbed some of her mother's orange powder into the gash. The exposed muscle quivered as she tore a strip from her tunic with her teeth before binding it tightly around the wound. The whole process was over in a matter of moments.

Talera shoved her panic down, keeping alert as she picked her way over the uneven terrain, limping slightly. She adjusted the pack and bow slung across her back. Talera reached down into herself, a soft sob escaping her lips as she felt her magic's familiar presence. A calm pool of moonlit water, her Faelyn rippled through her. She took another steadying breath as her senses heightened and strength flowed through her limbs again, her delicately pointed ears picking up a hum beyond the canyon.

She kept her sword out, drawing small circles with the point. Her eyes cut back and forth, looking for threats, her body tense as she made her way to where the chasm opened up. Along the basin were jagged rocks jutting up at odd angles as if smashed by a great fist. Ash hovered everywhere, stagnant in the bleak sky that yawned above her. The canyon walls began to widen, and Talera stopped short as the rock walls split open to reveal a valley.

A vast city sprawled across the barren rock, stretching

several leagues before it pressed up against an enormous plateau. Disjointed structures, derelict towers, and ruined architecture.

This will all be explained. This is some type of wizard's illusion or a poison-induced hallucination.

Her fingers and legs were beginning to tingle, and somewhere in the back of her mind she knew she needed to take deeper breaths, but that didn't seem important at the moment. She stumbled forward, her injury keeping her from sprinting outright.

The buildings loomed larger as she neared. Half-finished paintings on the sides matched the colors of the canyon walls. There were crumbling sculptures littered throughout, their placement seemingly without rhyme or reason. The sound of a lyre being plucked drifted through the air, flat and dissonant.

How long had she been wandering around? She needed to do something. Why hadn't she done anything? She needed to find answers.

A man walked by with wings of black feathers, and she saw several others with leathery, membranous wings. A woman passed with wings wreathed in lighting. Talera could have sworn that someone invisible brushed past her at some point.

The assault of the unknown broke over her in waves again and again—short-sleeved tunics in cuts she'd never seen, stiff blue pants made of an unknown material, skin of every color.

Anxiety surged through her, and Talera scrambled to grab the arm of a passerby. The man cried out and tried to wrench his arm free, but he couldn't break her grasp. "Tell me where we are. Tell me."

The man gave her a jeering look.

"Please." Her voice cracked on the word.

"Piss off."

Talera wanted to break his jaw, wanted to hurl him to the ground. She clenched her teeth and gripped the front of his shirt, pulling him closer as she snarled, "I asked you a question."

A warning went off in her mind, but she ignored it. She reached for her Faelyn, and the magic roared in her ears. The man's eyes went wide as her pupils dilated in response to the magic.

His face and neck flushed red as he tried to twist out of her hold. Talera squeezed his arm tighter, knowing she'd leave a bruise. His gaze darted to the weapons at her side, but he jerked his chin up in defiance. "You think you're better than me?" Contempt laced his tone, but a sheen of sweat covered his forehead. "You're just the same as me. The same as all of us."

Talera worked her jaw, trying to rein in her anger. People around them had stopped to stare, though it seemed to be more out of boredom than concern or interest.

"What is this place?" Talera's heart pounded, and she loosened her hold. Slightly.

He spat at her feet.

She rolled her neck. *Easy, Talera, no need to break his jaw.*

But then he leaned in, his breath hot and foul in her face as he said, "You're just as wretched as the rest of us. Best you accept that, princess."

A broken arm, then.

With a vicious twist, Talera snapped his bone. He screamed and dropped to his knees, cradling his arm.

She crouched down to look him in the eye as she growled, "Not a princess, asshole."

Ignoring the looks of horror from those around her, she brusquely straightened and stalked away.

The ground shook as a giant man, naked except for a small cloth around his waist, pushed roughly through the crowd. A creature with two heads passed by, one head in conversation with a cloaked man while the other talked to a half woman half cat. A group of children huddled against a deteriorating wall, their eyes distant, lost. One of them had green scales covering their body from the waist down.

Talera pressed a hand against her temple.

A bone-chilling screech made her instinctively duck and cover. A huge winged creature flew overhead, its scales a mix of reds and golds.

Talera was rooted to the ground.

A dragon.

A *real* dragon.

The large beast landed on a nearby roof, its dark eyes fixed on Talera, piercing and intelligent.

This isn't possible.

The dragon snorted puffs of smoke through its nostrils. It flicked its tongue, and she caught a flash of its teeth, each the length of a spear.

"It's considered rude to stare." The dragon's voice was deep and grating and shook every bone in Talera's body.

Some primal sense took over, and Talera slowly lowered her gaze in deference.

This can't be real.

She didn't notice her legs were giving way until she was on the ground, clutching her chest. Passersby threw curses at her as they moved around her.

She stayed where she was, her ragged breaths wringing out her body.

Mother, where are you? Where am I?

Tears burned her eyes. Her hands shook. Cold seeped beneath her skull, down her neck.

"Go to the Library."

Talera dragged her head up slowly. A small boy—one she'd spied earlier—was crouched a few paces from her.

His eyes darted around as if he wasn't sure he should be speaking to her. Then he licked his lips and said again, "Go to the Library."

CHAPTER FIVE

No Redemption

IT HAD BEEN NEARLY one thousand days since Rehnir had tasted Fear.

Barely tempered rage drummed in his veins, and his muscles pulled taut with it as he strode from the Library of Manuscripts.

The streets of the Abandoned Realm were as crowded as they were depressing, but the throng always seemed to recoil from him allowing him to move easily. Rehnir took a puff of his cigar. The crack of bone breaking cut the air as he passed a brawl—if it could even be called that, as the fight was so one-sided—between an elven woman and a burly man.

In his mind, he kept replaying the words that'd just been hissed at him. *Now I know what a monster you really are—beyond redemption, even more of a monster than your father was. You went down this path because you are weak.*

He flexed his fingers, a deep itch crawling through his limbs as buzzing static rose in his ears, his long-dormant magic imploring to be released.

Monster, a voice purred in his mind.

Rehnir clenched his jaw, picking his way through the throng of fellow characters in the Realm. Every last one of them had been found wanting, blotted out, and discarded.

I know what you are.

Monster.

He inhaled deeply, savoring the smell of Fear. It was distinct, the cloying scent smothering the offensive reek of this place they'd all been banished to. The sweet aroma drilled into his skull.

Weak.

Monster.

Rehnir brought the cigar to his lips again, the strong smell allowing him to regain control. Nearly one thousand days without feeding. He ignored the sickly pallor of his hand and the way it trembled. The bone-deep fatigue ate away at him.

You needn't be weak anymore.

Show them.

"No." Rehnir practically growled the word.

But even as he did, the seductive voice in his mind crooned, *What have you gained by refusing to feed? Why deny yourself your powers? They'll never see you as anything more than a monster. That's who you really are. Stop pretending and show them.*

I know what you are.

The voice grew louder.

The Fear was coming off the other characters in heavy waves, relentless, begging to be tasted.

He needed to get out of the city, away from the crowds.

He stepped over the corpses of two unfortunate characters who'd succumbed to the blight afflicting the Realm. Their fading flesh and rotting innards sent a chill down his spine.

You think you can save yourself? This place?

You are beyond redemption.

Rehnir fled to the outskirts of the city.

CHAPTER SIX

What Feeds Your Soul

BEX'S PHONE RANG, shattering the silence. She groaned, fumbling around on the nightstand, squinting to check the screen. As she answered the call, a smile tugged at her lips. "It's entirely too early to be speaking."

"Well, good morning to you too, kiddo!" Her dad's voice was annoyingly chipper.

"Mmmm-hmmm. What's up?"

"Can't a dad just call up his favorite daughter to say hello?"

Bex stifled a yawn. "You know, it doesn't get you extra points to say 'favorite' when I'm the only one. Technically, I'm also your least favorite." Bex propped herself up on an elbow and flicked on the lamp by her bed.

"Semantics. Besides, we haven't caught up in what feels like ages."

"I know, work's been hectic. We just did the Sherlock

Holmes event, so things will slow down for a bit before StoryCon. Speaking of which"—Bex rubbed the sleep from her eyes—"I have a present for you. From Peter and me."

"For me?"

"Yes." Bex grinned. "I have a ticket for StoryCon with your name on it."

"No," he said, unable to mask the excitement in his voice.

"Yup."

"It literally says Grant Harmon?"

Bex rolled her eyes and climbed out of bed. "Daaaad."

"Bex!"

She laughed as she padded toward the kitchen. "So you'll get to see the Arthur Huxby in the flesh."

Her dad let out a whoop. "When I said you were my favorite before, that was a lie. But now you've officially earned the title!"

"You're going to give me whiplash with all these demotions and promotions." She turned on the coffeepot, the percolating sounds comforting.

Her dad's easy chuckle felt like a gentle squeeze around her heart.

"Any news about the job hunt?"

Glad he couldn't see her face, she tried to force

cheeriness into her voice as she told him about her upcoming interview for the editorial position, leaving out the detail about calling her mother. Asking for the favor had been embarrassing enough; she didn't need her dad to know how miserably she was failing too.

"That's great, sweetheart. They'd be fools not to hire you."

"Thanks, Dad."

"And I am dying to hear more about your book."

Bex swallowed wrong and stifled a cough. "Well, there's not much to tell," she said as she fiddled with the drawstring of her pajamas.

"Oh, come on."

"No, really." Bex kept her voice even and shrugged. "I stopped writing it." She poured herself a mug of coffee, not waiting for the full pot to brew.

"What? Why?"

Bex took a sip. "You told me there were plenty of stories *you* didn't finish in college."

"We're not talking about me, Bex, we're talking about you."

"Dad, there's no point, okay? It was a silly story, and I know you think I'm going to be this author or something, but…I'm not. I'm just not." She slouched over her mug.

"Bex," he said, his voice calm and infuriatingly gentle.

"Dad." She mocked his tone.

"Did you happen to talk to your mother recently?"

Bex wrinkled her nose. "Yes, but what's that —"

"I can always tell when you've spoken her you because you become inexplicably down on yourself."

Bex huffed but had nothing to say.

Her dad clicked his tongue. "Bex, your mom…" He paused as if searching for the right words. "She's not the warmest woman in the world. I know she thinks she's showing you that she cares in her own dysfunctional way, but listen, kid—she's not the authority on what matters in life. Do you know why you write?"

"To avoid having to talk to people?" Bex grumbled, knowing what was coming next.

"You write because it feeds your soul. You don't do it because you're the best at it or because you owe it to anyone. You don't do it to prove anything. You don't write or dance or make art or sing to make money. I mean, yes, sure, sometimes that ends up happening, but that's not why you do those things. You do them because those are the things that matter in life. They feed our souls."

Her muscles tensed at the familiar words, and she rubbed her neck. "It's not that simple, Dad."

Her dad sighed. "Why is it that you can see the good in everyone around you but not yourself? What if Owen told you he wasn't good enough to write a book?"

Bex rolled her eyes again. "Well, first off, Owen doesn't care about writing a book, but if he did, I'm sure it'd be amazing. He's annoyingly good at everything. Anyway, that's beside the point. I'm fine with stopping. Really. I'm going to focus on other things."

"Other things," he repeated flatly.

"Yes, other things." Bex took another gulp of coffee. "Dad, it's not a big deal. So I didn't finish the story. I've never finished one." She shrugged. "It is what it is. My soul will be fine." She made a mocking flourish with her hand.

"All right, all right. I can take a hint." He paused. "Well, who knows, maybe when you're a big-time publisher, inspiration will strike again."

Bex grimaced at his misplaced confidence. "Editorial assistant, Dad. And it's not about that. I need a better job so I can afford to live."

"Ah, to be young." He changed the subject. "If Owen did write a book…do you think he'd put me in it?"

Bex snorted. "I'm one thousand percent sure he would."

"Excellent."

Bex looked at the clock. "Speaking of Owen, I've got to go. He's meeting me here for a run in a few minutes."

"Only Owen could get you to say yes to running."

"It's good for my health. Or something."

"Uh-huh. Well, tell him hello for me. Love you, sweetheart."

"Love you too, Dad."

It was just past lunchtime, and Bex stood staring at the shelves in the corner of the bookstore, head tilted to the side as she tried to envision the display she wanted. At her feet were the top sellers by the authors who were going to be speaking on panels at StoryCon.

For hell's sake, Bex, just pick a book and start shelving. Nobody cares about the display. Bex gave her head a shake and let out a sigh, then grabbed the stack nearest her and began arranging.

Her dad's words that morning had found that foolish hope in her heart, that wish she attempted to contain at all times to guard against inevitable failure. But his words had loosened her strangled hold on it, and now the dream unfurled in front of her as she shelved.

Her mother would prove helpful, and she'd nail the interview and get the job at Lynx. There was nothing sexy about textbooks but this job would be a foothold in the industry. Maybe the connections she'd make would lead to a spot in a literary agency. Being surrounded by talent and creativity would force inspiration to strike, and she'd finally, finally finish writing something.

Then she could shove her success into her mother's face: *See? It wasn't a waste of time. You were wrong.*

Her chest swelled at the thought but deflated almost instantly as the sharp voice in her head said, *You don't even have the job yet, Bex. Get a grip.*

A pair of women came around the corner, both wearing scrubs under their jackets, looking haggard as they browsed, each holding a large coffee.

"—longest shift. I don't know how you do it," the taller woman was saying.

The other woman, who had dark circles under her eyes, shrugged and said something about how working in the trauma unit had prepared her for the endless hours. She pulled a book out lazily, looking at it blankly before sliding it back onto the shelf.

"I always thought people were exaggerating about the Fading." The taller woman leaned against the bookshelf.

The shorter woman snorted. "Still think it's exaggerated?" Her companion shook her head, a haunted look on her face, and the two of them fell silent.

Bex cleared her throat, and they turned to her. "Sorry to butt in, but you two work at the hospital with Fading patients?" When they nodded, Bex found herself telling them about Benny. The look they exchanged made Bex's stomach tighten.

The taller woman checked her watch, groaning. "Shit. I have to get back." She looked at Bex. "What's your friend's name? I'll keep an eye out for him."

Shortly after they left, Bex felt her phone buzz. It was a text from Owen, reminding her about the last session of their jujitsu class that weekend. A bit of the tightness in her chest eased, and she returned her attention to the display.

CHAPTER SEVEN

LIBRARY OF MANUSCRIPTS

THE LIBRARY WAS LINED with columns with strange, intricate patterns etched into the stone. Talera craned her neck to look at the large building that was the focal point of the square. People littered the stairs leading up to the double doors. Talera fought down her revulsion at the number of corpses among the dejected-looking souls. She could see, through torn clothing, that the translucent skin of the dead revealed graying and shriveled organs beneath. It was as if all the color and life had been sucked out of them, leaving behind only faded husks.

The dread built inside her with every step up to the doors. With a shaky breath, she crossed the threshold.

The Library swallowed her whole. Talera stumbled, trying to take it all in. Rows and rows of bookshelves stretched to the ceiling like ancient towering trees. Mounds of tattered books, piles of parchment, and loose pages clogged the shelves and cluttered the floor. Dust lay like a heavy shroud everywhere she looked. Talera shivered.

It was like a tomb.

A soft fluttering and thumping noise punctuated the silence, but she couldn't tell where it was coming from.

She went deeper into the Library, stopping near the center at a huge dais. Like the bookshelves, it was nearly buried beneath stacks of paper of all different sizes, bound together in various ways: twine, metal fastenings, paste. Talera's pulse hammered against her skull as her eyes snagged on the deep scratches in the gnarled wood.

A woman sitting crossed-legged on the floor cradled a thick bundle of papers. She didn't seem to notice Talera as she approached, just continued to stare blankly ahead. Her face was streaked with tears. A man paced nearby, speaking in a fast guttural language that Talera couldn't understand, though his rage was evident.

She stepped up to the dais and leafed through the pages, taking in all the different lettering, ink colors, and document lengths.

Bloody gods. What were all these? Her blood thrummed in her ears. Every few minutes, a stack of papers dropped from above, landing on the dais with a loud *thwack.* Talera gawked at the ceiling, but there was nothing to indicate where the bundles were coming from.

A whirring noise caught her attention. A self-propelled metal box on wheels was rolling toward her, lights flashing. Two metal rods protruded like arms. The thing stopped just short of the dais, and the arms extended with a clicking sound, scooping up several notebooks. As the arms retracted, a small door on the face of the machine opened, and the pages disappeared inside. The machine blinked and beeped a few times, then began to roll back in the direction from which it had come.

The hair on Talera's neck rose.

Footsteps scuffed behind her.

With Faelyn-enhanced speed, she spun, drawing her bow and nocking an arrow as she did. She aimed directly at the heart of the man approaching her.

"Who are you? And where in the Seven Hells am I?"

The man licked his lips, sputtering. His skin was a warm reddish brown, and his dark hair was cut short, giving Talera a clear view of his human ears. Dressed in a simple white coat and trousers, he looked harmless, albeit strange. Talera lowered her bow slightly but kept the arrow nocked.

The man sighed and held his empty hands out before him. "I'm sorry for startling you," he stammered quickly. "My name is Guy. You must be new here."

"Where is *here*?" Talera practically growled the words.

"Let me guess—you were doing something very normal and mundane, and now you're suddenly in this place. Is that right?"

A flash of irritation pulsed through Talera. "I'd hardly call it normal or mundane. But otherwise, yes, that's accurate."

Guy nodded, slowly dropping his hands. "That's how it happens for all of us here."

"Explain."

"It's not an easy thing to explain. Well, no, explaining it is easy, I guess. It's the *believing* that's hard." He rubbed the back of his neck.

"Out with it," Talera snapped, her anger barely reined in.

Guy sighed, looking upward. "Right, then. The long and short of it is, you are a figment of someone else's imagination. Your life is—was, rather—a story someone was writing. And now you're here because they're not going to finish your story."

Cold seeped through her body. Talera blinked rapidly.

"This is the Abandoned Realm."

Talera stood motionless. It felt like she was being

pulled into the stone floor.

"To be fair, not everyone calls it that," Guy said, not seeming to notice her deathlike stillness. "I'm still waiting for it to catch on with the rest of the characters, but—"

"Enough." Talera's voice rang hollow in her ears.

This can't be happening. This isn't real.

"I don't know what you're playing at, *Guy,* but I'm starting to lose my patience. Tell me who the sorcerer or warlock in charge of this bloody illusion is, or I'll put an arrow in your thigh." She raised her bow pointedly.

The color drained from his face. "I promise you, I couldn't make this stuff up—"

Talera pulled back harder on the bowstring. Her arm shook.

"Please! I can see that you come from a world with magic and that you are"—he swallowed—"not afraid to use that bow. But I can explain. I can show you. I happen to rather like my legs, even in this shithole." Talera clenched her jaw a few times, and he exhaled sharply when she finally lowered her bow. "Oh, sweet mercy, thank you." He licked his lips before gesturing behind her. "May I?"

Her hands began to tremble, and she gripped the bow tighter, glancing down at her blood-soaked leg.

How much blood have I lost? Not enough for this type

of hallucination, surely?

Guy stepped carefully toward the dais. "Everyone arrives here without warning, myself included. We're ripped from our worlds the moment our stories are discarded. I'm truly sorry to say that whatever life you knew is gone."

Pain throbbed in Talera's chest, twisting like a knife. She couldn't get enough air into her lungs. Her fingers and toes prickled.

The life you knew is gone.

No.

Had she said the word aloud or merely thought it?

Guy was rifling through the pile of pages, muttering to himself as he seemed to catalogue her clothes. She couldn't make herself move from her spot.

"Here."

Talera looked at the black book in his hands. He handed it to her almost reverently. Her fingers whispered over the pages, smoothing out the crackling wrinkles from a dried stain. The handwriting was small and slanted. The ink color alternated between blue and black. Dread gripping her stomach. She began to read.

Her whole life was spelled out on the pages. Her childhood; her lessons with the elders on the magic of Faelyn; detailed accounts of the first time she'd held a bow, learned to hunt, learned to wield a sword.

This isn't possible.

What she'd once thought were hazy dreams or foggy memories were sections that had been crossed out. Her most intimate thoughts and inexplicable truths were laid bare in that godsdamned scrawl. She'd never once uttered her fear of letting her mother down, had barely allowed herself to think it. She hadn't told anyone about her desire to prove herself with her combat skills since she was a miserably inadequate healer. And yet those fears had been ripped from that hidden dark place inside her mind and scribbled into existence.

The Library spun.

There was a flash of white in the corner of her eye, and then Guy was kneeling beside her, a hand on her shoulder.

She was sitting on the floor. Was that gasping sound coming from her? Her hands were now clenched tightly. She tried to relax them but couldn't.

"You have to breathe," Guy said, his voice gentle. "It's all right. Come on, do it with me." He locked eyes with her and took a long slow breath in. Talera tried to mimic his rhythm as he slowly breathed in and out.

"How—"

"I'll explain everything, but you just need to breathe for

now." He eyed her warily. "It would help if I knew your name."

"Talera." Her voice was strained.

"Talera." He inclined his head. "You're in the Library of Manuscripts." He surveyed her for another moment, chewing his bottom lip.

All she could do was focus on breathing.

Breath in. Breathe out.

A whimper escaped her mouth at her mother's voice in her mind.

"Water," Talera croaked.

Guy winced. "Yes, well, we don't have water here." At the horror that surely bloomed on her face, he rushed to explain, "You don't actually need it."

With trembling hands, she picked up the notebook again. She was outside her body as she devoured the words.

Moments passed. Maybe hours.

Guy came and went a few times, taking away armfuls of stories as he did, while she sat transfixed. Tears obscured her vision, dropping onto the words she and her mother had exchanged the night before they'd left, when her mother had practically begged Talera not to go. But Talera had refused to listen, and now…

And now…

Oh gods.

An ache rose in the back of her throat as she reached the final page.

It was the battle at the ruins. The man calling her an elf bitch. The last moments she'd had in her world.

Adrenaline pumped through her veins, her senses heightened as the Faelyn coursed through her. Where was her mother? There was no sign of her at the edge of the forest, and Talera didn't know if that should comfort or alarm her. Dodging the slice of another blade, she spun in a tight pirouette, eliciting a cry of frustration from her foe.

She saw her bag and her mother's next to their scattered fire, pouches of healing herbs strewn across the dirt. Talera crouched, scrambling to gather it all, squinting at the tree line through the sweat and blood in her eyes.

At an enraged howl, she glanced over her shoulder. One of the men, her dagger still lodged in his chest, was dragging himself along the ground. He raised himself enough to cock his arm back.

As the wicked-looking metal star sank its jagged points into her calf

The writing abruptly stopped there. A harsh line slashed across the words. Talera ran her finger over the indentation from the pen.

There was finality in that stroke.

Another sob escaped her lips. Her thoughts rioted in her skull, leaving bruises and tearing at her sanity. Her body didn't seem to remember how to breathe properly, the air kept getting stuck in her lungs or pressed spasmodically down into her stomach. Every time a new manuscript hit the pile, the sound was like a nail being driven into a coffin.

Guy was speaking to her, something about the inscription on the bottom of the page about her *author*. She stared at the damning epitaph. He kept talking as if her world had not been ripped from under her, as if it mattered why she was here, as if she cared about the person who'd sentenced her to this place—

"—the most common reasons are fear, doubt, and death."

Death.

Mother.

She scrambled to her feet, backing away from the notebook as if it were a snake.

I have to find Mother.

Guy called after her, but she ignored him.

This can't be real. This can't be real.

She burst through the doors and ran.

Ran through the streets, past all the people—no, the

other characters—not caring that each step was agony in her leg. She let the hurt burn through her. She screamed her mother's name until her throat was raw from the loud, guttural cries. Tears and sweat mingled on her face. She gripped her hair, pulling it until it hurt.

"Talera!"

Chest heaving, she spun around to see Guy running after her.

"Where is she?" Her voice was hoarse. "My mother? If I'm here, she must be too, right?"

A haunted look flashed in his eyes. "No one…no one has ever found anyone else from their world." He took a hesitant step toward her, hands raised in that same nonthreatening gesture he'd made in the Library.

Her laugh was tinged with panic.

"Our theory is that only the main characters are sent here. That's the only explanation we've been able to come up with. We can't speak to where everyone else is, if perhaps there's another realm they're sent to or if they just—" His mouth pressed into a thin line.

Talera's legs threatened to buckle.

Guy exhaled sharply. "We try to piece together as many clues as we can from the manuscripts that arrive, but with everything that's changed in the Realm, the Council's numbers are limited. We can't accomplish as much as we used to." Guy licked his lips. "Look, I know this isn't the life you had. But it is a life. This place hasn't always been like it is now. It used to be vibrant. Chaotic but alive. The Council of the Realm—we're trying to make the best of it, to get back to how it once was. You could join us—"

"I'm not interested in making the best of it," Talera snarled. "How do I go back?"

He hesitated for a moment. "You don't. When whoever was writing you stopped, you were sent here. You can't leave."

His words were like a knife in her gut.

"I know, Talera—truly, I know what you're feeling right now." Guy took a step toward her, his face earnest.

"Don't you dare presume to know what I'm feeling."

Guy's face fell, and Talera almost felt bad. Almost.

He gave an exaggerated bow before turning to leave. But he paused after a few steps, looking over his shoulder to say, "It doesn't have to be an ending, Talera. If you change your mind, come find us in the Library."

Her rib cage ached, and standing suddenly felt like an impossible task. Talera sank to her knees. Her vision narrowed to one small section of the ground. He was wrong. This was an ending. She didn't care that this place, this realm, had once held something other than palpable despair.

You're not real. You're not real. You're not real.

A pitiful, low moan was coming from her, a sound she'd never made before. Distantly, she thought it sounded like an injured and dying animal.

Come back to me in one piece.

Her moan rose to a wail as she remembered her mother's last words to her. Talera gripped her stomach and doubled over, letting the agony overtake her.

CHAPTER EIGHT

A RIPPLE

REHNIR PACED ALONG THE edge of the battered city. The landscape was a mirror of the inhabitants of the Realm—faded, inadequate, and hostile. Beyond redemption.

"You thought you could wash your hands of what you've done?" His voice was brittle; his control over his mind was slipping. He needed to say the words aloud. To give them weight, to anchor his voice in the desolate landscape. "Of the monster you've become?"

His hands shook. Something roiled beneath his skin, lurked at the back of his skull.

There was no story in which he could be redeemed.

You're even more of a monster than your father was. The words—his own words? He was having trouble remembering—echoed in his mind.

Memories, long buried, resurfaced.

He tasted the coppery tang of blood in his mouth.

The smell of Fear drilled into his brain.

The ache and pain of his beaten body subsided as his power roared to life.

The raving cruelty in his father's eyes drained away, replaced by horror.

Euphoria exploded through him.

Monster monster monster

Rehnir took a long drag of his cigar, wrestling to stay grounded as the flashbacks threatened to pull him under.

You needn't be weak anymore.

His resolve was crumbling swiftly. The darkness in his mind was like the tide dragging him back out into the ocean.

Unrelenting.

Inevitable.

Futile to resist.

They'd never see him as anything more than a monster—today had proven that much.

Show them.

Monster.

This time the word fell like a mantle on his shoulders, and something deep inside him sighed.

"If I'm the monster here, then so be it."

Rehnir sank into his power. It was like dipping a quill into ink. The crackling frequencies of the cast-off characters reached for him immediately, and he latched on to their vibrations, tapping into and shackling their Fear.

An electricity moved seductively through the mental tether and into his veins, a promise of the euphoria to come. A faint exhale escaped his lips. Characters cried out in alarm as Rehnir pulled on the connection. A man curled up against a crumbling wall flinched in his sleep. A woman who was pacing stumbled, clutching her head. A muscle twitched in Rehnir's cheek. He held his hands up and watched as the sickly pallor of his skin burned away, blue light dancing like lightning across his arms. Strength bloomed through his limbs.

Why had he denied himself this feeling for so long? Rehnir laughed as a tightness in his chest eased.

This is who you really are, the voice purred in his mind. *Show them.*

Rehnir closed his eyes, concentrated on the pulsing magic in his mind, and reached out to pull once again. *Let's see what these fools fear most.* He smiled to himself, pausing in anticipation of the mental images from his victims, their worst fears and nightmares laid bare before him.

But nothing came.

Rehnir furrowed his brow. He hadn't fed since arriving in the Realm, but surely his powers should work the same way here. He tugged harder on the tether. The characters around him were all visibly in pain, but he saw none of the blood or wounds he usually saw when he fed. A ripple of unease went through him. Had refusing to feed cost him the ability to do so? Or was it merely this place?

Unease gave way to simmering rage. The vibration building in his body mocked him. He was barred from the power—*his* power. A low growl came from his throat. That exhilarating feeling was there, just out of his reach, begging to be claimed.

Rehnir flexed his fingers, yanking on the mental connection.

A few charred black tendrils spread underneath the skin of those writhing on the ground—the mark of dark magic from a shattered dimension. But still, the power he sought was contained behind some invisible dam.

Cursing, Rehnir thrust his hands out, channeling what little power he had into a blast of anger. The crackling energy shot out from his palms, the lightning dissipating as the magic left him. Before he could turn on his heel, a sharp crack reverberated, and in front of him…the air rippled.

Rehnir blinked as realization began to unfold. A memory—he'd heard talk of the boundary that kept this realm separate from the world that had fabricated every character's existence. Whispers of a portal…

My abilities must be limited here, he thought, *because all I can feed on is a shadow of real Fear. If there were a portal and I had access to pure, undiluted Fear...*

Rehnir scanned the street around him. There were easily a hundred characters in view. Characters who, like himself, had been deemed useless.

Well, not totally useless.

He wasn't completely cut off from accessing his power. He just needed to gather enough to channel it into the boundary's weakness.

"I think I'm going to enjoy this," he said, stretching his arms wide, inhaling the smell of Fear. A shudder went through the crowd as the connection formed again.

The magic was still weak, but as the black marks spread over his victims, dark tendrils and veins seeping under their skin, Rehnir felt his reserve slowly grow. A wave was building inside him. He fixed his attention on the air before him.

Hands outstretched, the air thrumming as blue light crackled from his fingertips, obscuring his vision, he willed the magic into the weakness in the boundary. There was resistance, and he steadied his stance, fingers strong as his hands formed a sequence of shapes. He pressed his will and intention into the Fear that was being quickly siphoned from him. A ripping sensation skittered over his bones, the landscape warping and distorting.

A tear split the atmosphere.

Rehnir fought to gather more Fear, his hands shaking with effort. The smell of blood filled the air as screams and moans rose in a crescendo. His head began to throb, and something warm and slick trickled from his nose, but he ignored it. Holding tight to his anger, he fed until he'd forced the tear he had formed into a shimmering portal. He didn't so much as breathe, his whole being focused on the portal and what he could see on the other side.

The sky beyond was a vibrant deep purple that bled into a fiery red on the horizon.

It was a city like none he'd ever imagined, bursting with noise and color.

The old fool was right…

Houses were crammed against each other, stacked high along steep roads. A large train car rolled up a hill, and metal carriages with no horses pulling them sped past. The street was teeming with people. In the distance was a large body of water with an immense burnt-orange bridge stretching across it. Rehnir's chest constricted as his eyes struggled to process the bright colors. He held open the window to the other world for a few heartbeats before he felt his power begin to strain. He didn't have enough strength to keep it open permanently. A warm breeze that smelled of saltwater blew through the tear, washing over Rehnir's face and carrying with it the cloying smell of Fear.

It was overwhelming, palpable, and intoxicating.

But his hold on the portal slipped away even as he tried to connect to the power beyond the boundary. It snapped shut, sending Rehnir stumbling back, a deep ache in his gut as the power he'd tasted was violently ripped away. A low growl tore from his throat as he kicked a fallen man beside him. Seething, Rehnir took in his victims. That world beyond the boundary was rank with Fear.

His lip curled back, and he bared his teeth.

"Let's try again, shall we?"

CHAPTER NINE

HALF FINISHED

JUDGING BY THE CYCLE of the moon—if that could be trusted—Talera had been in the Abandoned Realm for a fortnight. She'd spent the first few days in a haze of panic and rage. She hadn't slept, though it seemed she didn't need to any longer, and had spent countless hours searching the city for her mother or anyone else familiar, pleading with and sometimes interrogating the citizens of this place. She'd been met with jeers, pity, and scorn and was sometimes flat-out ignored.

She leaned against a large boulder, staring numbly at the empty wineskin in her hands; she'd just consumed the last of what had been tucked in her cloak when she'd arrived. Her fingers tingled from the alcohol.

A figment of some fool's imagination. Not even worthy of an ending.

Her head reeling a bit, Talera staggered to her feet and

began wandering back from the expansive canyon toward the city. Her body felt heavy with the truth of her circumstances, bogged down by the implications of this never-ending exile. When she'd realized that Guy had told the truth and her mother wasn't here, something had dimmed inside her.

You can't leave.

She reached the city limits after a time, everything around her cloaked in despair—the smell in the air, the ruined buildings, the dried blood smeared across the ground that no one cared to clean up. The rattling breathing of the despondent characters around her, the whimpers of the wounded that everyone ignored, and the delirious mutterings of the distraught combined to make the collective dirge of the Abandoned Realm.

Though Talera tried to ignore it, she could see evidence of the past glory of the Realm that Guy had spoken of. The art was now scratched and faded, half-finished buildings left to collect dust, and every instrument she could fathom seemed to be strewn throughout the city. A small part of her wondered at the beauty that had once been created here even amidst such despair.

This place had the ability to break anyone and everyone. How characters looked when broken varied slightly, but Talera could see that there were really only three outcomes: pain so dark there was nothing left that resembled life; anger so bitter that no act seemed too heinous; or willful ignorance of one's own insignificance that bordered on insanity. Talera couldn't decide which option was worst.

Guy had approached her several times after that first day, trying to explain the good she could do here, the life she could cultivate. He'd gone on and on about the damned Council and different occupations she could have: librarian, restorer, architect, or healer.

Talera's laugh had been acidic. *I'm not a healer. I'm not a hero. I am not* anything.

After that, Guy had left her alone.

She turned down another street, her footsteps unsteady, talking aloud to herself. "You think I'd choose to be a healer in this hellscape when I didn't even choose it in *my* world?"

Her foot caught on something heavy, sending her sprawling across the ground. Blinking slowly, Talera craned her neck to find the offending obstruction.

The corpse was fresh.

The woman's empty eyes were frozen wide in pure terror. Dried rivers of blood stained her mouth, chin, and neck. Dark marks ran across her flesh like a spiderweb of tar. Her skin looked burned and boiled in places, covered in angry discolored welts.

The stench of burned flesh assaulted her, and Talera turned her head and vomited. With a trembling hand over her nose and mouth, she looked around. Dead bodies were everywhere, the street silent and empty of any movement. An evil presence hung in the air, sending tremors through her body.

This wasn't like the death she'd seen in the large square in front of the Library of Manuscripts, the slow sickness of the Realm itself. It wasn't like the death she'd seen back home. This was malevolent.

Something was very wrong. All of her senses screamed at her to run, run and not look back. To get as far away as possible from what had happened here.

She had to warn someone…anyone.

A tightness took over her chest.

Who? You're not real. None of this matters.

But she couldn't shake the warning bells in her mind. If Mother was here…

An ache rose at the back of her throat. She'd told Guy that being banished here meant she was as good as dead. But that was a lie. It seemed there was a truer death that could still befall her here.

The life I knew is gone…but this is still a life.

She wasn't trained to heal, not like her mother was. But she wasn't completely inept either.

Her thoughts were still foggy as she started heading toward the center of the city. Breaking into a jog, Talera gave her head a shake, trying to piece together a plan. The movement helped clear her system; her lungs expanded and contracted, reminding her that she was still alive, even if that meant something different from before.

Setting her jaw, she solidified her decision.

She had to find Guy. He was the only one in this depressing place who seemed not to have given up—him and that blasted Council he'd been going on about.

She turned down several wrong streets before she finally found the square in front of the large Library. Her body burning off the remaining alcohol, she ran up the steps two at a time. The doors slammed open loudly, causing several people to cry out in alarm as she barreled into the Library.

"Guy?" Her words shattered the silence. "Guy? Where is Guy?"

Several people looked at her blankly, and her temper snapped. "Guy! His name is Guy, has anyone—"

"Talera?" Guy looked stunned as he appeared from behind a bookcase, followed by another man. "What are you—"

"Do you know about the people who died at the edge of the city?" Talera tried to keep her voice even. "With the dark marks branded on them?"

Guy blanched, and her chest tightened.

"There are at least a hundred fresh corpses in the street." She swallowed against the violent images bombarding her. "All of them…it's like their blood turned black in their veins."

"Dark magic," the man beside Guy whispered, holding her gaze intently over the rim of his glasses. His eyes were piercing. Dark cloudlike hair formed a halo around his ebony face.

"Talera, this is Branson, he's the head of the Council—"

"Where?" Branson cut off Guy's introduction. "Where exactly did you see—"

Screams erupted from outside the Library doors. Talera's blood turned to ice, and the hair on her neck rose. She cast Guy and Branson one glance before rushing toward the noise, toward the doors.

The square outside was in chaos.

Terror-laced shrieks assaulted her ears as people clamored over fallen bodies to flee the carnage—butchered corpses covered in entrails, bones jutting through the skin slick with blood, all with the same nightmarish marks marring their stiff forms. A ringing filled Talera's head, and she tasted metal.

CHAPTER TEN

FEAR

MAGIC AND PAIN WRENCHED through every muscle in Rehnir's body as he fed. His mind groaned in protest under the strain of maintaining so many mental tethers at once, but he didn't yield. He didn't know how long he'd been feeding, but still his legs carried him through the streets, following an invisible pull.

Now the dead fell at his feet as he stood in the square. Those lucky enough to flee did so, weakening the Fear he was channeling. His euphoria was lessening with every passing moment, replaced by smothering fatigue.

Panic gripped him at the thought of losing the power now flowing through him.

The boundary held against his onslaught, refusing to yield. He planted his feet wider, his whole body braced with the effort.

More more more—

And then an icy, greedy awareness gripped him, his back arching in response. His very bones seemed to bend toward the intense pull, forcing his attention over to the Library steps. Rehnir panted, honing in on the overwhelming source.

An elven female stood erect as a lodestone.

He recognized her as the elf who'd broken that man's arm. The pull was coming from her, a well of essence radiating from her. It wasn't the same frequency as the Fear he pulled from the others.

Rehnir sucked in a breath, clawing at the palpable magic rolling off of her.

Power crashed into him.

The fatigue pressing down on him vanished in the frenzied wake of the magic. With a fluid motion, Rehnir spun and sent a blast of power straight into the weakness in the boundary.

The world fractured.

CHAPTER ELEVEN

ALDAR

SHE WAS DYING. THIS was what dying felt like.

Her Faelyn was being sucked away, ripped from her body. The sensation was agony, like her soul was being shredded.

Air was wrenched from her lungs, and an oppressive weight shoved her down, down, down, crushing her organs. There was only darkness, all the warmth leached from her being. She was drowning in a cold, piercing terror.

And then the invisible claws in her mind and at her throat vanished. The ground trembled, then gave a resounding crack. Blue light exploded in the air, and the world split. Against the light, a dark shape moved and then disappeared.

Choking, gasping for air on all fours, Talera shook violently. Somewhere above her, Guy was yelling to Branson. Her ears rang.

She tried to call up her Faelyn but was met with a void.

Panic thrummed through her as she took in the scene before her. Though no one else near her on the Library steps had keeled over, everyone in the square had been struck down. Guy reached down to help Talera to her feet.

"It's not possible," Branson said.

Still shaking, Talera followed his gaze.

There, pulsing with light as if it were blood coursing through a vein, towering twice her height, was a distinct iridescent archway.

"Branson," Guy said slowly. "Is that…is that what I think it is?"

Talera knew, knew in her bones before Branson replied, what it was.

A magical portal.

Apprehension wound its way up her spine and around her throat. It felt like her soul had been invaded, the absence of her Faelyn a fresh wound. Had her power been used to make the portal? It was horrifying to consider.

Where does it lead?

"It would appear that the boundary has been torn." Branson's voice was far away, his eyes fixed on the shimmering door.

"What do you mean? What boundary?"

But before anyone answered, a woman shouldered past them, her brown skin glowing with cool jewel undertones. Her hair, twisted into dozens of tiny braids, was swept up, showing off her delicate pointed ears. Another elf, then.

"Don't just stand there doing nothing!" She cast them a furious look as she reached into the folds of her tunic, pulling at a chain that hung around her neck. On the end was a glass bottle the length of her hand, filled with a glimmering liquid.

Her words jolted Talera back into motion, and she swiftly followed the elven woman as she knelt next to one of the wounded. The same black markings Talera had seen on the other victims crept up this woman's neck, covering half her face. The woman clutched at her stomach, blood slipping between her fingers.

"Please…help…" Her breathing was shallow.

The elf quickly uncorked the bottle, pouring a small amount of the bright liquid onto her finger before smearing it over the marks on the woman's face.

Talera gripped the woman's bloodied hand, prying it away so she could see the wound, and swore softly. There was a gaping hole in the woman's abdomen. There was nothing to be done for her. Talera tore her eyes from the horrific wound as a rattling breath escaped the dying woman's lips. Then a jolt went through her as she took in the woman's features again.

Beneath the shimmering liquid, the marks were disappearing.

Talera had seen her mother use herbs and poultices countless times to heal, but this…

"How did you…what is that?"

The elven woman's face was drawn as she stared at the dead woman. A moment passed before she answered. "It's called Aldar. It comes from my homeland's sacred Runan trees. They weep it like sap." When Talera continued to gawk, she said, "It was just a guess that it would work. Everyone and everything interacts in different ways here, depending on how we were written. I thought the Aldar might counteract whatever strain of dark magic this is."

Talera's mind jumped back to how she'd felt only moments ago—like her life force was being ripped away. That deathlike hold on her magic…she shuddered. Her reserve of Faelyn had been completely depleted.

The other woman clicked her tongue. "I shouldn't have wasted it on her."

Talera's heart constricted as she looked around at the slaughter. The elven woman moved quickly to another victim, taking a little extra time to inspect their wounds before deigning them fit to receive the healing ointment.

Talera's hands were numb as she stepped into the role of a healer. Her eyes flicked back to the portal as she tied a crude tourniquet around a man's leg, wondering again where it led.

But she kept quiet, keeping her swirling thoughts to herself as she smeared orange powder into a laceration to stave off infection. She ignored her mother's voice in her head telling her to use the powder again on her own leg. She couldn't afford to think about her mother right now, when she needed her composure. Still, swallowing became difficult, and her grief lodged in her throat as she moved from one victim to the next.

A deep, constant vibration hung in the air, the magic of the portal refusing to be ignored.

Talera watched as a group of characters stepped up to the portal, hesitating momentarily before passing through. It was another detail she filed away for later. Later, when she could think and breathe and figure out what in the Seven Hells was going on.

Covered in blood, her back tight with tension, Talera worked feverishly alongside the elven woman. The hours pressed on as she stanched blood and clumsily set bones, only to hear that death rattle over and over. She closed the eyes of another dead woman and turned her attention to the man sprawled next to her. His wounds, if tended to immediately, could be treated. But he shoved her hands aside as she reached for him.

"No." He shook his head, the motion causing more blood to gush from the wound in his neck. He winced in pain but said, "I'll be damned if I let you take away my chance to leave this hell."

Confusion must've been plain on her face, because he said, "Don't you know? Violence and that damned blight are your only hopes of leaving this place." His grip tightened on her wrist, keeping her from stopping the bleeding. "Please."

"But I can—"

"Please." A tear slipped down his cheek. If she didn't get pressure on that wound—

His nails dug into her skin…and then the light in his eyes went out. A chill ran down her spine, and she stumbled away.

Only violence or that damned blight.

Her stomach turned to lead as she understood the implications. Here, she wouldn't grow old and die naturally. She wagered the blight he referred to was the one causing characters' skin to turn translucent. Those were her options: rotting away from sickness or being slaughtered, either by her own hand or another's. Otherwise she'd be here, cast aside and forgotten, for eternity.

Choking on her horror, Talera staggered toward the edge of the square.

I want to live. I want to live.

If she repeated it enough times, maybe some of the panic would ease. She squeezed her eyes shut. Wanting to live and accepting the realities of this realm were two separate things. Was she doomed to live forever without her family, without a shred of familiarity, surrounded by the destitute? What would her purpose be in this world?

"Talera." She opened her eyes as Guy strode toward her. "Are you all right?"

Dried blood was caked on her hands, arms, and face. "How do you stand it? I've only just gotten here, and I already feel myself unraveling." She pointed behind him. "That man begged me—*begged* me—to let him die. Before, when I found you in the Library, a survival instinct had kicked in, but now…" She trembled, shaking her head. "How can you stand so much apathy? Are you really okay with just existing here for the rest of time?"

Guy looked at her with such sadness and pity that a small tug of irritation broke through her weariness.

"Am I wrong?" she snapped. "If we don't die by

violence or whatever that damned blight is, we're stuck here forever?"

Guy's voice was soft when he said, "We don't age here. We didn't get ill either until this sickness started claiming lives." He put his hands in his pockets, let out a heavy breath, and continued, "There is a boundary between this realm and the real world. Branson suspects that it's been weakening over the last several years, the result of which is the blight." His eyes had a haunted look as he went on. "The sickness—or contamination, or whatever you want to call it—it's like a virus that causes our tissues to destroy themselves. People's bodies rot away from the inside, and their skin turns translucent.

"I was trying to tell you before about how things used to be. It wasn't always like this. Branson speaks of a time when people still had ambitions and will to live after they got over the initial melancholy that happened when they arrived. But recently the number of manuscripts arriving has surged, the blight has appeared, and things have been changing. The Council has far fewer members than it used to; there's hardly anyone left besides myself and a few others in the Library sector. Even though it's only been a few hours, with the portal ripping the boundary clear open the number of people showing the effects of the blight has risen alarmingly. I fear it's only a matter of time before—" Guy cut off his impassioned speech, rubbing his forehead.

Talera's eyes skated over the many corpses around them with translucent skin, and she suppressed a shudder.

Guy continued after a moment, face weary but determined. "This place hasn't robbed me of my eyes or intuition. I saw what you're capable of." He swept a hand behind him, indicating the square where she'd been tirelessly working. "The part of your heart that makes you human"—Talera arched a brow, and he corrected himself—"sorry, elven. The point is, what you just did was obviously instinctive for you. Acting from your heart is never a waste or a mistake, Talera. And it matters a great deal more than actual skill, in my opinion."

Talera pursed her lips, turning the words over in her mind. "Why should I care about this place, about anyone here, if no one else does? Why do I matter if I was so easily thrown aside?"

"You're still here, aren't you? Even after being discarded. We. Are. Still. Here. So why shouldn't we care?"

Something tugged in her chest at his words. Desire? Purpose?

I have to prove myself.

That need to demonstrate that she was worthy, good

enough, throbbed in her chest. Wasn't that what had driven her all her life?

But if none of that was real…

We are still here.

So why shouldn't we care?

Maybe…maybe she could still find it. Fill that piece of herself.

Talera squared her shoulders. "What exactly do you have in mind?"

CHAPTER TWELVE

Show Them

Darkness pressed in with icy cold hands.

And then—

Rehnir was on the other side of the portal.

The smell of Fear drilled into his brain. The bridge he was standing on was immense, stretching off in both directions, connecting the land on either side of the large body of water below. His clothes clung to his body due to the sudden wind and the moisture in the air. A steady roar filled the sky as what looked like metal carriages hurtled across the bridge just on the other side of the rail he gripped tightly. Laughter and loud voices caught his attention, and Rehnir turned to watch a group approaching him on the narrow walkway. A vibration thrummed in his chest, and he inhaled sharply, catching the smell of Fear rolling off their bodies. None of them had noticed that he'd stepped through a doorway from another world.

Rehnir kept his face calm and cool as he reached out the tether of his mind to that invisible vibration found in every sentient being. A pulse, a faint brush of the frequency—if he pulled from that Fear, they'd get mild abrasions, headaches, or nausea. But if he tapped deeper into the frequency, found their deep-seated fears and traumas—

Rehnir kept his eyes trained on the four friends, the vibration sending chills up and down his spine. His connection to their frequencies was immediate and strong, so much stronger than all those he'd made in the Abandoned Realm. A shiver of pleasure passed through him, and he flexed his fingers, a familiar blue light sparking from his palm.

A snarl curled Rehnir's lips as one of the men faltered, his eyes going wide. The wind whipped Rehnir's cloak as he pulled on the tether between his mind and theirs.

The man stopped abruptly, clutching his throat as the color drained from his face. He fell to his knees, causing his three companions to trip over him. Rehnir's whole body hummed with power, and he reached out his mind to grip the other tethers tighter. He pulled, feeling their life force rushing out and slamming into him. Bones snapped and blood sprayed into the air. Shouts of panic came from behind him, and he saw people frantically turning back.

Rehnir walked toward the group of four, a hunter stalking his prey.

He reached the bodies, three sets of eyes unblinking as they lay in a growing lake of their blood. Rehnir surveyed the dead for a moment before shifting his focus to the remaining woman. She whimpered in pain, trying to pull her broken body away from her friends' carnage, black tendrils coiling up her neck as the dark magic spread its poison. Her hands were covered in burned flesh, large oozing sores that bled.

Rehnir caressed the tether between their minds softly, and the woman flinched, her cries rising to a scream. "Let's see what you're afraid of," Rehnir mused as he sorted through the mental images that flashed in his mind. Her nightmares, fears, and traumas splayed out before him like a deck of cards.

He *tsk*ed. "I'm disappointed. Drowning? Your mother's sickness returning? The man who lives next to you?" Rehnir knelt so he was at eye level with her. "I will show you what fear really is."

Rehnir's grasp on the tether tightened, like talons and claws ripping into flesh, and he pulled the remaining Fear from her. The woman's shriek of horror filled the air, and every muscle in Rehnir tensed with the power flooding his system. The magic coursed through him greedily, boundless. He'd never tasted such power. A roar erupted from his throat, and his arms swung wide, the power needing a release, a purpose, a target.

Energy flared out of his body, rippling through the air before finding its victims.

Rehnir gasped as the wave of power crashed around him. The smell of smoke and blood mingled with the Fear. He surveyed the bridge, waves of heat billowing from the metal contraptions that were now licked by flames. Horns blared while shouts of confusion twisted into horror.

He barely registered the other characters emerging from the portal, their malice palpable.

Never again would he be weak.

Monster.

The word was a declaration, not damnation.

Show them.

The thrill of the feed consumed him.

CHAPTER THIRTEEN

Grappling With Feelings

"I HATE THESE THINGS—I feel like I'm wearing a bathrobe." Owen tugged at the belt of his gi.

Bex shushed him, eyes on the instructor. It was the last of their jujitsu classes, and with the blue sky and perfect weather, she couldn't blame Owen for complaining. She was uncomfortably warm in her rash guard and the stuffy gi now that the morning fog had burned away.

Thick blue mats covered the grass, the cheerful noise of weekend parkgoers around them, the Golden Gate Bridge tall in the distance. A light breeze kissed her face, curling under her collar and tickling the wisps of hair that had fallen out of her ponytail during the first half of the class.

The girl Bex had been paired with whispered something about needing to duck out early as the instructor rambled on. She squeezed Bex's elbow and discreetly gathered her things. Bex turned her attention back to the demonstration, resisting the urge to sigh.

Oh good. More *rolling on the ground.*

They'd spent the last six weeks learning different positions—mounts and guards—and practicing shrimping to escape being trapped under someone. It wasn't until after she'd spent the entire first class on the ground that Bex had realized she wasn't going to be learning any of the takedowns she'd envisioned when she'd signed up.

Another thing to add to her list of time wasters. Bex had been tempted not to come at all today, considering she'd abandoned Talera's story, but she still hadn't told Owen about throwing the manuscript out, and an hour of grappling seemed preferable to having that conversation.

Preoccupied with her thoughts, she hardly registered what was being said until the instructor pointed between her and Owen. "Hmm? Sorry?"

The instructor looked irritated at her obvious lack of attention. "You two—pair up."

Her mind stalled. *Oh.*

Today Owen had been paired with the instructor, but now with Bex's partner gone, there was no longer an uneven number of students. It wasn't unusual to do coed grappling, but Owen and Bex had yet to be partnered.

"We've got about fifteen more minutes, and I want to

see you working that whole time. I'll be coming around to check technique." The instructor clapped his hands together in dismissal, and the rest of the class paired up. Bex tried to force a normal smile as she turned to Owen.

He grinned, rubbing the back of his neck. "Looks like we're together finally."

"Looks like." Her stomach fluttered with nerves. *It's just Owen. It's just Owen.*

Owen reached out, gripping the lapels of her gi. His knuckles brushed against her collarbones, and he gave her a playful shake. "Let's see your elf warrior moves, B."

Bex scoffed, ignoring the shiver that ran down her spine.

They knelt on the mats. The couples around them were in various guards or starting to roll.

Owen's hair fell across his forehead in the breeze. Bex's palms were sweaty, and her mind was infuriating empty of all the things they'd been learning.

Don't make this weird. Why are you making this so weird?

Owen quirked an eyebrow. "Top or bottom?"

Heat rose in her cheeks. "Eh, let's just start from knees."

"Don't think I'm going to go easy on you."

Bex rolled her eyes, adjusting so she rested on her toes as well before giving the customary hand slap start. Owen's hand shot out, snaking around her wrist and grabbing hold of her gi. He yanked her arm across her body, pulling her off balance and closer to him. Bex dropped her shoulder, tucking her chin as she pressed against his chest. Owen's stance was steady, though, and his other hand came around to grip the fabric at her hip.

With a sharp twist, he flipped her onto her back, the matt softening the impact. His grip was secure, and before she could react, he'd straddled her hips, pinning her. Bex grabbed at his collar, trying to use the leverage of the gi to pull a collar choke, but Owen batted her attempt away.

They both panted slightly, breath hot between them as they fought for control. Her heart was pounding against her ribs in a way that had nothing to do with the grappling. Her thoughts scrambled.

Bex bucked her hips, driving her heels into the ground. It was enough. Owen pitched forward, hands landing on either side of her head to catch himself, and she took advantage of the new position to capture his arm, then drove her hips up again to unseat him.

Owen's laugh was close and low in her ear as she flipped him over. She needed to pin his arms, but he was moving so quickly, eyes dancing and a grin on his face. His hands came up behind her and grabbed her pants, pulling hard on her hips.

"Shrimp!" He laughed as he shimmied out from under her. The next attack had her flat on her back again: his knee holding her hips down, his torso pressed tight into hers, his forearms under her neck. His jaw moved against her temple, each breath pressing their chests together, his calves squeezing her hips.

She wriggled beneath him, trying to move him. His chest rumbled against hers as he laughed again. And even though she was trying to escape, it felt more like pulling him in than pushing him away. His breath skated between her gi and the bare skin of her neck, the sensation overwhelming, her mind short-circuiting.

They both froze, the moment stretching.

Bex tapped his arm in submission.

Owen pulled back, blinking rapidly. There were freckles splashed across his nose, and a lock of hair stuck to his forehead. The air between them was hot, and Bex couldn't seem to take a deep enough breath.

A drop of sweat dripped from his nose…right onto her face.

"Oh my god, *gross*, Owen!" Bex scrunched her nose,

and Owen sat back, reality snapping back into place. He rolled onto the mat beside her, wiping his face with the crook of his elbow with nonchalance.

Bex's traitorous body cataloged the absence of his weight as an unnatural state instead of the way it had always been and always would be.

A loud clap of thunder cracked the air. Bex whipped around just as a flash of lightning painted the Golden Gate Bridge a vibrant blue. Something shifted in her bones.

"What the hell was that?" Owen's voice was loud in her ear, straining to be heard over the tremendous noise coming from the bridge: cars screeching, horns blaring, a cacophony of screams. Bex's blood ran cold, and a wave of nausea rolled through her.

Someone was saying something about tornadoes turning the sky dark blue.

Green, Bex thought, not tearing her eyes from the bridge. *A* green *sky can happen before a tornado.* Of course, it was hurricanes they needed to worry about here, not tornadoes. She didn't bother explaining any of this, though, just waited and watched. The sky was still clear with no signs of rain clouds. Her heart beat to the words *what happened what happened what happened.*

For a few moments, it seemed like everyone in Crissy

Field was enchanted, unable to look away. An undeniable, invisible string pulled the whole city's attention toward the bridge, pulsing with energy, pulsing with magic.

Then the unspoken moratorium on reality lifted, the people around her shifting their focus, breaking the spell. Bex was left feeling like she'd missed a step going down the stairs, like she was the only one who hadn't heard the recess bell and was now alone on the playground. Did no one else feel that ache in their chest? Was she the only one desperate for the mystical to be explained?

Disappointment seeped through her body. Everyone resumed grappling, the sound of sirens in the background blending into the city's usual soundtrack.

Owen's eyes flickered with an emotion she couldn't place as she turned back to face him. Heat climbed up her neck. She just needed to survive the remainder of the class without making a complete fool of herself in front of him.

CHAPTER FOURTEEN

Hope in the Library

A LINGERING UNEASE HAD TALERA scanning the stacks as she followed Guy deeper into the heart of the Library. Her leg throbbed. At Guy's insistence, she'd applied another coat of the orange powder from her mother—nearly all used up on treating others—and dressed it with clean bandages. She deserved the ache and the slight limp, as it was sheer luck that infection hadn't set in while she'd stubbornly ignored it.

A tall man in a wide-brimmed hat rounded a bookshelf, yelling obscenities over his shoulder. Guy grasped Talera's elbow, steering her the other way.

Talera yanked her arm back. "Unhand me!"

Guy removed his hands but kept edging her down a different aisle. "Trust me, you don't want to meet that odious man."

"And who exactly is he?" Talera matched his slightly

hushed tone.

"His name is Duke Decker." Talera snorted and Guy nodded. "Trust me, I know. He's been here for a while and has never really warmed to the place. He's definitely in the camp of 'I'm angry about what's happened in my life, so I'll make everyone else miserable too.' I once made the mistake of trying to give him some light reading materials. You know, Wild West adventures?"

Talera stared at him blankly.

"Oh, er—right, I forgot. You're fantasy. He's from the western genre—he's a cowboy. Rides horses and shoots guns." Guy made a strange gesture with his pointer fingers and thumbs before rolling his eyes. "It doesn't matter. Anyway, he got annoyed and ended up tying me to shipwrecked remains and leaving me there for several days."

Talera bristled. "He did *what*?"

"Come on, the others are waiting for us."

When they arrived, Branson and the elven healer were conversing in hushed tones. A large manuscript was in Branson's hands.

"I haven't found Sekzelt yet," Guy said by way of a greeting, "but I did find another to join us. Talera, you haven't formally been introduced—this is Branson and Adaira. Branson was an atomic physicist who was in the middle of a dinner party with a Russian ambassador and his colleagues when he abruptly arrived in the Abandoned Realm some ten-ish years ago."

Branson inclined his head slightly.

"And Adaira here, as you may have guessed," Guy continued, "was an elven healer who was about to inherit the crown of her people when she woke up here." Adaira's heart-shaped face was solemn, her green eyes piercing. "This is Talera, an elf who—er—" Guy looked at her, quirking an eyebrow.

Talera gave him a withering look. They all looked at her expectantly, and she sighed. "I was on my way to compete in the Challenge to gain entrance to a school where I'd further my skills with my magic and train as a warrior. The company I was traveling with was ambushed on the road when…" She trailed off, her throat tightening, and turned to Guy. "And you?"

"I'm Guy, as you know. I think my author meant to come back and give me a proper name when he thought of one, but he died before he ever got around to it. I was a scientist—a botanist, specifically." He gave a small flourish of his hand.

Talera gaped at him. "That…that's why your name is Guy?"

Branson sighed and cut in, "Fascinating as these synopses are, we have more urgent matters to discuss." He held up the manuscript in his hands. "I think we figured out who made the portal."

Adaira nodded. "His name is Rehnir."

Guy's eyes went wide. "As in…Rehnir the feeder?"

"You know him?" Talera asked.

"I like to read all the manuscripts," Guy replied absently as he shuffled closer to Branson, craning his neck to see the words on the pages. As if his suspicion was confirmed, he swore softly.

"What exactly is a feeder?" Talera wrinkled her nose at the term.

"One of the foulest abominations in this wretched place." Branson spoke with such vehemence that Talera flinched.

"Are you familiar with how brain waves function?" Branson asked. Talera shook her head, glancing sideways at Guy, who looked like he might be sick. "Well, the basics will be enough to understand how his powers function." He cleared his throat, and his posture shifted to one that appeared more scholarly.

"There are five different types of brain waves." He ticked them off on his hand. "Delta, theta, alpha, beta, and gamma. Each of these has its own frequency range. Theta waves occur most often when we sleep. This is where fears and nightmares lie, where past traumas and troubled histories are stored, as well as intuition and imagination.

"Rehnir's ability allows him to access people's theta waves even while they are awake. When he locks onto a frequency, he's able to tap into the very energy source that creates those brain waves and use it to generate power. That drains the life from his victims and leaves them dead or wounded, depending on how long he feeds on them."

"He literally feeds off people's fear," Guy said weakly. "According to his story, he resisted the call of his abilities for a long time, but it eventually won out. Enter evil mentor who showed him the ways of the feeders. Rehnir began killing in earnest and gaining more and more power. He got greedy and wound up killing his master—a very common storyline, mind you, and a bit of a cliché."

No one said anything for a moment.

"Right, sorry." Guy rubbed the back of his neck. "Not the time—I see that now."

"That's how he was able to penetrate the weakness in the boundary?" Adaira asked. "By feeding?"

Branson nodded. "It would appear so. My guess is that he wants to exact revenge on the world that banished him to this place." He rubbed his eyes.

Talera furrowed her brow. "Where does the portal lead?"

Adaira met her gaze. "It opens to the real world."

"But the sheer amount of power he needed to penetrate the boundary is staggering," Branson said.

"Well, this place is full of fear and trauma. I imagine that gave him plenty of sources to pull from," Adaira said.

Talera shifted her weight, steadying herself. If they noticed her reaction, they didn't show it.

Branson rubbed his chin. "Unfortunately, I'm afraid that with a boundary this weak and an open portal, the cross contamination between worlds will spread rapidly." He looked them each in the eye in turn. "It's only a matter of time before the Abandoned Realm is fully destroyed, and us with it."

CHAPTER FIFTEEN

INTERVIEW

"WHERE DO YOU SEE yourself in five years?"

Bex plastered a fake smile on her face as she gave the interviewer, Stephanie, the polished answers she'd practiced at home—solid career in publishing, student loans paid off, working toward being an editor. She left out the things she really thought she'd be doing—loathing herself for leaving Between the Lines, wishing she could hack it as an author, and most likely watching Owen get married to Heidi or someone equally amazing.

Bex scraped her thumbnail along her palm as she navigated the conversation. Stephanie was kind, and Bex had to remind herself that the fact that she knew her mother shouldn't count against her. Lynx Publishing had an airy office with big windows looking out onto a busy street. It really wouldn't be a bad place to work, all things considered.

"Tell me what drew you to this position."

Seems like a nice enough place for my dreams to die? It's time to grow up? This was less intimidating than other listings because my mom had a connection?

"I have a real passion for editing, and I love project-oriented jobs." Bex's cheeks hurt from smiling, and she could feel dampness under her arms. "The bookstore was a great place to work during college, but I'm ready to transition into publishing."

Stephanie nodded. "Well, it's not always the most glamorous of jobs, but it's a skill set there will always be a need for."

At the end of the interview, they shook hands. Stephanie promised to be in touch; she said they had a few more applicants to meet with but that she felt confident Bex would be a good fit for the team.

As she turned to leave, Bex's eye caught on a copy of an Arthur Huxby novel sticking out of Stephanie's purse. Her heart lifted a bit. *Maybe this won't be so bad after all.* "Huxby fan?"

Stephanie's brows pinched together, and then she saw what Bex was referring to. "Oh god, no. My girlfriend got me that as a joke." Her laugh was delicate and lovely, and Bex hated it. "I'm almost exclusively a thriller reader. The only fantasy author I can get into is Tom Hallen. I'm obsessed with his Truthsayer books."

Bex's mouth formed an O shape. *You have got to be kidding me*, she wanted to say, but she held her tongue. *Tom Hallen? Really??* She groaned internally, this horrifying development giving everything Stephanie had done in the last hour new context.

Seeming blissfully unaware of the havoc her words had wrought on Bex's morale, Stephanie chatted about Tom Hallen's latest excuse for a novel as she led Bex out of the office.

CHAPTER SIXTEEN

Through the Portal

"WHAT YOU CALL MAGIC in your world is what we would describe as science in ours. But in the real world, they are the same," Branson said. "That realm is the product of the magic and power that's in thoughts and words. You see, when someone in the real world writes a story, their words have a magical ability. They create a frequency—a vibration, if you will—and that frequency has a physical effect on the world. This whole realm exists parallel to the real world."

Talera swallowed her annoyance at Branson's penchant for monologuing. He'd already spent a quarter of an hour explaining his science background and that his story was set in the real world, both of which apparently made him the expert in charge.

"Now, I believe that what powers the boundary that separates us from the real world and keeps us alive even after our authors have stopped writing our stories is the belief in magic. It's people believing that what they think and say carries weight. That there is magic in their words."

"Indeed," a voice said behind them.

Guy yelped, and Talera spun to see an old man robed in deep blue leaning heavily on a gnarled wooden staff. "In the First Language, the words for *magic* and *speak* were the same. But humanity has long since stopped believing in actual magic, so the idea that their words and thoughts carry that power has mostly been forgotten."

"Good god, Sekzelt." Guy clutched at his chest. "Don't sneak up like that!"

"Apologies," Sekzelt said in a tone that was in no way apologetic.

Talera turned back to Branson. "So you're saying that you think this lack of belief in magic out there"—she gestured to where the portal stood outside—"is weakening the boundary that keeps our worlds separate?"

"Not just separate—*alive*," Branson said. "I've been here a very long time. We didn't used to get sick, and we can't age. It's like we're stuck in time. Barring death at the hand of others or ourselves, we've always simply kept on existing. We cannot procreate, but our numbers continue to grow, as newly abandoned characters are arriving all the time.

"But as the boundary has weakened, the blight has spread, as if the increased exposure to the other world has contaminated our realm. Characters are now fading and dying, rotting away from the inside. As the contamination has grown, so has the number of new manuscripts. It's easy to see that the world out there has stopped believing in magic, which has weakened the boundary even more."

Sekzelt cleared his throat. "It seems not everyone is content to wait around for the boundary to disappear. A great many characters are crossing through the portal."

"Let them go. Our chance to save this realm is more tenuous than ever, and each of them is a drain on the boundary," Branson said.

"Can we go back to the part about the portal destroying our realm and erasing all of us forever?" Guy asked.

Tension was thick in the air.

Adaira broke the silence first. "Surely there's a way to close the portal?"

Sekzelt snorted. "Best of luck trying to figure out how. Do you know how many different versions of portal magic there are here?" He waved a wrinkled hand around at the vast library for emphasis.

"Four thousand, eight hundred and ninety-two.

Approximately."

Everyone turned to Guy. Color bloomed on his neck and cheeks. He shuffled his feet. "L-last I checked, anyway."

"So we read them. Process of elimination." Adaira leveled Sekzelt with a withering glare. "Do you have a better idea?"

Sekzelt puffed out his chest as he opened his mouth to retort.

"Arguing will get us nowhere." Branson dragged a finger across his lower lip, eyes distant. "Adaira makes a valid point. But we need a contingency plan. We need to seriously consider moving those who wish to live farther into the Realm, away from the portal."

This statement elicited an uproar among the Council members.

"And go where?"

"You can't possibly be serious—"

"It could buy us more time—"

"Everything we've worked for is here!"

"You said yourself that there's nothing out there—"

Talera rubbed her temples as the bickering continued, but she wasn't listening.

The real world. The portal led to the real world.

She chewed her bottom lip. She wanted to live, she was

sure of that now, and it was becoming increasingly clear that this place wasn't guaranteed to survive much longer. Her body itched to be in motion. There simply wasn't time to stand around and argue with these people, who obviously had no idea how to fix the situation any better than she did. Her blood buzzed with adrenaline.

That first day in the Library, Guy had mentioned the inscription on each story indicating its author. At the time, it hadn't seemed important, not when she was trying to comprehend everything else he was saying. But now…

Her mind was made up.

"…put every spare person we can on reading portal magic manuscripts," Adaira was saying, "and Sekzelt, you'll be the one to work through each method. We'll eliminate possibilities until we find one that works."

Branson scoffed. "I still say we need to focus on finding those who stand a chance and moving them deeper into the Realm."

"Those who stand a chance?" Talera asked, unable to stop herself.

Branson turned to her, surveying her over his spectacles. "When you've been here as long as I have, you learn to be realistic."

Talera let out a snort at the irony of the word choice.

She watched Guy's lip twitch and knew he'd heard it too. "I can see this conversation is going to continue to go in circles, so I'll see myself out." She gave a mocking bow. "I'd say it's been a pleasure, but the truth is that this whole experience has been rather unpleasant. Best of luck to you all."

Talera smirked as she turned on her heel and strode toward the dais.

"Where are you going?" Guy called out.

"Through the portal."

Guy's rushed footsteps pattered across the floor. "Have you lost your mind?"

"Can I technically lose it if I'm not actually real?"

Guy, it seemed, was not in the mood for her dry humor. "Why?"

"It's clear you all aren't going to be able to fix the portal. I'll take my chances with finding my author and reversing this whole nightmare." She shot Guy a look. "You can't tell me you aren't the least bit curious to see the real world. You could find your author too and try to get out of this place."

"My author's dead."

Talera flinched. "I—I'm sorry, I forgot."

Guy flicked his hand impatiently. "I'm not saying it for

sympathy. You mean to tell me you're just going to waltz on through and…what? Say to everyone you meet, 'Hello, excuse me, do you know of anyone who was writing a story and stopped? I'd like to have words with them.'"

Talera kept up her swift pace but nodded in acknowledgment of his wordplay. "No, that would be rather tedious to explain over and over." They'd reached the dais now. She scanned the pile for a moment before grabbing the notebook containing her story. "But this has the name and location I'm looking for, yes?" She flipped to the back page. "Bex Harmon. See?" She glanced at the words below the name: a date, the coordinates of something called Between the Lines, and the reason Talera was here: fear.

Guy chewed on his lower lip, but she could see the wheels turning in his head.

"You've accepted this place as home," Talera said gently. "I haven't gotten there yet. So I'm going to go through and demand that she finish my story and set this right."

Guy eyed her. "I'm not sure it works that way."

"You said yourself that you don't think we'll figure out how to close the portal. And if it doesn't get closed, we're all dead anyway."

Guy fidgeted with the sleeve of his jacket, looking torn.

"Fine. I'm coming with you, then."

It was Talera's turn to balk. "What?"

"If they want to read every portal story here and try to convince everyone to flee in the meantime, that's their choice. But there's a chance the answer is on the other side of the portal. If the people in that realm are the ones who invented us, surely someone there must know how to close the portal. And since I was never given a quest or a mission, I should very much like to seize this opportunity." He lifted his chin. "Besides, the likelihood of you succeeding in the real world with your fantasy background are slim to none. You're going to need me."

Silence hung between them for several moments, punctuated every few seconds by more discarded stories dropping onto the dais.

Talera narrowed her eyes. "You'd risk contamination or death for the small hope that we might find a way to close the portal?"

Guy's smile was tinged with sadness. "Hope is my purpose. I wasted enough time not allowing myself either of those things. And if death is coming for us all, then I choose hope and purpose until that time comes, no matter which side of that portal I'm on."

Talera sized him up. "All right, then. Are you going to

tell your precious Branson your decision? He might not like it."

It was Guy's turn to roll his eyes. "I don't do everything he tells me. Only side characters do everything someone tells them. I'm the main character in my story, remember?"

"Gods help us," Talera muttered as they headed toward the exit. A thought occurred to her. "What about Rehnir's story? Couldn't we just go find his author and ask how to close the portal?"

"No, his author is also dead."

"How in the Seven Hells do you remember that?"

Guy laughed and tapped a finger to his temple. "I told you, I read all the manuscripts. How else do you expect me to pass the time here?"

Talera grunted begrudgingly.

Guy's eyes gleamed as he said, "Besides, even when left unfinished, stories are the best places to find hope."

CHAPTER SEVENTEEN

Welcome to San Francisco

Thanks to the Realm's lack of water—really, how could Guy consider this place home?—Talera wasn't able to rely on her Faelyn Fog to refill her magic source. Sleep it was, then.

She scowled up at the starless sky, the hard ground beneath her digging into her back as she tried to will her brain to shut off.

Her mind was stuck on the interaction they'd had with Branson a few hours ago, despite Guy's insistence that he didn't need to inform the man of his every action. The older gentleman had thought their plan "foolish and suicidal" and had made sure they understood in no uncertain terms that when they figured out how to close the portal, they wouldn't wait for them to return before doing so.

She and Guy had left Branson, along with Sekzelt and some other Council members Talera didn't bother to introduce herself to, pouring over manuscripts in the Library.

Meanwhile, the exodus of characters through the portal continued; they were surely bent on unleashing their revenge and anger on the other side.

Guy had prattled on in more detail about different schools of thought in the Realm, but Talera had paid him little attention—it was rather pointless, since she'd be leaving this place soon. Besides, it didn't take a lot of imagination to guess the very polarizing opinions people—characters—might hold when faced with the eternal damnation of this place. You'd either give up entirely, as she had done herself; rage at everything and everyone around you (a certain broken arm attested to this); or delude yourself into grasping for some semblance of a life, spurred on by the visceral fear of death. The latter appeared to be the least popular. Talera had experienced the entire gambit of emotions since her arrival. It seemed not everyone moved from one to the next.

Talera squirmed, trying to get comfortable.

An impossible task.

She expelled an irritated breath.

Focus, Talera.

Breathe in.

You'll find your bloody author and go home.

Breathe out.

You will go home.

I'm coming back, Mother.

It was a long time before sleep finally took her.

Her dreams were a blur of torn pages and invisible talons. She could hear her mother's screams behind her, but every time she tried to turn, to look, to go to her, the mental claws dug in.

You're not real.

You're not real.

Not. Real.

Talera reached for her sword but instead drew a long featherless quill coated in thick black ink. The ink began to stain her hands. It spread up her arms, across her torso, and up into her mouth. Then down her throat, forcing its way into her nose and eyes, suffocating the scream of terror tearing from her.

Talera jerked awake, clutching at her heaving chest. Cold sweat covered her body.

She lay alone at the edge of the Abandoned Realm. The sky had begun its dismal approximation of a sunrise.

Her breath sawed in and out of her lungs as she waited to regain composure. Her muscles were stiff, but her Faelyn was replenished, thank the gods. She quickly donned her cloak, which she'd used as a makeshift pillow, feeling in an inside pocket to make sure the black notebook was still there. She slung her pack over her shoulder, made sure her bow and arrow were strapped on securely, and buckled her sword at her hip.

Right. Steeling her nerves, she made her way back into the city.

There was a buzz in the air from the magic surrounding the portal leaking into the Realm. A coppery tang filled Talera's mouth as she got closer to the center of the city. Guy was waiting for her at the foot of the Library steps, a hesitant smile on his face. The pair of them were quiet as they made their way to the portal. The vibration thrummed in Talera's bones and made her ears pop. The sense of pressure bearing down on her increased the closer they got.

Guy cleared his throat. "You've still got your manuscript?"

"Yes." Talera swallowed, tearing her gaze from the iridescent doorway to look at him. "Ready to go on an adventure?"

Guy cracked his knuckles and smoothed the front of his white coat. "Yes, this sense of foreboding and excitement seems to match the descriptions I've read of what heroes feel when their journeys begin. I can't tell if I'm going to be sick or pass out."

Talera snorted, sweat beginning to bead on her forehead. "I'm quite sure some of that is because of this blasted tear between worlds." Indeed, the color had drained from Guy's face, and her limbs were shaking from being so near the portal.

"Right, then. Shall we?" Guy quirked an eyebrow as Talera breathed deeply through her nostrils to quell the roiling in her stomach.

"Let's."

Guy hesitated, then whispered "Bollocks" and stepped through the portal.

Talera was right on his heels.

The ringing in her ears deepened. The air was ripped from her lungs. There was nothing but endless darkness and cold. She stumbled, and the next instant the world dropped back around her.

Waves were crashing. Horns blared. The cool breeze made her shiver as it whipped her hair across her face. Talera craned her neck to stare at the vast structure they were on. It was a metal bridge, a burnt-orange color, stretching out in both directions. Guy gripped her by the elbow and pulled her along.

Life and color filled the sky again. Talera's eyes stung from the brightness of the sun. There was so much *noise*. The ground rumbled as strange wheeled contraptions whipped past them on the bridge. Birds called overhead, and Talera tripped on some rubble when she looked up to watch them. She would've fallen if not for Guy's hand steadying her. He was talking, but Talera's mind was reeling too much to hear him. Each breath was painful and wonderful.

Tears rolled down her face. She hadn't realized how bland and dreary the colors of the Realm had been. How had she forgotten what colors should look like in only a few days? But now, bombarded with the vibrant hues around her, she felt as if she'd spent a lifetime there.

Talera tossed a look over her shoulder. The portal was barely distinguishable, just a blurry smudge against a metal pillar.

A man dressed in wickedly short trousers and nothing else was running straight toward them, sweat glistening on his body. Talera called out in alarm, reaching for her sword. But Guy shoved her up against the railing and out of the way. The man spared them a brief glance as he maneuvered around them and continued sprinting.

"What—what the bloody hells?" Talera pushed Guy off of her.

"He's just jogging, Talera," Guy practically hissed, much to her chagrin. "Honestly, you might need me more than I thought." He eyed her. "Lesson number one—try to blend in. Any hope we have of finding your Bex and fixing this mess will depend on not getting arrested. Surely you had some type of authority in your world, guards or the like? Prison? The stocks? Er—dungeons?"

Talera growled. "I'm not completely inept, Guy."

Guy spread his hands. "Wouldn't dream of implying otherwise. But if the people here think we're baddies, you can kiss your homecoming goodbye."

Talera raised her chin, sneering. "And if one of the actual baddies from the Realm attacks us?"

"I give you full permission to save our skins if Rehnir or any other baddies attack us. But otherwise, we need to keep a low profile."

Talera rolled her eyes. "Fine. And stop saying baddies. You sound like a child." She turned on her heel and stalked off.

They continued toward the city at the end of the bridge. One tip of the island was packed with incredibly tall buildings, like steel imitations of the Shanrun Forest back home. Sloping green hills dipped down to sandy beaches and rock walls that broke the waves. A slight fog clung to the ground. Gusts of wind continued coming off the things whizzing past them on the bridge.

"What are those, anyway?" Talera asked quietly.

"Cars—automobiles," Guy said.

The small walkway was rather crowded with people—some who had stopped to look out over the water, several more who were jogging, and a few on two-wheeled contraptions. The majority of people were flowing in the same direction they were going. Talera noted several people with drawn faces, touching their heads or muttering to their companions that they didn't feel so good. Judging by the tension on Guy's face, he was observing the same. The presence of the portal, though not as visible from this side, was still affecting people, repelling them with an unknown force.

"Oh yes!" a woman called to Talera, her smile wide. She wore a boxy sort of top hat with large metallic spectacles balanced above the brim. Her coat was long and covered with sashes, chains, and several dangling medallions. "Love it!" She made a sweeping gesture at Talera, head to toe, and elbowed her companion in the ribs. "See, I told you people are already dressing up."

The woman's companion was wearing plain slacks and a short-sleeved tunic that looked similar to the clothing Guy was wearing. The woman gave Talera two thumbs up as they passed.

Talera waited until they were out of earshot. "What just happened?"

"I believe she was a steampunk cosplay enthusiast." Guy glanced over his shoulder at the retreating couple. "Fascinating." He caught Talera's look. "Don't look so surprised—the range of subjects in the Library of Manuscripts is extensive."

They'd reached the far side of the bridge by the time Guy was done explaining the concepts of cosplay and steampunk. Talera's head was beginning to hurt. Unfortunately, the experience of the bridge was only a small taste of the shock that was to come as they traipsed through the city.

Shops lined the streets, children and adults swarmed the walking areas, and the automobious things were everywhere. She kept seeing small devices people would either hold to their ears or tap their thumbs on frantically. The clothing styles matched some that she'd seen in the Abandoned Realm. There were huge signs in the sky every fifty or so paces, each vying for attention.

STORYCON IS COMING THIS MONTH! BE THE HERO OF YOUR STORY!

TOUR ALCATRAZ ISLAND!

SWITCH TO VERIZON TODAY!

Talera lost track of time, the ache in her feet the only indication of how long they'd been walking the increasingly steep streets. Guy kept muttering to himself, looking at the small street signs. He stopped an elderly man to ask a few questions, but Talera didn't bother to listen. Red, yellow, green, and orange open carriages hooked to thick cables above passed by steadily. Talera nearly walked right in front of one, its ringing bell blending into the overwhelming noise in her head. Guy tackled her out of the way as it barreled passed.

She swayed, her mouth painfully dry. "I think I need to sit down." Guy looked stricken as he nodded.

They veered onto a smaller street, and the crowds and noise lessened ever so slightly. They stopped at a bench next to some grass. Talera closed her eyes, trying to will the dizziness away. She gripped the cold metal of the bench and took several deep breaths. "Remind me why I thought this was a good idea?" Her voice was strained.

"Well, your options were this or staying in the Realm, hoping we could close the portal and possibly dying a slow and painful death as you rotted from the contamination."

Talera cracked an eye and looked at him.

"Or from boredom after listening to Branson's long-winded lectures." Guy smiled weakly.

"Yes, he does like to hear himself talk, doesn't he?" The tingling sensation in her limbs was dissipating. She tipped her head back. Branches created a soft canopy over them, and she took comfort in the familiar sight.

"The good news is that your author lives in this city," Guy continued, as if sensing that talking was helping to ground her. "Bit of luck, that. According to that gentleman, the address in your manuscript is a well-known bookshop a little farther into the city."

Talera nodded vaguely. "How are you handling this so well?"

"It helps that the world I was written into was based on this one," Guy said. "We can head that way after we rest for a moment. We have time."

Talera grunted. They didn't have time. She stood, brushing off her trousers. "No. Let's keep going." She just needed something to focus on, some way to keep her mind on their goal. "Tell me about Rehnir's story as we walk."

Guy appraised her for a moment before apparently deeming her fit to walk. Irritating human. The moisture in the air made her clothes stick to her, and she adjusted her pack as she followed him.

"Well…" Guy rubbed his chin. "If I recall correctly, his story started when he was a kid. Around nine?" He pursed his lips before snapping his fingers. “Yes, that’s right. Nine is when feeders’ abilities manifest. His dad was a drunk bastard who beat him and his mother and eventually killed her in one of his rages. Rehnir’s powers manifested the next day when his dad was beating him.”

Talera clenched her jaw, recoiling slightly as he continued.

“As Branson said, he can tap into people’s brain waves and siphon power from them. His dad was dead before Rehnir understood what was happening.” Guy grimaced. “It was a really gruesome opening scene.”

“That’s horrific,” Talera said. They stepped around a line of people waiting for gods knew what and headed up a cross street—another hill.

“Yeah, he was terrified by what he’d done and at first tried to refrain from feeding, like I mentioned in the Library.”

“And now he’s running around feeding here. Brilliant,” Talera said sullenly.

“Yes. He and all the other baddies.” Guy smiled.

Talera rolled her eyes and cracked her neck. “The sooner we find Bex and figure out how to close the bloody portal, the sooner I won’t be subjected to your terrible humor.”

CHAPTER EIGHTEEN

WORLDS COLLIDE

WITH THE CONVENTION NOW only a few days away, Between the Lines was buzzing with activity. Bex and Peter were doing their best to keep up with the influx of business StoryCon enthusiasts brought in, finalizing preparations for the booth as well as staying on top of the day-to-day shelving, inventory, and communication with publicists.

It was late afternoon, and there was a rare respite from their onslaught of patrons, which meant Peter was reading his favorite newspaper. He let out a sound of disgust. "Well, this is just terrible."

Bex looked skyward, knowing he was going to continue regardless of her interest, and said, "What is it this time?"

Peter looked up at her from his perch at the front counter. "You'd think it was the end of days or something."

"No one says 'end of days' anymore, Peter."

He ignored her comment. "Look here—the number of Fadings has skyrocketed this week, and hospitals are near capacity. Do you realize how many hospitals we have just within a five-mile radius? It's close to twenty! And *all* of them are near capacity?"

Bex furrowed her brow as Peter rubbed his temples and continued. "They think there may be some new strain. People are coming in with these terrible black scars. Did you see this?" He held up the paper, pointing at a picture.

Bex cringed, peering closer. "Are those burns?"

Peter shrugged. "Hell if I know. And then there's the whole accident on the bridge."

The bell above the front door rang as a few customers came in. Bex gave them a half smile before shifting her gaze back to Peter as he tucked the newspaper away.

"I'm just saying," Peter said in a low conspiratorial voice, "nearly everyone on the bridge having simultaneous seizures and crashing their cars? How does that even happen?" Bex shrugged as he continued muttering to himself. "Hospitals overrun with the Fading, freak accidents all over the city, not to mention the crime rate going up—"

"All right, Peter," Bex hissed through a clench-toothed smile, eyeing the nearest patrons. "Take your doom and gloom to the back before you scare away all the customers."

Peter held his hands up in surrender and obliged.

Bex's anxiety had been increasing all week; she didn't need Peter to add to her stress. For days she'd been seeing people in cosplay for the convention, but despite her usual thrill at seeing various characters traipsing through the city, this time it set her on edge.

As if her thoughts of the convention were a summoning charm, Between the Lines began to fill with people who were obviously planning on attending. Bex hardly had time to think about her worries during the next hour as she rang people up, chatting with each of them about what part of StoryCon they were most excited about.

Her phone buzzed on the counter next to her with a text from Owen.

Run tomorrow?

Bex sent a stream of thumbs-ups and hurriedly put the phone away as she heard the bell jingle again. Two people strode into the store decked out in cosplay. The dark-haired man was dressed as a scientist, though she couldn't tell from which books. But then her eyes moved to the woman, and she was suddenly transfixed.

The woman's long hair was pulled away from her face in intricate braids, so blond it was nearly white. Her pants were tucked into knee-high leather boots. She wore a leather jerkin and bracer on her left arm and had a baldric slung across her chest, holding a quiver and bow in place. The sword and handful of daggers at her hip looked uncomfortably real.

Bex smile apprehensively as she cleared her throat. "Welcome, guys. We've got all the books by all the authors who'll be at StoryCon this weekend just over there, if you want to pick up any copies to be signed."

"Oh, eh—okay. Thank you." The man smiled warmly, taking a few steps toward the counter. "Actually, we're wondering if you could help us find someone. We're looking for Bex Harmon?"

Bex raised her eyebrows in surprise. "I'm Bex."

"Oh wow, would you look at that," the man said as he gave the woman a look.

"Can…can I help you?" Bex glanced between them.

"You're Bex Harmon, the writer?"

"The—er, no, no, I'm not a writer," Bex stammered quickly as the woman neared, trying to figure out where she recognized the costume from. She dragged her focus from the clothing to the woman's face and froze.

Her eyes were violet.

They're just contacts. Bex gave herself a mental shake.

The woman reached into her cloak, pulled out a black notebook, and tossed it on the counter. "So you didn't write this?"

A knot tightened in Bex's stomach as she looked at the notebook in front of her. She opened her mouth.

Peter, reappearing out of nowhere, said, "Oh, I just love your costume!"

Bex and the man in the lab coat jumped, though the woman seemed unfazed.

"Are you getting ready for StoryCon?" Peter reached out to touch the bow strapped to the woman's back, and in a blur of movement, she had him by the wrist. A strangled noise squeaked out of him. "Okaaaay, so you're in character," he drawled with a nervous chuckle. "Sorry, I don't know the etiquette." He pulled his hand out of her grasp, gingerly holding his wrist as if she had burned him. "I see Bex here is already helping you, so I'll just leave you to it." He narrowed his eyes slightly before he retreated.

"I am so sorry about him. It, uh—it is a great costume, though," Bex finished.

The woman tapped the notebook, ignoring the

comment. "Did. You. Write. This?"

"I don't know what—" Bex choked on her words as she flipped the pages open. Ice shot through her veins as she recognized her notebook. "H-how did you get this?" Warning bells rang in her mind, and she looked at the woman again. *Oh my god—*

Her ears were pointed.

"My name is Talera. I'm a wood elf warrior trained in Faelyn magic. I was in the midst of fighting for my life when I was abruptly pulled from my reality, only to be informed that I'm a character from someone's imagination." She practically bit out each word. "Someone who gave up on my story, dooming me to rot in the abyss. And according to this"—she rapped a knuckle on the notebook—"that someone is you."

Bex gripped the counter as the floor tilted beneath her. The sounds of the shop became muted, and her jaw went slack. "I'm…I'm sorry…what?"

The woman—the woman claiming to be Talera, her Talera, the character she'd written—was breathing heavily, her chest rising and falling. The man was biting his thumb, the other hand on his hip as he looked on. Bex rubbed at her throat, which was suddenly dry.

A bored-looking teen, oblivious to the tension between

the three of them, strode up to the counter. "You're out of the new Arthur Huxby's book in the display."

Bex gave her head a small shake. "We have more in the back, if you just head there. Peter can help you."

The kid rolled his eyes and stomped off.

Light-headed, Bex looked back at Talera and the man. "Is this some kind of joke?" She still had one hand braced on the counter, the other white-knuckling the notebook—her notebook, the one she'd tossed in her recycling bin at home—and a frantic laugh bubbled up in her throat. "How did you even— Listen, I don't know how you did this, but the joke's over, okay?"

"It's not a joke, Bex," the man said. "We wish it were. But we've come through a portal between our worlds to find you."

Her heart slammed into her ribs. "A portal," she said flatly.

The two of them nodded, not looking away. Another laugh escaped Bex's lips.

"We need your help," Talera said.

The phone rang before she could think of anything to say, and her hands shook slightly as she picked it up. "Thanks for calling Between the Lines Bookstore, can you hold for a moment?" Bex covered the mouthpiece and whispered, "I don't have time for whatever this is."

Talera narrowed her eyes at Bex as she turned her attention back to the phone call, slipping the notebook under the counter and out of their reach. Bex turned away as if by not looking at them, she could make them disappear.

They did not disappear.

Bex hung up the phone, stalked away from the counter, and began reshelving discarded books. They followed.

"You can't ignore us," Talera hissed through an opening in the shelves. Bex thrust a book into the space to block her from view.

The man rounded the shelf into her aisle. "You don't understand—lives are at stake," he whispered urgently.

This has to be anxiety-induced delirium. Bex's hands trembled as she turned down another aisle. *Oh god, am I having a nervous breakdown right now?* She collided with a display table and sucked air through her teeth. Hip smarting and eyes stinging, Bex steered herself toward the break room.

Unfortunately, the EMPLOYEES ONLY sign didn't deter them.

The man cleared his throat, and Bex had to crane her neck to look him in the eye, as he was standing entirely too close. "We understand that this sounds…impossible." He lowered his voice. "Trust me, it seems just as impossible to us. But our situation is very real."

Bex pointed an accusatory finger. "Stop it. How did you get my notebook?" A headache was building behind her eyes.

"When you stopped writing my story, the notebook was dropped into the Library of Manuscripts in the Abandoned Realm, as was I," Talera said.

"That's impossible. I threw it away."

Talera's nostrils flared. "You what?"

"Easy," the man said, shifting in front of Talera as she made a move toward Bex. "Let's just take a breath here. We're all rational people, and even though this is a very peculiar predicament we find ourselves in, I am sure we can figure it out." He narrowed his eyes, looking closely at Bex again. "You threw away your notebook at home?"

"Yes," Bex said. In her mind's eye, she could see the full recycling bin in her front room that she'd been meaning to empty out for days.

The man clapped his hands together. "Well, there you go. Your notebook must still be there since our copy came from the Library of Manuscripts. So if you could just verify that you do indeed still have it, thereby proving our story is true, we can move on to other matters." Bex scoffed and he raised an eyebrow. "Unless you have another idea?"

There was no way this was real. "Fine," Bex growled, eager to wipe that smug expression from fake Talera's face.

"Lead the way," Talera said.

Bex barked out a laugh. "What, *now*?"

"As we said, lives are at stake." Talera's stare was deadly.

Bex raised a shoulder, feigning nonchalance. "Well, I'm here for another hour, so if you'd rather, you can just end this little prank now and save yourself the time."

Talera opened her mouth, but Guy said quickly, "We'll wait. Thank you."

Bex glared at them for the remainder of her shift as they roamed the store. She kept stealing glances at the notebook, assuring herself that it was indeed hers. Finally, her shift was over, and they followed her home in tense silence. She was almost impressed by their dedication to seeing the prank through. Almost.

"Let's get this over with," Bex said as she impatiently slipped the key into the lock. "Wait here." She didn't bother to look at them as she strode inside. "As I said, I don't know who put you up to this, but this is—"

Her reprimand died in her throat as she upended the recycling bin, and the walls seemed to be closing in on her.

The notebook thumped onto the floor.

"That—this isn't possible," she stammered, fumbling to pull the black notebook from the pile of scattered trash. Heart pounding, she reached into her bag and pulled out the other notebook. They were identical, down to the dried coffee stain, bent pages, and scratched-out phrases. "Impossible. This is impossible," she repeated, running a hand through her hair. Time seemed to stretch as she compared the two notebooks, and her brain tried desperately to process what was happening. Finally, eyes wide, she looked at Talera and the man. "You're telling me that…that you're…that I…?"

Talera merely nodded, a muscle twitching in her cheek.

Bex sagged against the wall. The two walked slowly into the apartment, leaving the door slightly ajar.

"It's a bit overwhelming at the beginning," the man said gently.

Bex blinked rapidly. "So if I…if she's Talera, who—"

"Don't worry, someone else wrote me." He gave a crooked smile. "I'm Guy."

Bex swallowed, her knees suddenly weak, and she pushed off the wall and headed toward the couch. "I think I need to sit down."

A knock sounded, and the door eased open a few more inches. "B? Did you know your door is open?"

Relief flooded Bex. "Owen." She returned to the door and opened it farther. "What are you doing here?"

"Hey." He was out of breath, and his voice was edged with nervousness. "Sorry I didn't call, but I have to talk to you—"

Just then, he spotted Talera and Guy behind her. "Oh." He paused, his expression closing slightly as color rose in his cheeks. "I didn't realize you had people over, I should've—"

Bex grabbed his wrist and pulled him into the apartment, closing the door with her heel.

Owen raised a hand to Talera and Guy, a polite but confused smile on his face. "Hey. I'm Owen. Sorry to barge in." He rubbed his palms on his jeans and looked at Bex, his brows pinching tighter as he scanned her face. "What's going on? Are you all right?"

He was waiting for an explanation, an introduction, a joke, anything to clue him into what was going on.

Bex chewed her bottom lip. "They have my same notebook."

Owen quirked an eyebrow, glancing at Talera and Guy. "Okay…"

Bex's fingers trembled as she gripped the two manuscripts. "No, Owen, they have my *same* notebook." She thrust them into his hands, unsure how else to explain, afraid to say the words aloud: *I wrote her, and now she's real.* Her chest threatened to burst from the excitement and horror those words evoked.

I wrote her, and now she's real.

Owen looked at the notebooks in his hands, brows furrowed. "This is your book."

Bex nodded.

"And there's two of them," he confirmed, confusion seeping into his expression.

Talera sighed heavily. "I'm Talera."

Owen paused. "Okay, so she's who you got your character's name from?"

Silence.

"Not exactly."

"All right…"

"I've possibly lost my mind, but there's a chance that she…is…my character."

Owen looked at her blankly. "I'm sorry, what?"

Guy stepped forward. "Bex was writing Talera's story, and when she quit—"

Owen jerked his head toward Bex. "Hold on, you quit

writing?"

"So not the point," Bex said, gesturing frantically to Talera and Guy.

"Er, yes, so when she quit, Talera was sent to the Abandoned Realm, which is a world parallel to this one. It's where all discarded fictional characters end up. The boundary between our worlds has weakened, which allowed someone to make a portal." Guy and Talera exchanged a quick look. "We came to find Bex to figure out how Talera can reverse the magic and seal the boundary."

"Ideally before contamination destroys both our worlds." Talera's teeth flashed as she sneered.

Bex was definitely losing her mind.

A ringing filled her ears. Sweat slicked her palms, and she shook them out. "Is it hot in here?" Her voice sounded far away, and she plucked at the collar of her shirt.

"Contamination?" Owen looked between Talera and Guy.

Bex paced, eyeing the notebooks in Owen's hands. "Am I hallucinating right now? Do I have some sort of tumor in my brain? Those can cause hallucinations, right?"

"I think it's highly unlikely that we are both hallucinating this exact scenario," Owen said.

"And this isn't you pulling some joke?" Bex whirled on

him. "Is this some elaborate prank to convince me to keep writing?"

Owen glared at her. "You think I could come up with this?" He waved the notebooks under her nose. "Plus you never let me read any of it, B."

Bex pressed the heel of her palm against her forehead.

"As enjoyable as it is for me to watch your reality shatter," Talera said loudly, "we unfortunately don't have much time."

"The contamination from the boundary weakening puts us all in danger," Guy said, answering Owen's question. "Anytime someone in your world stops writing a story, the character is banished to the Abandoned Realm. But the boundary between our worlds is deteriorating, so they're essentially leaking into each other. That cross contamination causes characters to rot from the inside, and their skin turns translucent…and judging by the looks on your faces, I'd say the results on this side are the same?"

"The Fading," Bex and Owen said in union.

Guy let out a low whistle. "Damn, that's a cool name. Wish I'd come up with that one." Talera scowled at him, and he held his hands up. "Not important, you're right. Bottom line is, now that the portal is open, the annihilation from the contamination will be absolute."

No one spoke for several moments. Bex rubbed her chest, her heart beating feverishly.

"So close the portal," Owen finally said, sounding angry.

Guy cleared his throat. "We were hoping Bex could help us with that."

She let out a strangled noise that might've been a laugh. All eyes turned to her. Her face grew hot, and she bit the inside of her cheek hard. "What?" The rapid fluttering in her chest sped up even more when no one contradicted Guy. "Why would I know how to do that?"

"Surely you know about magical portals? And how to reverse the magic?" Guy said.

Bex choked on her laughter. "No, I don't know anything about magical portals! None of this is real—"

Bex was suddenly slammed up against the wall, her head banging into it sharply. Talera's fingers dug into her throat, cutting off her air as Bex pawed at the forearm pressed into her collarbone. It had happened so fast that Owen and Guy hadn't been able to react other than to cry out in alarm.

Talera's violet eyes bore into Bex's. "I found out my entire existence is a lie. My world, my family, everything I care about—gone." She tightened her grip, the pressure causing Bex's eyes to widen.

"Talera." Guy's voice was strained.

Bex tried to swallow. Talera didn't move as she said with deadly calm, "You don't get to refuse. Villains and monsters are now running rampant in your city. Every moment you waste means more people will die. You did this to me, and you will do something about it."

Movement caught Bex's eye, and she croaked out, "Owen, don't—"

But it was too late. Keeping Bex pinned with her forearm, Talera shot out her other hand to grip Owen's wrist as he lunged. Bex's lungs burned as she gulped down air. Talera twisted Owen's arm sharply, halting his attack, and Owen swore, bending and arching to try to accommodate the unnatural way his arm was being rotated.

"Oi, Talera!" Guy waved his arms rapidly. "What are you gonna do, eh? Kill them all? Bloody hell, let them go. Everyone just take a breath!"

With a snarl, Talera released them and began to pace with clenched fists. Bex held her throat as she watched Talera move like a caged animal. Owen rubbed at his wrist, ever so slightly angling his body between her and the seething elf.

"Fighting and blaming each other will get us nowhere."

Guy blew out a breath. “But Talera’s right—the longer we take to solve this, the more lives are at risk. I highly doubt Rehnir and the others are playing nice.”

Bex crossed her arms tightly, chewing her bottom lip. She shuffled, a weight settling on her chest and shoulders.

Unable to look at Talera, she said, “Who’s Rehnir?”

CHAPTER NINETEEN

I'LL BE YOUR MONSTER

THE SHARP PULL OF Fear had lured Rehnir to the alleyway where he now watched a vampire drain the life from a middle-aged woman. He leaned casually against a dumpster, greedily observing the debauchery while he lit a cigar. The small cigar shop was one of the first places he'd stopped after coming through the portal. The Fear was so much stronger here on this side, the pull almost unbearable; it reminded him of the frenzied years just after his abilities had awoken. The uncontrollable urges to feed, the intoxicating thrill of euphoria that begged to be claimed again and again. The pungent taste and smell of cigars was how he'd controlled those desires back then.

Rehnir took a deep inhale, letting the smoke fill his mouth before exhaling slowly. He flicked the cigar gently with his thumb, and a bit of ash crumbled to the ground. The buzzing in his head began to crescendo as he tethered himself to the frequency of the dying woman. With another drag from his cigar, he siphoned her Fear with a lover's slow touch, enjoying the sensation.

The vampire drained the last mouthful of blood and raised his head. Rehnir frowned, but not at the sight of the blood covering his chin or the deadly fangs. He could see through the vampire's skin. They held one another's gaze.

Rehnir inwardly cursed. In his frenzy of feeding, he'd forgotten all about the contamination. Of course it was happening on this side of the portal as well. He turned on his heel, stalking toward the street as he inspected his hands. Yes, he could sense it now, the strange weakness he'd attributed to his hunger to feed or perhaps a shift in his powers in this world. His eyes roved over the people on the streets, all of them moving through their days, all unaware of the monster walking amongst them. His head mostly clear, the edge of his hunger dulled for the moment, Rehnir debated where to go next. He walked for a while, taking small pulls of Fear off of those he passed, his cigar long gone.

He'd just crossed the street and entered a large crowd of pedestrians when a sharp pang of need sliced through his stomach. The smell of Fear crawled up his nostrils and into his brain just as his focus landed on a man with a young boy.

A father and his son, judging by their resemblance. Rehnir took in the man's clenched jaw, the tight grip of his fingers around the boy's upper arm. The boy's barely perceptible flinch as his father whispered something through gritted teeth.

The potency of the Fear rolling off the boy…

Rehnir's vision tunneled, and suddenly he was no longer standing on the street. His mind was back in a cramped cabin room. His face still stung from the blow, and his bones ached in anticipation of the next, fear and terror clawing at his senses. He heard his own broken whimper as he begged for unconsciousness to take him.

A sickly sweet smell filled the room.

The blow didn't come.

Strength bloomed in his body, banishing the aches and pains. The room righted itself, and his hands lifted of their own accord, his mind reaching out—

Blood pooled at his feet, and his father's lifeless body hit the floor with a sickening fleshy smack.

A whip lashed Rehnir back to the present as his powers extended, tethering to the man gripping his son. Confusion filled the man's face, and his eyes darted around, trying to find the source of the danger he sensed.

Rehnir's whole body thrummed with rage and need,

and he was at the man's side in an instant. Blue light crackled in his palms as he wrenched the man's hand off the boy. There was a roaring in his ears, blocking out the angry words the man began to yell.

"Do not lay a finger on him again." Rehnir's voice was deadly cold. The man sneered, but something like shame and panic flooded his eyes. He pulled away from Rehnir but didn't touch the boy again, just called for him to follow.

The boy looked stricken, head swiveling between his father and Rehnir. "Th-thank you," he said before darting off after his father. The whispered words pierced something behind Rehnir's breastbone.

He didn't release the tether between his mind and the retreating father's. A soft, sinister laugh brushed against his skull.

You still think you can redeem yourself?

I know what you are.

You know how this story ends.

That boy will go on to become a monster

just

like

you—

Rehnir pressed his tongue against the backs of his teeth, his body quaking, begging to give in to the pull of the

Fear. His fingers twitched, wishing for a cigar to hold.

It's better this way.

You're doing him a favor, really.

Nostrils flaring, he inhaled deeply, sucking the intoxicating tang into himself. *I can save him from this fate, this fate of becoming a monster. I'll be his monster...*

The darkness crooned gently as if it too knew it was a lie.

"Don't thank me just yet," Rehnir whispered.

And pulled on the tether.

Twenty paces ahead, the man fell to his knees, cupping his head. A scream of pure terror ripped from him. Rehnir was moving, unable to stay away. The boy stumbled back, eyes wide, and the crowd began to panic. As he neared, he could see the blood pouring from the man's nose, splashing onto the ground. Rehnir held his arms out, his veins pulsing dark against his pale skin. Magic poured from him, snaking through the streets with a life of its own, destroying everything in its path. The darkness expanded in his chest in a rush that bordered on painful.

Smoke and screams and the bite of blood filled the air. He shackled the minds of the crowd to him, siphoning their essences. His own mind was overrun with their dread and terror, and he staggered under the deluge of images that threatened to swallow him whole.

Rehnir flung his hands wide, the power demanding a release, refusing to be contained even as he tried to rein it in.

His eyes fell on the boy, tangled on the ground as he tried to scramble away. Rehnir stalked toward him as everyone fled in confusion. The boy's mouth hung open, paralyzed with fear, and Rehnir crouched down beside him. The boy's gaze flickered to his father.

Rehnir cocked his head, smiling. "You don't need to fear him anymore." The boy just stared at him, chest heaving. "It's better this way." The words fell easily from his lips, but the voice didn't feel like his own.

A flash of dread crossed the boy's face just as Rehnir ripped into his mind.

The boy was dead before Rehnir whispered, "I'll be the monster."

CHAPTER TWENTY

ALPHA AND THETA

BEX SAT WITH HER legs tucked up to her chest, squeezing her knees together painfully. "Brain waves," she repeated hollowly, looking between Guy and Talera. Next to her on the couch, Owen had gone very still as the other two explained to them how Rehnir's power functioned.

Guy nodded.

Bex's whole body flushed hot. Her chest was painfully tight.

"Shit."

"Yes, our thoughts exactly," Guy said.

"No, not just that. It's just—shit." Bex bit the inside of her lip so hard she tasted blood. She couldn't force herself to look at Owen, knowing that if she saw her own fears confirmed on his face, she'd fall apart.

The air grew tense.

"What is it?" Guy's eyes flicked between them.

"I think…it's possible that Rehnir was able to make the portal because of Talera," Bex said.

"What?" Talera looked murderous.

Bex pressed her hands into her knees to keep them from shaking. "I…I did all this research when I was writing about your magic. You know, just so I could explain it right and make sure I knew how it worked." Her mouth was dry, and she swallowed. "Faelyn is basically accessed in a flow state, which happens during deep meditation or when someone is in a creative zone. So it's either replenished by sleep or by dropping into that sort of deep meditation, twilight consciousness. It's the alpha wavelength that does that."

Talera made an impatient motion with her hand. "Yes, and?"

Bex finally dared to glance at Owen. The expression on his face told her that he did in fact remember the copious notes she'd taken and her long-winded musings several months ago.

"Rehnir's powers come from the theta wavelength." Bex's heart twisted sharply as understanding dawned on Guy's face. "Theta and alpha wavelengths border each other and can combine their oscillations in certain situations. So it seems that when Rehnir was feeding"—Bex wet her lips—

"You two fight like an old married couple," Owen said.

Guy snorted, and Talera glared at him. "You're not my type," he said.

"And what type am I? One who knows her own mind? Elven?"

"A woman," Guy said coolly, arching a brow as he crossed his arms.

Talera sniffed and turned sharply toward Bex. "Well? We don't have all day."

ᛞᚨᚦ

They were all situated in the kitchen, notebook on the table, pen in Bex's hand. Guy sat on her right, Owen to her left, while Talera loomed over her shoulder. Bex cleared her throat. "So how does this work?"

"*If* this works," Guy said, ignoring Talera's huff. He pursed his lips, studying the notebook. "Why don't you pick up where you left off. If nothing happens, you can start the story fresh from the beginning."

Bex nodded, biting her lip. She stared down at the pages, at the final lines she'd written and crossed out. She read them over, trying to unlock her inspiration.

At an enraged howl, she glanced over her shoulder. One of the men, her dagger still lodged his chest, was dragging himself along the ground. He raised himself enough to cock his arm back.

As the wicked-looking metal star sank its jagged points into her calf

The air turned stale and claustrophobic, and Bex stood abruptly, knocking her chair into Talera's shin.

"Sorry, I just…I can't write with you all watching."

She retreated to her room, and some of the tension between her shoulders eased. Leaving the door ajar, she slumped onto the bed. She tapped the pen on the page a few times and began. She stumbled through several paragraphs, wincing at the clumsy way the words fell onto the page.

See, she wanted to shout at them, *this is why I stopped. It always goes like this. I have an idea, and then I have no clue where to go with it and it just all falls apart.* Everything seemed pointless, contrived and cringe-inducing. There was too much going on in the plot, but nothing that mattered. Her fingers itched to throw the notebook in the trash again.

For the better part of an hour, she wrote, peering into the other room every few sentences to see if Talera had magically returned to her world. But she was still very much there and very much annoyed.

"Shouldn't something be happening by now?" Talera snapped at Guy.

Guy bit the tip of his thumb, then called to Bex, "Try starting over from scratch."

Bex obliged by flipping several pages to make the delineation clear and began the story anew. With a measly page written, she looked up. "Feel anything?"

Talera groaned. "No."

Bex couldn't sit still anymore. She didn't want to think about her writing or what it meant that Talera was still here. When she strode into other the room, Talera and Owen were sitting on opposite ends of the couch, Guy still at the table. Owen looked up from his phone, his lips pressed tightly together and a line between his brows. He caught Bex's questioning look and gave a single shake of his head. *Later*, it seemed to convey.

Oh god, it was probably Heidi. Bex had nearly forgotten that anyone outside of this room existed. She felt so disconnected from the regular world. But if this was all truly happening…

She turned to Talera. "What happens to everyone else? From the story, I mean. Where's your mom or those men you were fighting? Are they all in the Realm as well?"

Talera didn't respond, but a muscle twitched in her

cheek as she glared at the worn carpet. Bex picked at her nails, pain in the back of her throat as she inwardly cursed herself for bringing up Talera's mom.

"Only protagonists are sent to the Realm, as far as we know," Guy said. "Just the heroes, no one else."

"Rehnir sounds like a villain," Owen said.

"Oh, he absolutely is," Guy said.

Owen frowned. "But you just said it's only the heroes who get sent to the Realm."

Guy spread his hands. "Well, yes, they're all heroes at the start. But the Abandoned Realm does something to even the best people. It sometimes breaks them and twists them into something ugly and cruel, or it destroys their will to live so utterly that they may as well be dead. It's actually rather poetically tragic. People always think they're the good guys in their stories, that the world revolves around them and all their actions are justified. But circumstance and choice can still shape them into villains."

The words skittered over Bex's skin. "And other villains have come through the portal too?"

Guy met her gaze. "Yes. And most are here with the sole intent of rectification."

"Rectification," Bex repeated.

"To make things right," Talera said.

"I know what rectification means," Bex snapped.

Guy cut in quickly, "They want to exact revenge on the world that sentenced them to the Realm. They think it'll even the score."

"But we didn't mean to! They were all just supposed to be stories!"

"Unfortunately, intent is irrelevant." Guy's face was somber.

"We could argue about this for hours." Talera ran a hand over her face, and Bex noted the dark circles that had appeared under her eyes. "Even if we manage to stay clear of the hoard of villains, the contamination will wipe us all out eventually." She looked at Bex. "You might not have intended any of this, but it's what's happening. This isn't just some story. This is real."

Owen blinked, sitting up straighter. "But stories come from somewhere." They all looked at him as he scooted to the edge of the couch. "Think about it. All stories start somewhere and have some kernel of truth to them. B, how many books have we read where there are portals and witches and vampires in the normal world? If all of this is real, the Realm, the boundary…" He licked his lips. "Maybe something like this has happened before. Maybe there's someone else who can help us."

CHAPTER TWENTY-ONE

GENIUS AND INSANITY

"THAT'S CALLED A LAPTOP computer," Guy whispered loudly to Talera. "It's an electronic device that functions like a book or an archive or—okay, you get it."

Talera fixed him with a glare, and Guy hunched his shoulders to his ears.

The corner of Owen's mouth twitched as he cleared his throat. "Right, so we're looking for anything about portals, multidimensional travel, alternate realms…" A light tapping filled the apartment. Owen had disappeared for a few minutes to retrieve his laptop from his car, and Bex had grabbed hers from the bedroom.

Feeling useless, Talera let her eyes wander over the bookshelves. The bitter truth was slowly sinking in. She couldn't go home. Guy had warned her, but that hadn't stopped her from holding on to her desperate hope. There was a heavy hollowness in her chest. Grief threatened to cave in on her again.

She waved her hand at the books. "Is there anything useful in any of these?" A dull burning sensation simmered through her body, reminding her that she was not meant for this world.

Bex looked up, lips pursed. "Actually, there might be. Guy, do you know how to work this?" She gestured to the laptop.

Guy nodded emphatically, his fingers practically twitching as Bex vacated the chair for him and walked over to Talera. After a few moments of scanning the shelves, Bex began pulling out books and stacking them in Talera's arms.

"I have a lot more portal magic books than I realized," she said.

"That's because you know those are the best stories," Owen agreed in a singsong voice.

Bex shoved a few more books into the crook of her own arm. "This should be a good starting place." She motioned for Talera to follow her to the couch and began spreading the books out on the small coffee table.

As the minutes slipped by, Talera was oddly reminded of the Library of Manuscripts, only these were stories that had been deemed worthy. The light coming in from the windows slowly dimmed, the shadows elongating.

Owen let out a small gasp.

"What is it?" Bex asked.

Owen held up a finger, his eyes rapidly moving back and forth over the screen. Finally he leaned back in his chair and looked up.

"So this guy Michael Moorcock is big in the science fiction and fantasy arena. He was the first to coin the term *multiverse*. But in this article, he talks about how the sci-fi and fantasy community was unknowingly developing theories about the multiverse at the same time scientists were discovering evidence to support those theories. Listen to this:

"'Sometimes what happens is that you are imagining these ideas in the context of fiction while the physicists and mathematicians are imagining them in terms of science. I suspect it is the romantic imagination working, as it often does, perfectly efficient in both the arts and the sciences.'"

Owen looked at them, eyes bright. "He's basically saying that stories come from some type of universal truth."

"That still doesn't tell us how to find the people who know the truth," Talera said.

"This might be something," Guy said, rubbing his chin. "I found a site that has what it calls fan fiction? There's this

Owen snagged another mug and poured in a dark liquid from the pot on the counter. Talera took it, warming her hands on the porcelain as she cleared her throat. "Thank you."

Bex squirmed in her seat, and Talera knew she was searching for something to say. Bex's discomfort shouldn't have pleased her, but it did.

At a low moan, the three of them turned to see Guy rising, arms stretched overhead. A bit of spit still trailed down his chin.

"You may want to wipe your mouth," Talera said with a smirk.

Guy's hand went to his face, and he chuckled. "Well, that's not a great impression."

Talera remained still, the heat against her palms anchoring her to the present as the nightmare gradually released her body. Owen filled another mug and passed it to Guy as he joined them. Guy stared down at it, scratching at the back of his head. "You know…it's the strangest thing, but in the Abandoned Realm, we…don't really eat or drink."

"What?" Bex and Owen asked in unison.

"I mean, logically I know my body needs food to survive, but there…" He shrugged, brought the cup to his lips, and took a hesitant sip. His eyes grew wide. "Oh my. This is just plain coffee?"

"Uh-huh." Owen raised an eyebrow at him. "So you're saying you've…never had anything real to eat or drink?"

"Well, to be fair, even if he had, it wouldn't have been real," Talera interjected as Guy took another long sip of the coffee.

A soft sigh escaped him before he continued. "See, most people don't think about writing essential but normal and mundane things like eating, drinking, menstruating, flatulence, defecating, and the like." Guy shrugged as Owen snorted into his mug. "So even though in theory we all do those things, we're not compelled to in the Abandoned Realm. I suppose we could, it's just not compulsory."

Seeming horrified, Owen looked at Bex, who shrugged sheepishly. "I guess it just never crossed my mind to write those things in? Well, except for cramps!" She pointed triumphantly at Talera.

"Yes, thanks for that. So glad that bodily function made it into my reality." Talera finally raised her mug to her lips. The coffee was dark and rich with hints of hazelnuts and a spice she didn't recognize. It warmed her down to her belly. She brought her fingers to her lips, savoring the taste. When a smile tugged at the corner of her mouth, Bex looked so day…I can't remember exactly how the conversation went, but we found this site talking about portals to other worlds and them being tied somehow to Huxby's sanity or creative genius? But we couldn't figure out exactly how." Bex was squirming a little. Talera resisted the urge to sneer at her inability to lie.

"You kids don't know?" Grant's eyebrows shot up as he looked at them, their faces blank as they shook their heads. "Oh my—what planet are you from?"

A strangled laugh came from Guy as Bex shuffled her feet. Grant playfully nudged Bex.

"I guess I have only myself to blame—I'm ashamed to have failed at my fatherly duty to pass on all my nerd knowledge."

Talera watched as Owen grinned and folded his arms.

"So, back before Arthur Huxby was *the* Arthur Huxby, he was just a kid living in England somewhere." Grant's whole face was alight as he spoke. "After a trip to London, his parents admitted him to a psych ward when he started repeatedly—and publicly—claiming to have traveled through a portal to another world."

The air in the apartment was suddenly charged. Talera sat up a little straighter.

"He was in the psych ward for several months, if my

memory is correct, and was super adamant that he wasn't crazy." Grant shrugged. "But eventually he must have agreed it was some type of psychotic breakdown, because he went through treatment."

Bex had gone pale. "The quote we found was someone talking about how geniuses are usually insane."

Grant's brow furrowed. "Well, that's in poor taste. Unfortunately, there's always been stigma around mental health issues. I don't think it's something to be ashamed of—most everyone deals with them in some way. But I do agree that it's partly why Huxby's such a brilliant writer. He's not constrained by our limited view of reality."

"How come we couldn't find any of that online?" Owen asked.

Grant rubbed his chin. "You know, I think I remember hearing that Arthur is actually his middle name. Back when he was trying to get his first book published, there was a lot of backlash and ridicule from critics who weaponized his mental illness and treatment. He had to hire a PR rep to help bury the story so that people would stop talking about it and he could just get on with his writing career." Grant shrugged again. "As I said, the whole thing happened years before he was trying to get published."

Talera blinked, trying to keep up with all the unfamiliar

terms.

"That's terrible," Bex said.

"It's a shame, really. I'd have thought that after so much time, people would have gotten over trying to discredit those who are open about their mental health." He sighed and waved a hand. "Anyway, I could talk about Huxby for hours, but I've got to go. I'm meeting an old friend for breakfast before work." When they all continued to stare at him in stunned silence, he added, "Does that answer your question?"

Owen gave Bex a small nudge. "Oh—uh—yes. Yes, it does. Thanks, Dad. For the book, too." She held it up. "That was really thoughtful."

"You're welcome, sweetheart. I'll see you at StoryCon." Grant pressed a kiss to the top of Bex's head and uttered a few more goodbyes, but Talera wasn't listening. Her mind was reeling.

Someone else had used a portal. Used a portal and gone to another world.

Bex shut the door with a click. Slowly she turned to face them, her eyes wide.

Talera planted her feet in a wide stance and jabbed a finger at her. "You're taking us to that convention."

CHAPTER TWENTY-TWO

DUKE DECKER

"IT'S NOT THE WORST idea I've ever heard," Owen mused.

Bex glared at him, and he spread his hands on the table. Her dad had left about fifteen minutes ago, and they'd all been arguing since then. "Look, everyone there will be dressed up, so they'll fit right in."

Bex rolled her eyes. "And we're supposed to do what, exactly? Walk up to one of the most popular fantasy authors of all time and say, hey there, Professor Huxby, big fans. Listen, remember that one time you said you found a portal to another world and no one believed you, most definitely leaving you traumatized? Cool, we just were wondering if you know how to close a portal like that?"

Owen smirked over his mug. "I'd say it more eloquently than that, but yeah, something along those lines."

"But tickets have been sold out for weeks!" Bex

countered.

"I don't understand why you still think this is up for debate," Talera said. "We're going. End of story."

Bex flinched at the words and the double meaning they held. Guilt coiled in her gut. *What else are you going to do, Bex? This is all your fault. Don't be such a coward.* She swallowed hard. "Okay. You're right. We'll…we'll come up with something."

"Are there any more Between the Lines T-shirts?" Owen asked.

"I think so. Why?"

"Let's snag a couple of those for the convention." Owen jerked a thumb at Guy and Talera. "We'll pretend they're employees helping to run the booth ."

"Yeah, I guess that could work." She rubbed at the tension in her forehead when something occurred to her. "It's Thursday," she said.

"Yes." Owen raised an eyebrow.

"So don't you have lunch with Heidi today?" Usually Heidi had to work late at the firm on Thursdays, so they had a standing lunch date.

Owen brushed something off the table, leaning back in his chair. "Uh, no, not today." From the bag at his feet, he pulled out some folded clothes. He slid them over to Guy.

"Thought you may want a change of clothes so you can blend in a bit more."

Guy grinned as he held the clothes up. "I would like a change of clothes!" He cocked his head, reading the print on the baggy shirt. "Weezer. Sounds fantastic. Thank you!"

Bex's eyes slid to Talera. "That's not a bad idea…"

Talera straightened and arched an eyebrow. "I'm not changing."

ᛞᚨᚦ

With the arrival of autumn, it was a cool, pleasant temperature outside as they made their way to the bookstore. Bex shoved her hands into her jacket pockets. The fresh air was helping to dispel some of the anxiety lodged tightly in her chest.

Talera walked a stride or two ahead of Bex with confidence and purpose. Bex self-consciously tightened her ponytail and brushed a few stray hairs away from her face, eyeing Talera's frosty blond hair. Talera carried herself in a way that made any imperfections fade away, like a trick of the light.

Owen was talking to Guy ahead of them with his usual gentle ease. Guy blended in much better than Talera did. His change of clothes and nonchalant conversation with Owen in no way betrayed that he was from another world.

They crossed a smaller street, weaving around a few people walking in the opposite direction. Bex cringed inwardly at the awkward silence, not sure what to say to start a conversation with the very real figment of her imagination. Just then, someone slammed into her shoulder hard, sending her stumbling to the side, trying to regain her balance.

"Hey!" she exclaimed, turning back to give the perpetrator a scathing look.

She quickly swallowed her retort as she saw the man turn, his hand resting on a holstered gun. He looked at her from under the brim of a dark cowboy hat, his face weathered and his eyes shadowed. Guy let out a soft moan, and Bex felt Talera step closer to her.

The cowboy's mouth twisted into a snarl, and he pushed his jaw out, gesturing to Guy. "Well, I'll be damned. Didn't think I'd see you in these parts." His words were so comically cliché that Bex would have laughed if not for the blood splattered on his clothes. A lot of blood. Bile rose in her throat.

"Duke," Guy said, his voice strained.

A villain from the Abandoned Realm.

Former hero turned villain, Bex corrected herself as

Talera took a step toward him, rolling her shoulders back to move her cloak out of the way.

"Seems like you're already stirring up trouble on this side." Talera gestured to his soiled clothes. Her voice was casual, but her stance was anything but.

Duke sneered at her. "Wasn't nothin' they didn't have coming."

"How is killing and terrorizing innocent people going to make things better?" Guy asked.

The cowboy stepped close to Guy, looking down at him menacingly. "I died a long time ago." He spat, and Bex saw Owen's look of disgust out of the corner of her eye. "These sons of bitches here are the reason. So I reckon it's an eye for an eye—and it feels mighty good. The way I see it"—the contempt was heavy in his voice—"if you're with them, you deserve the same fate as they do."

People passing by stared at the group. Bex glanced hesitantly at Talera, whose eyes burned with barely tempered rage, silently willing her not to do anything stupid.

"I suggest you turn around and go back through that portal before you regret it." Talera's voice was deadly cold.

Duke's hand hovered over his holster, and his lip curled into a snarl. "I'd like to see a little elf bitch like you try to make me."

Talera's fist collided with his jaw, the crack disproportionately loud given the slimness of her body. Duke reeled back, dazed. Talera launched herself into the air with disconcerting speed, her legs scissoring around his neck. She threw her weight backward, hands connecting with the ground, and whipped Duke into a forward flip like a rag doll. Bex's brain stuttered at the smack of his back on the pavement.

"Talera, no!" Bex shrieked.

Talera's breathing was even as she produced a dagger from her boot and pressed the point under his jaw. Owen swore as he pushed a hand through his hair.

Talera's eyes cut to Bex for a moment. "He has *murdered* people, Bex."

"You can't just—" Bex sputtered, gesturing frantically. "This is the real world. You can't just…kill him!"

Talera exhaled sharply through her nose. After several tense seconds, she rolled her eyes and removed the dagger from the cowboy's neck…and proceeded to deliver a decisive blow to the back of his head with the hilt.

"Satisfied?" Talera pulled a small coiled rope out of a pocket inside her cloak and dragged the heavy man a few feet with chilling ease.

"Not exactly the word I would use." Bex pressed a palm

to her forehead, her heart beating erratically as she watched Talera tie the cowboy to a bike rack.

Talera brushed her hands on her thighs. "Right, then, shall we?"

Owen started to laugh, an incredulous sound. "Ho-ly shit!" He said it as three separate words. "Are you kidding me?! That was amazing! You just—and he—you kicked his ass!"

"It's probably a good idea to vacate the area," Guy said, and Bex followed his gaze to the crowd forming across the street, muttering and pointing. Guy said sharply to Talera, "He's not dead, right?"

Talera's shrug was noncommittal.

"Let's get out of here, then, before the cops come." Bex was shaking as she once again took in the amount of blood on the cowboy's clothes. "I'm sure they'll be glad to take him in."

The others agreed, quickly leaving. But Bex stood still, unable to move until she felt Owen's firm grip on her arm and he steered her away.

She'd just witnessed a come-to-life character from her imagination very easily incapacitate a come-to-life villain.

A murderer, Bex thought, *judging by the blood on him.*

Adrenaline still roared in her ears by the time they

reached Between the Lines. Peter had rented a van to transport all the boxes to and from the convention.

"Just…go wait over there and don't do anything," Bex said to Talera and Guy, pointing toward the café. "We'll load all the stuff quickly, and I don't want Peter asking any questions."

Bex followed Owen to the back room, giving a few hellos to customers they passed. She tried to erase the mental image of the cowboy's bloodied face. She pushed the shock and horror to the back corner of her mind. They didn't have time for that right now.

Looking around to make sure no one else was in sight, she quickly snagged two extra Between the Lines shirts and tucked them into an open box. It took her and Owen longer than she would have liked to get the van completely loaded with all the supplies for the booth. As she walked back inside for another trip, her phone buzzed. Bex's stomach flipped when she looked at the number. She ducked off to the side, pressing the phone to her ear.

"Hello?"

"Bex! How are you? This is Stephanie from Lynx Publishing."

Bex clicked the volume down a few notches, casting a glance over her shoulder as she exchanged pleasantries.

"Well, I don't want to take up a lot of your time," Stephanie said. "I just wanted to call and offer you the job."

This should feel exciting, right? This is what I wanted. Bex swallowed, mouth suddenly dry. "Oh wow, thank you."

"We don't need you to start for a few weeks, of course, like we talked about."

Bex chewed on the side of her thumb. "Mm. That's…yeah, that's fine. I still need to give my notice at the bookstore."

"Excellent."

Is it?

Stephanie prattled on, confirming the salary they'd discussed and her exact start date. Bex did some quick mental math. She'd have to give Peter her notice right after StoryCon. She could enjoy the weekend, pass Talera and Guy off to Huxby, and then come Monday, adult reality would start.

They said their goodbyes, and Bex reentered the bookshop.

With cosplayers all over the city, Talera and Guy looked almost normal and, thankfully, bored as they sat in the café. Bex jerked her chin toward the doors. "Come on. Owen's bringing the van around." Peter had suggested they park it at her apartment since it was closer to the convention center and they could avoid some of the traffic tomorrow. Bex was about to follow them onto the sidewalk when Peter called her name.

She turned back as he hurried toward her. "Oh good, you're here."

Bex smiled and tried to look casual.

Peter looked her up and down. "Are you all right?"

She flushed. "Uh, yes, just didn't sleep great."

"Well, make sure you get good sleep tonight. I won't be able to make it over to the convention until the afternoon tomorrow, so it will just be you and Owen in the morning. Can you handle that?"

"Yes, of course. We can definitely handle it." Peter eyed her again, and she tried to rein in her awkwardness. "Any news about Benny?"

"Stable for now." Peter lifted one shoulder.

Bex absently picked at her nail polish.

"Okay," Peter said after a moment. "Well, I'll see you tomorrow, then."

Bex nodded. "Tomorrow."

CHAPTER TWENTY-THREE

FOGGY FEELINGS

EVEN THOUGH TALERA HAD promised to be on her best behavior, Bex still insisted they take a longer route back to the apartment to avoid "the whole cowboy situation." Talera grudgingly agreed with Bex's decision, considering she had no qualms with going back on that particular promise if need be.

Talera pursed her lips, taking stock mentally as they walked. Her automatic instinct to protect her comrades had never felt surprising, but her ferocious need to keep Bex and Owen safe? That was…interesting. Why should she feel compelled to protect these people who hadn't cared about her existence until forced to do so?

She didn't know how to feel about the shift happening inside her. Restless anxiety buzzed just beneath her skin.

She could feel Bex eyeing her, and then she cleared her throat and asked, "How are you feeling?"

The way Bex held herself reminded Talera of a skittish deer.

Talera scoffed. "How am I *feeling*? It's hard to say, really. In a matter of days, I've gone from being torn from my home to seeing a dragon to dodging these ridiculous death traps on wheels." She waved a hand at the busy street beside them. "I can feel my body slowly decaying thanks to the contamination, and we only have one bloody clue as to how to fix the portal. So I dunno, Bex. You're the author here, why don't you tell me how I'm feeling?"

Bex flinched.

Good. She should be the one to feel bad, after all.

"Easy." Owen's voice was an octave lower than normal as Bex blinked rapidly.

Guy cleared his throat. "Let's keep in mind that we're all on the same team here."

Talera huffed out a breath. "Fine."

Rationally she knew that Bex hadn't intentionally made her and then cast her off. Being curt wouldn't do any good, wouldn't send her home or fix any of this. Chiding herself for her attitude, Talera rolled her shoulders, trying to relieve some of the tension she held there.

But by the gods, maybe if Bex spent less time worrying about what other people thought of her, I wouldn't be in this situation.

Her emotions were a knotted mess lodged in her chest. Why did it fall on *her* to help Bex see that?

"What is it you're afraid of?" she said.

Bex whipped her head around. "What?"

"Every manuscript that comes to our world is marked with the author's name, location, and reason that the story was discarded. Yours—mine—listed fear as the reason. So I'm asking, what is it you are afraid of?"

Bex's mouth moved silently for a moment, and then she snorted. "I'm not—it has nothing to do with fear. The system must have malfunctioned or something, because that isn't what's going on."

"What, like fear of failure?" Owen asked. "Fear of not being good enough?"

Bex glared at him.

"What? I'm sorry, but you get in your own way a lot, B." He leaned away from her slightly, hands shoved deep in his pockets, and chuckled. "I've said it to you million times. You don't give yourself enough credit. Just because your mom is evil, her opinion shouldn't shape your opinion of yourself." Owen gave her an apologetic smile

Bex grumbled something unintelligible, looking at her shoes as they walked. Owen and Bex gravitated toward each other. It reminded Talera of how clouds looked sometimes before she realized there was a distance between them that she couldn't see from where she stood: their connection seemingly inevitable but never realized.

Talera turned her face to the sky, taking a cleansing breath. The waning light cast bruise blue over the sidewalk. The evening fog slowly sank from the clouds, bringing with it the smell of salt and ocean spray. Vibrations from passing cars rolled up through her feet. The four of them squeezed together as they walked, elbows brushing as they maneuvered around other people. She tuned out the faint nausea and trepidation over what tomorrow would bring, focusing instead on the noises, tastes, and textures of this strange world.

CHAPTER TWENTY-FOUR

SHOUTS AND SHAME

EVERY HUXBY BOOK BEX owned had been pulled from the shelves, splayed open, and dissected. The laptop had been passed around so all four of them could read various articles. Scrap paper littered the kitchen table with hastily written and half-formed plans. Hours had passed, and Bex had swapped her work clothes for a baggy threadbare T-shirt and sweats. She rubbed her heel against her ankle.

Bex scanned the computer screen again. On it was a short news article about a wealthy family from England whose son had spent six months in in-patient facilities for "delusions." She tapped the keyboard lightly, turning all the details over in her mind. Had Huxby actually thought he was crazy, or had he finally just said what he needed to say to get out? Had his portal led to another realm entirely? Why had it opened?

"Huxby definitely has a theme that spans all his magic

systems." Owen sat opposite her on the couch, tapping her old copy of *The Orithian Sword* on his lap. "Belief is important for things to work. And remember that whole chapter in *The Herald's Return* where Dar is struggling to control his powers? He keeps emphasizing that it's the lack of belief that's holding him back and causing the incantations not to work."

"That goes hand in hand with Branson's theories," Guy said. "He thinks that's why the boundary weakened in the first place."

"Is anyone else seeing anything about traveling through portals?" Talera stood up from the table and began to pace again. "This one"—she turned the book over to look at the dragon on the front—"keeps mentioning a ritual that has to happen to open and close one. Do you think Rehnir had to do something like that?"

Guy shrugged. "Don't know. I'm not sure if anyone close enough to see him make it survived. What sort of ritual?"

Talera scanned the pages. "An incantation and a hand gesture that ends with a flick of the wrist? Sounds like the fingers have to be placed just so, but I can't figure out—"

"Like this." Bex held up her hand, palm out. Her ring finger bent down while she barely curled her index finger and thumb, as if holding an invisible ball between them, leaving her middle finger and pinky extended. Then she gave a quick flick of her wrist.

Talera blinked, then glanced down to consult the book. "Yeah, that's it."

Heat bloomed in Bex's cheeks as Owen raised an eyebrow and Guy gawked at her. "That book's one of my favorites." She shrugged, fussing with the pages of her own.

"But is that just made up, or do you think it's actually part of opening a portal?" Owen asked, stretching his legs out and stifling a yawn.

"I don't think we can know that for sure until we ask Huxby." Her stomach fluttered.

"Right. Well, I know you two don't really need to eat, but I'm starving," said Owen. "Pizza?"

Bex nodded, and he pulled out his phone. Bex rubbed a hand over her face and tried to work a kink from her neck. The book Talera had just read from, *The Skeur*, had come out close to a decade after Huxby's stint in the psych ward when he was nineteen.

A book filled with magic and doors to other worlds. It had to be connected.

He has *to be able to help us.*

Owen sat back down on the couch, closer to her now.

"Pizza is on its way. I got Hawaiian with extra pineapple." He glanced sideways as she rolled her eyes, then gave her a soft nudge with his shoulder. "Obviously I got half pepperoni, half sausage. Figured we could blow their minds." He nodded toward Talera and Guy, who'd gone back to pouring over their books.

Bex huffed out a laugh.

"Show me that hand thing again."

Bex flushed and reached out to shove him, but she wasn't quick enough. Laughing, he snatched her hand, blocking her attempt, and damn her, but her stomach fluttered in a way she had no right to feel.

"I'm serious!" Owen said as she shifted to set the laptop down. "I may have to close a portal soon. Come on, B."

"Uh-huh." But Bex held up her hand, arranging her fingers once more.

Owen held his own hand up, his fingers looking more like a misshapen claw. "Wow." He gave a short derisive laugh. "That's not it at all." He grabbed her hand so casually that Bex's breath hitched. "Let's see," Owen said, molding his fingers around hers to create the same shape. A callus on his palm scraped gently across her skin.

Her pulse danced, and she remembered how his body had felt on top of hers in their class the other day.

After a long moment, he slowly pulled his hand away, trying to maintain the shape. "How's that?"

"Well, I wouldn't quit your day job." Bex licked her lips, tucking her hands into her lap.

Owen leaned back against the couch, rocking his knee slowly back and forth, tapping hers as he did. Schooling her features, she clamped down on the flicker of heat his touch elicited.

"I feel like the whole world has turned upside down," he said softly, looking at the ceiling.

Bex's eyes slid to the column of his throat as he swallowed. *You have no idea.*

"A week ago, we thought Benny was just sick with some variation of the flu, and now we know it's really because the boundary between our world and another is deteriorating."

"Yeah, decades of no one being able to explain the Fading suddenly makes a lot more sense." Bex picked at her fingernails as she situated herself in the corner of the couch.

Talera and Guy were conversing in the kitchen, both of them pale with sweat beading their foreheads. The dark circles under Talera's eyes were more pronounced than they had been that morning. Guilt tore at Bex's gut. *Arthur Huxby will know what to do.*

The next twenty minutes passed with the scrape of pages turning and soft conversation. It was surprisingly comfortable. *Well, no,* Bex thought, stealing a peek over at Talera. *Not comfortable. But less hostile*.

Guy stood, gesturing to the bathroom. "I think a shower would feel nice…well, I imagine it would. May I?"

"Of course." Bex grabbed him a towel, then showed him the trick to the hot water tap. As she closed the door to the bathroom, Talera approached her.

"I'm going out for fresh air. I'm not used to being indoors for so long."

"All right. Do you want—" Before she could finish, a knock came at the door.

Talera pulled it open and brushed past the pizza delivery man.

"Hey." Bex gave him an apologetic smile, taking the pizza box from him. "Thanks so much." Owen reached into his wallet, but Bex beat him to it, shoving her bills at the delivery man. "Nope, I got this." She kicked the door closed, eyeing Owen. "It's the least I can do for you in exchange for helping with…all of this."

Owen snorted, taking the box into the kitchen, then noticed her hesitating by the door. "Aren't you hungry?"

Bex tilted her head. "Do you think I should go with

her?"

Owen opened the lid. The smell of pizza filled the room. "I think she is perfectly capable of taking care of herself. Remember the cowboy?"

"That's why I'm wondering if I should go with her," Bex muttered, but she followed him to the kitchen, where they each got a plate and a slice of pizza before returning to the couch.

From behind the bathroom door, Guy began to sing an off-key tune. Owen and Bex looked at each other and smiled, trying not to snicker. As she took her first bite, Bex realized just how hungry she was. She closed her eyes, savoring the taste of the pizza, exhaustion finally seeping into her body. They ate in companionable silence.

StoryCon was tomorrow. They'd meet Arthur Huxby somehow and convince him they needed his help…somehow. Then this wouldn't all be on her shoulders. Someone more capable would sort out the mess she'd caused, and everything would go back to normal. She could return to real life.

She wouldn't make the same mistake again. She'd never start another story so she'd never have to abandon one. Which meant she'd never again banish someone to literal hell because she couldn't damn well do anything right—

Owen's heavy exhale snapped her out of her thoughts.

"I broke up with Heidi." His eyes darted to her face.

"What? Why? What happened?"

Owen brushed some pizza crumbs from his leg. "It just…wasn't working."

Bex blinked rapidly. "But…Heidi's perfect for you." *Perfect for anyone, really.* "She's smart and funny and nice—"

"I mean, on paper, she's great." Owen studied the carpet. "She's just not….I don't know."

A hollow feeling ran through Bex. If Heidi wasn't enough, then what did that say about her?

"I didn't want to keep stringing her along when I knew it wasn't going anywhere. It wasn't fair to her."

Oh shit. Guilt seized her. "When did you break up?"

"Last Saturday."

"Oh." Saturday, after the disastrous grappling class where Bex had made a fool of herself. *Oh my god, this is because of me.* "You should've said—"

"I meant to when I showed up last night. I just got a bit distracted." Owen finally met her gaze. He blew out a breath. "Compared to a magic being real and a portal that's about to dissolve the world, it doesn't matter…but it felt weird that I hadn't told you yet."

Bex swallowed hard, dropping her chin to her chest. "Yeah, everything's pretty messed up right now."

In their silence, the tightness in her chest spread, gripping her.

You did this, you did this, you did this. Talera's words reverberated through her. Now that the room was devoid of chatter and fictional characters, the horrible truth she'd been ignoring reared its head.

"This is all my fault." The whispered confession burned her throat.

She felt Owen shift on the couch, but she kept her eyes averted as the words tumbled out. "You heard what they said. Rehnir was only able to make the portal after…after I sent Talera there." Emotion clogged her voice, and she finally dared to look at him. "People are dead, Owen. It's all my fault, and I don't know how to fix this. I can't fix this."

"Hey, hey." Owen scooted closer and grabbed her hand, his fingers warm against her suddenly cold skin. "Bex."

Tears spilled down her cheeks. Words lodged in her throat. *I'm sorry, this is my fault, I'm sorry I got carried away and made you feel so awkward you broke up with Heidi, I'm sorry, I'm sorry.*

"You didn't do anything wrong. It sounds like it was

only a matter of time before this happened, with or without you. The Fading's been around since before we were even born." He smiled weakly at her, giving her too much credit, too much grace. "There's no way you could've known what stopping your story would do."

"You don't get it, Owen." Her voice came out louder than she meant for it to. She tugged her hand back, curling into herself.

Owen stiffened as she shoved off the couch. "Bex, c'mon, calm down—"

"Don't tell me to calm down," Bex snarled, letting loose the tumult of emotions that had been building in her.

"All I'm saying is that you didn't know what would happen." Owen was on his feet now.

"That doesn't change the fact that I'm responsible for all those dead people and—"

"*You're* not responsible for that, Bex! *Rehnir* is." He was standing so close she had to crane her neck to look at him as he gripped her shoulders. "Why are you always so set on blaming yourself for every little thing—"

"Because it is my fault!" Hot shame flooded her body. "You don't get it! When you mess up, it's like…like breaking up with Heidi, not dooming the whole world."

Owen's jaw tightened, and he lifted his hands from her

to cross his arms. "So it's a mistake to break up with someone I don't love?"

"No one's ever good enough for you, Owen!"

He let out a harsh laugh that washed over her face. "And you're the expert on relationships, now?"

She flinched and her nostrils flared. Owen's expression fell.

"I didn't— That's not what I meant, Bex." He threw his arms out. "I don't even know why we're arguing. I'm just trying to help you feel better." His breath was hot on her face.

"Well, stop. I don't need you to make me feel better," she snapped, crossing her arms as well.

"Yeah, you've made it pretty clear you don't need me, Bex."

The bathroom door slammed open, and they leapt apart.

"That," Guy sighed, a towel around his waist, "was heavenly."

Bex cleared her throat and briskly flicked the tears from her cheeks. "Glad you enjoyed it. There's pizza here, too." She gestured to the kitchen, carefully avoiding Owen's eyes, before grabbing a plate from the cupboard for him. She threw a slice on it and thrust it at Guy, mumbling, "Here you go."

Guy had enough sense not to ask about the awkward tension that was palpable in the air and instead focused intently on the pizza.

"Talera just went out for fresh air, so make sure to save some for her," Bex said, watching as he greedily devoured the slice.

"Bex." Owen moved toward her.

Bex's stomach clenched, and she desperately wanted to be anywhere but here in her too-small living room with their words still hanging in the air. "It's fine, Owen. Don't worry about it." She waved a hand at him, shrugging into her jacket and moving toward the door.

"Bex—"

"I'm just going to go check on Talera, make sure she isn't cracking any skulls."

She forced a smile, eyes burning as she slipped out the door.

CHAPTER TWENTY-FIVE

LONDON FOGS

TALERA SUSPECTED SHE'D FOUND the one quiet spot in this godsforsaken city. The small patch of grass tucked between two streets seemed to be designed for people who had domesticated hounds. It was blessedly empty. Talera exhaled the bottled breath in her lungs. Once. Twice. She rubbed absently at her chest as she sat on the grass, the cool night air kissing her face. She hadn't been alone since they'd come through the portal, and as she sat in solitude, a bit of tension eased from her shoulders.

Her eyes closed, and she focused on a long inhale and exhale through her nose. It was a trick her mother had taught her when she was young, to use when she was feeling overwhelmed or angry.

Breathe in…

Breathe out…

She had hoped it would encourage Talera to turn to

healing instead of fighting, and look how well that had turned out.

But her mother had understood that being able to protect others from evil, being able to mete out justice…those were Talera's ways of healing things.

A lump formed in her throat as the pain of missing her mother—a literal, visceral pain—fractured something inside her.

Breathe in…

Breathe out…

She'd find a way to heal this wound. Heal the tear between the worlds, heal the fury of the Realm. For her mother.

Breathe in…

Breathe out…

Tomorrow I will find a way.

She would make sure the horde of villains was stopped before more innocent people died. She would help close the portal and strengthen the boundary so that she and all the other characters had a shot at living.

Talera returned her focus to her breath and let the state of stillness replenish her Faelyn. It flowed through her body, a cool wave washing over her, filling her up. The smell of the grass mixed with that of the crisp air. Stars once again peeked through the dark sky, so faint against the light from the city but winking there all the same. The ground beneath her became a part of her, the trees offshoots of her limbs, the moon a mirror for the power pooling in her veins. The insects buzzed alongside the vibration of magic in her bones. Joy ballooned in her chest as the familiar magic eased her heart. Her magic was still her own, still answered her call.

Slowly, Talera released her grasp, and the Faelyn sighed back and down, ready and waiting to be summoned.

"Hey."

Talera snapped her eyes open. Bex stood a short distance away, a streetlamp bathing her in a pool of light.

Like some unholy specter.

An illuminated reaper.

Bex rubbed her palms on her legs, hesitating.

Talera lifted a brow, keeping her face cool. "Yes?"

Bex shifted her feet slightly. "I just thought…maybe you'd want some company…or something."

Talera arched her eyebrow even higher and still said nothing.

Bex let out a huff and scowled. "All right, I knew you wouldn't, but I do."

Talera laughed softly and inclined her head…barely. "So sit."

Bex slumped down next to her and stared intently at the grass, idly picking at some small mushrooms. She didn't speak, and Talera found herself content to let the silence cloak them. Crickets chirped and the wind rustled the trees.

Several minutes passed before Talera finally said, "So, do you think that Huxby truly believed he was crazy?"

Bex's eyes were distant. "I hope he didn't."

Talera watched Bex closely, noting the tension in her forehead, her pulse beating in her throat, her eyes, heavy with guilt.

Bex worked her jaw a few times. "I wish I…" She seemed to lose her nerve and started again. "What Guy said about characters in the Realm wanting revenge—do you think more will keep coming through?"

"Maybe. Honestly, I don't know that I blame them. I imagine it changes you, being stuck there for as long as some of them have." Her thoughts turned to the bloodstained cowboy. "I don't condone the bloodshed, but…"

The implication hung in the air between them. Bex's head bobbed. "Thank you." Her words were so soft that Talera might not have heard them without her elven senses.

Talera snorted. "For what?"

"For not…killing me." Bex looked at her intently.

Talera pursed her lips, holding her gaze before giving a

curt nod. "I would be lying if I said I hadn't thought about it." She flexed her hand. "But I realized it wouldn't do any good. I'd prefer to put my energy and skills toward something a little more...productive." Emotion flashed across Bex's face. "What?"

Bex scrunched her brows, shaking her head. "It's just that...that's impressive, is all. You're impressive."

Talera knew from the droop in Bex's shoulders what she wasn't saying. "You don't think you'd do the same?"

Bex brushed her hair from her face, not meeting Talera's eyes. "I'd like to think I would, but..." She let out a long breath. "Honestly, I don't know. Meeting you has made me realize all the things I'm not. All the things I wish I could be."

Talera stayed quiet as Bex sifted through her thoughts. She could see it now, the way Bex had poured into her the abilities she herself lacked. Even when Talera's mother had fundamentally disagreed with the path she was taking, she'd never withheld love or wielded disapproval as a weapon.

The thought pulled at her protective side without her consent. "There's still time."

Bex merely picked at the grass. "We'll find a way to close the portal, and all will go back to...well, not normal, but something less awful than this." Talera waved a hand.

"And now you know that you just have to finish the stories you start. You'll have books on the shelves at Between the Lines in no time."

Bex's laugh was brittle. "No."

Talera stilled, her gracious thoughts depleting quickly.

"I'm not going to be working at the bookstore much longer. I took a new job, so I'll be giving my two weeks' notice after StoryCon."

Could Bex truly not see how flawed that decision was? That it was the antithesis of everything she cared about?

"Don't worry," she continued, "I've learned my lesson. I won't be writing any more stories, so I won't send anyone else to the Realm."

Talera began plucking mushroom heads off their stems and tossing them aside. "So you don't wish to be more like me. You just wish your mother were more like mine."

The look Bex gave her indicated that she didn't see the importance of the distinction. Talera's irritation rose in her throat.

"If what you admire about me is that I stick to my path even when others don't agree, then you'll keep writing. But if what you actually want is for your mother to change so you don't have to deal with feeling like a disappointment or acting against others' wishes, that's you being a victim. Not everyone is going to like you, Bex. Nor should they have to."

The mushroom caps left a residue on her fingers. She wiped them on the soles of her boots, ire simmering beneath her skin.

Bex's phone buzzed. "It's just Owen. He said he's going home to sleep and will meet us at the convention in the morning." Talera's harsh words still hung in the air. "I just meant…"

"If you have something to say, just say it."

Bex blushed. "I was thinking how strange it is to be able to talk with you. You're here and real and…in some weird way, it's like I'm talking to myself. Except you're very clearly not me, but I made you up, and…" Bex shook her head again, her words rushing out. "I just feel like my brain is going to explode. There's this part of me that's so damn excited—the kid in me feels so validated, like, I knew it, I knew magic was real! But I'm an adult now, and this isn't a game or a story. There are real consequences, and I don't know if I can handle them. I mean, the fact that I'm talking to you about this is the most meta thing I've ever heard." She barked out a laugh. "But who else am I supposed to tell? No one is going to believe us besides Owen, and he's pissed at me, and—" She cut herself off, the red in her cheeks flushing darker. "Sorry. And I don't just mean for the rambling."

"I'm not sure what *meta* is, but I feel like my brain might explode, too. So…we should at least be able to talk to each other about it." Talera caught a glint of silver in Bex's eye and squirmed uncomfortably. "Please don't cry."

Bex sniffed and gave herself a little shake. "I don't know what you're talking about."

After a few moments a thought struck Talera. "What's pizza?"

Bex laughed, the sound bright, and it eased the lingering tension in the air. Then she gasped softly, grabbing Talera's elbow.

"What?" Talera looked around for the source of Bex's alarm.

"Would you like some Faelyn Fog?"

Talera's heart skipped. "What?"

Bex was speaking quickly now. "Well, it's technically called a London Fog, but that's what I based Faelyn Fog on. I like to drink it before bed. I was so overwhelmed last night that I forgot, but we can totally make it now."

Something burned behind Talera's eyes, and she blinked to clear the irritation. "Yes, I'd like that very much."

CHAPTER TWENTY-SIX

LABEL IT

THIS WAS THE FIRST time StoryCon had come to San Francisco, and it seemed the whole city had turned up. Throngs of people dressed in various costumes spilled over the pavement as they waited in line to be let in. Bex had thrown her voice in with workers from other local shops and corporations who wanted the privilege of hosting the prestigious fantasy and science fiction event in their city, and she felt a small swell of pride as she took in the crowd. Attendees clutched copies of their favorite epic fantasy and sci-fi novels, ready to get them signed, buzzing with excitement. Strangers became friends as people recognized fellow fans. Fae creatures, wizards, goblins, vampires, superheroes, aliens, and warriors overran the city, beloved characters come to life.

With a jolt, Bex realized that they actually *had* come to life. Somewhere out there, all these characters existed. But not all of them had gotten so lucky. The familiar guilt rolled in her stomach.

Owen avoided looking directly at her as they wove around the long lines to the designated vendor entrance. Bex chewed on the inside of her lip as they approached the bored-looking security guard checking badges at the door. She offered a shaky smile as he gave their passes a once-over, nudging Talera forward. Talera flashed a grin and smoothly began conversing with the man, pulling his attention from the badges. After a few moments, he waved them in.

"Close your mouth, Guy. You needn't look so shocked," Talera said.

"I'd given Talera high charisma to influence people when needed," Bex explained. "I'd thought to use it more when she got to the Challenge."

"So this stubborn, prickly demeanor is just…fun for you?" Guy stared at Talera who in turn bared her teeth in a snarky approximation of a smile.

Their group walked down the large hallway toward the vendor area. Large banners hung from an upper level and nearly touched the floor. The smell of hot dogs filled the highly air-conditioned room, and the buzz of conversation and music pressed into their ears. Every booth and table was designed to vie for attention.

They arrived at their booth, and Talera quickly discarded her Between the Lines T-shirt, though Guy kept his on. After twenty minutes and four rounds of *higher on the left—your other left* as Owen and Talera tried to get their banner straight, they were ready.

Bex, her stomach still a jumble of nerves, began making tiny adjustments to a stack of books once again, though there was no need. She sipped the coffee Owen had brought for all of them as she studied Talera and Guy. They didn't look good. Talera's complexion looked even more ashen than before, and Guy had the same wan look to him.

Owen nudged her elbow. "Hey."

"Hey." She turned to face him. "Listen, I'm sorry about yesterday, I—"

Owen shook his head. "It's all right, don't worry about it. I'm sorry, too."

"No, Owen, I was a jerk. I'm not handling any of this well. I'm in no way equipped to deal with magically induced disease and other people's lives in my hands." Bex rubbed at a spot on her jeans. "But you're my best friend, and I can't do this without you."

He gave her a soft smile, though his eyes still looked a little dim.

"What time does Huxby's panel start?" Talera flipped

the schedule brochure back and forth, looking at it like it was written in a foreign language.

"In just over an hour. Doors open at nine, and the panel starts at ten sharp." Bex pointed to one of the many stages that had been erected on the convention center floor. "It'll be over there. We should make sure one of us is there early to get in the question line."

Guy plucked the pamphlet from Talera, pointing to Huxby's biography. "I still can't put a finger on why I know his *name.*" He leaned against the table for support, taking the last swig of his coffee.

Talera pulled a book from the top of the stack Bex had been fiddling with. She opened it up and began slowly turning the pages.

"That is one of my all-time favorites. I can recite nearly the whole first chapter by heart," Bex said.

Talera arched an eyebrow, intrigued. "How many times have you read it?"

Bex gave a small laugh. "Honestly, at least ten times all the way through. Sometimes I just read my favorite sections, though." Her smile fell a little as she tapped the author's name on the cover. "She's incredible. And then every time I pick up my pen to write…it never comes out even close to the brilliance of her or Arthur Huxby." She shrugged. "Then

I just get so discouraged, like what's even the point?"

Talera looked on quietly, only slight irritation showing on her face.

"Obviously, that was before…" Bex waved her hand at Talera.

"So it *is* fear."

Bex shifted uncomfortably. "I mean, if you have to label it—"

"Technically, it wasn't me who labeled it."

"Well, regardless, it all turned out badly." Bex glanced toward the stage again. "I just hope…he *has* to know how to fix the portal." She forced a smile. "Soon this will all be over, don't worry."

The doors at the far end of the room swung open and a rush of people flooded into the building as StoryCon began.

CHAPTER TWENTY-SEVEN

BESOTTED

TALERA WAS BEWITCHED. STORYCON'S every detail seemed crafted to celebrate the joy of fables, myths, and adventures, to tell tales of heroes and heroines, and to praise the weird, singular, and unique. The booth next to theirs sold recordings of books being read aloud. The one across from them had a lavish display of illustrated stories, most of which were quite graphic. Another boasted an array of hundreds of small figurines of popular characters. When Talera asked why anyone would want a replica of a fictional character, Bex looked at her stupidly, unable to articulate why such a thing was done.

Several full suits of armor stood at attention nearby, wicked jeweled spears clenched in their gauntlets. Next to a weapons vendor was a booth stacked high with hundreds of books with cheesy erotic covers that Talera was sure she'd seen at Between the Lines. A woman, presumably the author, sat behind a table signing copy after copy for a long line of people winding down the aisle.

Bex was complimenting the costume of a young girl who practically preened at the attention. Owen's eyes flicked over to Bex, and a small smile pulled at his lips when she laughed.

Talera shifted, her bow rubbing against her back and her short sword pressing into her spine. She'd left her long sword and more prominent daggers back at Bex's apartment. She blended in perfectly with this crowd. She realized with a start that aside from the scenery and the lively mood, she could just as easily be looking at the Realm. Vampires, warriors, fae, and wizards all milled about.

A mane of red hair snagged Talera's attention, and her chest squeezed. *I'll never see Mother again.*

Guy touched her elbow lightly, his eyes focused on her face. "All right?" he whispered.

She was shaking. "How you manage to stay positive is beyond me," she said quietly.

Guy nodded. "It gets…easier."

"Does it?" She looked him straight in the eye.

He took a moment to answer, but it came out soft and honest. "Not always."

Talera gave a short nod, turning her attention back to

the woman Owen and Bex were talking with. The woman was dressed as an elf.

Poorly, Talera thought. Those wax ears were positively insulting, and how she was dressed was in no way accurate to any group of elves—wood, sea, or winged—or fae.

"That's exactly how it happened." Bex was laughing hard. "He's just too embarrassed to admit it." She held her hand to her chest, trying to catch her breath.

"Not embarrassed—I just want history to be told correctly!" Owen said, his eyes alight.

The poorly dressed impostor laughed too, and her eyes finally stopped on Talera and Guy. "Oh, I'm so rude! Hi." She extended a hand. "I'm Alex. I went to school with these two."

Talera stared at her outstretched hand, brows pinching together.

"Pleased to meet you." Guy leaned in quickly to grasp her hand, shaking it vigorously. "I'm Guy. This is Talera."

The imposter, Alex, ran her eyes over Talera. "Wow, your costume is seriously amazing! Where on earth did you get it? Don't tell me you made it, because I made mine, and I might just give up if you say you made yours." She laughed again.

"Elvish clothing is made by fae couturiers—for wood

elves, that is. Some of the sea elves have become quite radical and have begun making theirs themselves." Talera picked at an invisible piece of lint on her sleeve, her cloak shifting with the movement to reveal the weapons strapped to her body. "But I'm partial to fae-influenced fashion myself. Much more comfortable in combat."

Bex laughed. "So in character, that one."

Alex gave a weird chuckle, looking slightly taken aback.

"Yeah, Talera is cosplaying a character Bex made up," Owen jumped in.

Bex open her mouth slightly and threw a very calculated look at Owen.

"Bex! That's awesome! I've always said you should write something. Very cool!"

"It's…a project I was toying with that I just picked back up." Bex stumbled over the words.

Talera raised an eyebrow at her.

"Just trying to figure out how to do such a great character justice," Bex added with a nervous smile, but her eyes were earnest.

"Cool." Alex's attention strayed to the convention swirling around them. "Well, it's good to see you guys. I have to go meet up with the rest of my kindred." With a goofy wave and one last glance at Talera, she shuffled off.

Talera watched her go, smirking. "Well, she's sure spirited."

"Honestly, though, Talera, *elvish clothing is made by fae couturiers*? We're trying to blend in here," Bex said pointedly.

Talera shrugged. "You're the one who made me this way." She grinned widely. "Oh, lighten up. I'm sure she just thinks you've found someone even nerdier than you to hang out with."

Bex looked skyward. "Dear god. Just let me get through today. And you"—she poked Owen in the chest—"can we not with the talking about writing and the revealing secrets and embarrassing things?"

Owen shrugged. "You started it."

Bex grumbled but didn't have a rebuttal, likely because she *had* started it. Owen playfully shoved her and then gave Guy and Talera a small wink when she turned away. "Anyway, Guy, we should get going."

"Right!" Guy pressed his palms together excitedly. "Ladies." He nodded to them both, and then he and Owen made their way toward the panel stage, Owen throwing Talera one more wink over his shoulder.

"He thinks his charm works on me the way it does on

you," Talera mused.

Bex snorted. "What? He doesn't…work stuff on me," she said, a blush rising in her cheeks.

Talera glanced at her sideways. "Oh no, it definitely works on you." Bex let out a huff. "Do you mean to tell me you don't see it? It's quite obvious to the rest of us."

"*The rest of us?* Who, you and Guy? You've been here, like, a day! And *what* is obvious?"

"He is obviously besotted with you." Talera sauntered over and leaned against the table, turning to face Bex.

"Besotted with me?" Bex's voice was shrill.

Talera waved a hand. "Besotted, smitten, in lo—"

Bex made a strangled noise, cutting her off. "He isn't—doesn't—Owen is my oldest friend. It's not like that at all." She turned to straighten a stack of books that was not askew.

Talera pursed her lips. "Interesting."

"It's not interesting, it's just…what it is, which is nothing other than friendship."

Talera cocked her head. "You said last night that talking to me is sort of like talking to yourself. Maybe your subconscious brain is my conscious brain."

Bex sputtered for a moment, the color in her cheeks darkening even more. "What?"

"Maybe my brain is the part of your brain that knows

that Owen is indeed"—she gave a flourish of her hand—"*besotted.*"

Bex opened and shut her mouth several times.

"Oh, relax!" Talera teased. "Gods, it's not like I'm telling you that you're a figment of someone's imagination and your life is over."

Bex pressed her lips into a thin line. "Touché."

"Huh?"

"Never mind. Just…you win on the bad news front, and just…please drop it about Owen."

Talera spread her hands. "If you wish."

CHAPTER TWENTY-EIGHT

StoryCon

Besotted, my ass, Bex thought to herself as she and Talera began to make their way to the panel. The booth had been mercifully busy since their ridiculous conversation, saving Bex from further embarrassment. She squinted, trying to find Owen or Guy in the sea of heads, but they were impossible to make out.

"They're over there." Talera nodded toward the right side of the stage.

Bex scanned the area again more closely and finally spotted Owen and Guy sitting next to each other near the stage. "How did you see them?"

Talera shrugged. "Elvish eyesight, remember? I could see them from back at the booth."

Bex attempted to cover her incredulous giggle with a cough.

The crowd started to applaud, jostling them slightly, as

the panelists made their way onto the stage. There were five of them total, men and women who spanned a range of ages and ethnicities.

"Which one is Arthur Huxby?" Talera whispered, lips slightly pursed as she studied the group.

"Two in from the left. That's him."

Arthur Huxby stood taller than most of the others on the panel, with rich ochre skin, close-cut hair, and a short beard peppered with gray. He had a prominent nose and deep, kind eyes behind glasses, and he was sharply dressed in slacks and a blazer.

The moderator, a woman in a smart pantsuit, walked on stage next, microphone in hand. "Welcome, San Francisco, to StoryCon!" The crowd gave an enthusiastic cheer. "We have quite the lineup for you today to kick off the con." The woman began introducing the panelists, pausing briefly after each one to allow for applause.

Bex's stomach was a jumble of nerves and excitement. Talera stood next to her, seemingly calm, but Bex could see a tightness in her expression that hadn't been there before. She focused her attention back on the moderator.

"We have San Francisco's own Tom Hallen, author of *Truthsayer*." The man sitting next to Arthur was probably twenty years younger than him and had pale skin and shockingly red hair. "Cynthia Madison author of the *Dark Kingdom* trilogy and the new *Battleborn* duology." The woman on the far right with bright lipstick and white hair gave a small smile and a nod. "And author of over two dozen fantasy books, most notably *The Orithian Sword,* Professor Arthur Huxby." Arthur grinned, smile lines creasing his broad face.

"The collective accomplishments on this stage are staggering. All of these amazing women and men are *New York Times* bestsellers, have outrageous fan followings"—the crowd howled and cheered excitedly again—"and have published some of our most beloved and influential science fiction and fantasy novels. Not to mention their impressive accolades outside of their writing careers. Their genius extends to the worlds of science, law, engineering, forensics, and philanthropy."

Bex shifted on her feet to scan the crowd for her dad. She sent him a quick message letting him know where they were in relation to the stage, and by the time he slipped through the crowd to her, the moderator had begun the panel discussion. He gave her shoulder an affectionate squeeze, his face split in a wide grin as he greedily drank in everything being said. The discussion lasted about half an hour before the moderator announced it was time for questions from the audience.

"We have microphones set up on each side of the stage"—she indicated with her free hand—"and we will alternate between the lines. So in an orderly fashion, please begin to form a line on either side." She raised her voice as the crowd began buzzing and people rushed forward, jumping from their seats to get in line.

Owen and Guy charged to the front. As people moved to line up, Bex, her dad, and Talera were able to shuffle forward a bit, getting a clearer view of the panelists.

"Uh, hi." The nasal voice came abruptly over the speaker system. "My question is for Cynthia Madison." He paused, breathing loudly into the microphone the way a child would. "What was your inspiration for the Dark Kingdom trilogy?"

Bex tapped her foot impatiently as Cynthia answered, her bright lips spread into a wide smile. When she finished, there was a smattering of polite applause, and Bex nudged Talera, nodding toward Owen as he approached the microphone.

He cleared his throat. "Hi, hello. I have a question for Arthur Huxby." He waved to Arthur, who in turn inclined his head. "You once said you believe that what you write has real-life consequences and can even create other worlds. I was wondering if you could elaborate on that a bit."

The crowd tittered as the smile faded from Arthur Huxby's face, and Tom Hallen subtly rolled his eyes. Arthur cleared his throat.

"Well"—he gave a small forced laugh—"someone's been doing a lot of research. That was a long time ago." He peered over his glasses to look more intently at Owen. "It is true that back then, I talked about the multiverse and my belief that there are infinite versions of our stories." He gestured to the audience. "And also the idea that the stories we write actually materialize." His eyes flicked to Tom Hallen. "Many of my colleagues don't agree, but…"

He paused, and Bex held her breath as she waited for him to continue. "I believe that what we create does exist in some other plane. That there are alternate worlds, universes, or realms where our creations, the stories we tell and the worlds we invent, come to fruition."

A few of the other panelists shifted in their chairs, and Tom Hallen didn't attempt to hide his smirk.

"Is there any way for someone from an alternate world to survive in ours?" Owen said.

The moderator glared at him for asking a second question, but Arthur didn't seem to notice, as he was already replying.

"There are a few different theories that are supported in the community regarding the multiverse and travel between realms. The one that aligns with my research best is that atoms become contaminated when someone or something from one universe travels to another. Unless you can alter the foreign atoms—calibrate them, if you will—that person or thing won't be able to survive long term." There was a haunted look in his eye as he spoke, and a chill ran down Bex's spine.

Tom Hallen let out a short laugh.

Arthur angled his body to face him. "Something you'd like to add, Tom?"

Tom spread his hands. "I just find it amusing that you've actually researched something so preposterous. I don't mean to offend, but come on, Arthur." His voice was oily, and he spoke with a slowed cadence, as if speaking to a child. "You ought to know that what we do"—he gestured to his fellow panelists—"is all made up. There's nothing real about it."

Arthur looked at Tom coolly over his glasses. "Yes, I imagine you would find it amusing that I've done the research. Research and world building are what give our readers a foundation to believe in what we write. Now, I don't mean to offend, but I think many would agree that the

Truthsayer universe could benefit from a bit more research."

Tom Hallen's face and neck burned red, and his mouth fell open, giving him the appearance of a nearly ripe tomato. The audience collectively gasped, several people emitting bursts of laughter. Her dad whistled. A few booed and a few cheered as Tom Hallen clenched his mouth shut.

"What just happened?" Talera whispered, just loud enough for Bex alone to hear.

"Tom Hallen wrote the Truthsayer Saga, and there's a lot of criticism from readers that there are discrepancies that make no sense. Not to mention that his magic system is really weak, so it's not very believable," Bex said softly behind her hand, trying not to laugh.

"Why is he popular, then?" Talera hissed.

Bex shrugged. "He writes some pretty graphic sex and gore."

The moderator was frantically trying to get the panel back on track, talking loudly into the microphone over the buzzing crowd, so when Tom Hallen was finally able to form words again, he had to shout into his own mic.

"The multiverse is a widely accepted and discussed reality in our community, and I can get behind that. But to imply that what we write actually materializes in some alternate world or plane is irresponsible and nothing short of a god complex!"

The moderator looked like she wanted to strangle the two men. Turning her back to the audience, she held her microphone down so no one could hear what she hissed at the bickering panelists.

The moderator smoothed her suit, a tight smile plastered on her face as she called for the next question. It was something inane about which of their own characters each author was most physically attracted to.

Bex impatiently chewed on a knuckle as she waited for Guy's turn to ask a question. She glanced at Talera, who was focused closely on Guy as he finally approached the mic, his usually cheerful demeanor replaced with an apprehensive one.

"Guy, was it?" her dad asked and Bex nodded.

Guy cleared his throat. "I'd also like to pose a question to Professor Huxby." Tom Hallen looked annoyed at the attention the older gentleman was getting.

"Going back to alternate realms, what about travel between them? When you went through—" Guy suddenly stopped short. Arthur Huxby was glaring at him over his glasses, and Guy wet his lips. "Er…what I meant to say is…when you went through the writing process, how did you decide how portals could be closed?"

Bex ground her teeth as Guy fumbled with his words. It was evident from his expression that Arthur didn't appreciate any mention of the event that had been seen as a psychotic break. He didn't answer for a moment, his piercing gaze fixed on Guy, who was making a pitiful attempt to replicate the hand gesture Bex had shown him the day before. Next to her, her dad folded his arms over his chest, brow furrowing.

Finally Arthur Huxby sniffed and said, "I was watching my two-year-old goddaughter make different shapes with her hands. That sparked the idea." He turned to the moderator and inclined his head slightly, signaling that he was finished answering, and the next question was called.

"Oh, but if you could just—" Guy was jostled aside as the line behind him moved forward. He looked crestfallen. Her dad was pulled into a side conversation with someone in chainmail as Owen and Guy pushed through the crowd to get to them. Briefly she wondered why she hadn't told her dad the truth, but she quickly pushed the thought aside. There was no need to worry him when she was about to have this whole mess handled and in someone else's hands.

Guy was shaking his head. "As an academic, I feel like I should've been able to articulate that question in a way that was less offensive to our only source."

"We just need to talk with him one-on-one," Owen said, keeping his voice low.

"Four-on-one, in this case," Guy muttered. He looked back over his shoulder. "It's driving me mad that I can't recall why I know his name."

Bex waved a hand dismissively, glancing over to make sure her dad was still preoccupied with the other conversation. "That doesn't matter right now. What are we supposed to do? Just wait for the panel to be over and then intercept him somewhere?"

The rest of them murmured in agreement.

Talera nodded to the stage, pursing her lips slightly. "Maybe they'll say something useful. Or maybe another argument will start." She smiled wickedly. "I quite enjoyed that."

CHAPTER TWENTY-NINE

To Celebrate Stories

SOMETHING WAS WRONG WITH the Fear.

Pain seared through Rehnir's body, and his mind felt like it was going to split in two.

This is wrong. This is WRONG—

He screamed the words in his mind, unable to speak aloud.

This is why we chained ourselves like rabid dogs—to keep from becoming monsters—why we—

All thoughts vanished as agony threatened to shatter his body, his mind, his very soul—

His breath sawed out of his chest as images assaulted his vision.

His father on the floor, shock and pain etched into his lifeless eyes.

Faces of those he had grown up with in his village, twisted in agony.

An entire family dead in a cramped and dirty home no larger than three men across.

Then hundreds more.

Rehnir lost track of time as the moments compressed, seconds or days or a year passing—he didn't know. All he knew was pain and revulsion and endless images blurring together in a torrent of gore and terror. A formidable wave of nightmares, slaughter, and horror—horror in those eyes and horror leaching from his own body, crashing over him, and then—

As abruptly as it had begun, it ended.

Cold sweat soaked through his clothes. He was shaking, his back pressed up against a brick wall on a deserted side street. His mouth was parched. Sounds coming from the next street over beckoned him. Three bodies lay at odd angles on the ground, blood pooling around them. With a shudder, Rehnir realized he couldn't remember running into the young men or feeding on them.

Fear had never affected him this way. His powers were mutating. There was a shifting darkness inside him, answering the Fear's demands, greedily accepting the cost of the reward. The bricks dug into his palms as he shrank against the wall.

Something was wrong.

He needed to get back to the Realm so he could regain control of his powers and this growing shadow inside his chest that so relished the slaughter.

But before he could move, the euphoria erupted.

The rampant panic and shame from only a heartbeat ago were dispelled as control and pleasure roared through him. His whole body pulsed with a heady vibration, a pleasant sensation of dizziness. He breathed deeply again, savoring the power surging through his veins. He staggered down several streets, an invisible force luring him. He shivered, every inch of his skin sparking and craving Fear's electric touch.

He was in a crowd, moving in a steady current. Eccentric body paint, billowing robes, and crude replicas of weapons and magical artifacts surrounded him. Boisterous voices and laughter cut through his delirium. The streets were flooded with people dressed as if they were in the Abandoned Realm.

But he wasn't in the Realm, he was—

A large winged man appeared at Rehnir's side. The man's wings were made of thousands of inky black feathers that seemed to suck light into them. His torso was bare, and his green irises swallowed the whites of his eyes.

The man fell into step beside him and dipped his head

to whisper, "You're the one who made the portal, aren't you?" The dissonance in his voice was startling—masculine and feminine, old and young, all at the same time.

There was a gasp as someone shouted to their friends to *check out this awesome costume*! The winged man gave a barking laugh. The roiling darkness behind Rehnir's breastbone was building, wearing down his restraint.

The massive wings twitched as the man hissed, "This is some type of massive gathering—all these fools are dressing up as people from stories to celebrate." With another laugh devoid of amusement, the man swept passed him. Rehnir followed him with his eyes and saw a huge building with enormous banners plastered to the front.

STORYCON: BE THE HERO OF YOUR STORY!
DON'T MISS OUR AUTHOR PANELS!
COME CELEBRATE YOUR FAVORITE STORIES!

The internal pressure was crushing, a roar was filling Rehnir's ears, and his steps stuttered. The pain turned into a wrenching blow that shot through his whole body. He moaned, doubling over, clutching his head as his vision blurred.

Hard concrete struck his bones when his knees buckled. Every muscle in his body pulled taut. Spittle gathered at the corners of his mouth, and his breathing was ragged. There was a painful pulling sensation in his stomach—not the usual hungry feeling that accompanied his desire to feed, but an acute, unrelenting demand. It consumed his mind. His nails bit into his palms, but he couldn't unclench his fists.

He needed more. Now.

Someone touched his shoulder. "Are you all right, man?"

Rehnir's eyes snapped open to focus on the man crouching down next to him. He lashed out his mental tether, leeching onto the man's essence. Rehnir snarled and watched the color drain from the man's face, fear registering in his eyes too late. Blood gushed from the man's nose as he slumped to the ground, a rasping breath escaping his lips.

The agony relented a fraction as the Fear rushed into Rehnir, a soothing balm. He ignored the tremble in his hands.

I can fix this. I just need more.

The pulling sensation began to swell again, drowning out the cautionary voice at the back of his mind. The Fear was too strong, the rush too exhilarating, the power too enticing.

Rehnir's lip curled. He inhaled the Fear deeply, letting it quell his nausea and anguish. Letting the building dark sentience within push him toward the mass of people ahead.

CHAPTER THIRTY

This Isn't Rivendell

BEX ALLOWED HERSELF TO listen to half the panel before guilt over neglecting the booth won out. When Guy slipped away to find out where the panelists would go next, Bex squeezed her dad's hand and left him with Owen and Talera. She spent the next half an hour trying to smile at customers, anxiously checking her phone every few minutes.

Professor Huxby hadn't seemed willing to divulge any information about portals. In hindsight, asking him at the panel hadn't been the best choice. It should've been obvious that he wouldn't admit to anything so publicly.

Her hope was faltering. She'd been so naive to think they could just demand an explanation in front of a crowd and then she could wash her hands of everything. She'd been so focused on shifting the responsibility to someone else that she hadn't even considered other alternatives. Her stomach quivered, and a sob—or perhaps a laugh—lodged in her throat.

The others finally returned, her dad and Owen animatedly discussing the paranormal detective series Owen was obsessed with. Bex rubbed her neck, searching Guy and Talera's faces. Talera gave a slight nod toward the back of the convention center.

Bex's stomach somersaulted. She half-heartedly listened to her dad prattle on about the panel while she waited for her moment.

"I've gotta say, this is one of the cooler conventions I've been to," her dad said, looking around.

"Do you think you could watch the booth for a few minutes, Dad?" Bex tucked a lock of hair behind her ear. "There's a booth Peter wants us to check out."

He gave her an easy smile and squeezed her shoulder. "Sure thing, kiddo."

"We'll be fast," Bex promised.

Grant waved them off. "I can handle it," he assured her, and the four of them set off, Guy in the lead.

"There's a lounge set up for the panelists on the upper mezzanine," Guy said quietly as he led them past fantasy set pieces, winged cosplayers, and the weaponry booth with full suits of armor they had to maneuver around. Huge banners hung from the upper level to the floor bearing gigantic images of various authors' faces and popular book jackets.

Upstairs it was much less crowded, and Bex was sure that even though there'd been no security at the steps, they weren't supposed to be in this area.

At the far end was a roped-off section with several cozy chairs and high-top tables. A small buffet with snacks and drinks for the panelists was stationed along the wall. The floor below was a veritable sea of fae folk, wizards, warriors, caped heroes, cloaked travelers, Renaissance knights, and masked monsters. Owen nudged her, and Bex pulled her eyes away from the costumes to see Arthur Huxby climbing the steps, having just extracted himself from the clutches of an enthusiastic fan.

As Professor Huxby approached, Owen and Guy shuffled away from the railing a bit—not enough to block his way, but enough to catch his eye.

He spotted them, and his lips pressed into a thin line.

Bex stepped forward and held out her hand, unable to stop herself. "Professor Huxby, it's truly an honor to meet you." Heat bloomed in her cheeks as he smiled kindly and grasped her hand.

"You're with these two, then?" He jerked his head

toward Guy and Owen.

"Yes, I am. We wanted to speak with you. You see…" Bex hesitated, unsure how to proceed. How was she supposed to explain to her idol that she believed he had indeed traveled to another realm and that there was another break in the boundary now? She wet her lips. "The reason they were asking about portals is that…well, there's one open right now between another realm and ours."

Professor Huxby blinked. He looked slowly at the others, then back at her. "I beg your pardon?"

Talera gestured to herself and Guy. "We're characters that people never finished writing. We came from the Abandoned Realm through a portal."

"A portal we think is similar to the one you went through all those years ago," Guy said.

Professor Huxby rapidly blinked at them. The four of them looked at each other nervously.

"I see." Professor Huxby's tone was clipped and flat. "And where did you say you were from again?" They hesitated, and he clicked his tongue. "Were you sent by the Oxford Committee? Perhaps the board?" His nostrils flared, and he waved to someone behind them. "If you'll excuse me, I don't very much feel like enduring another session of ridicule."

He made to go around them. A stocky security guard was making his way toward their group. Bex instinctively lunged, grabbing his arm. "Wait, please! It's true."

Professor Huxby turned and pointedly looked down at his arm, which she quickly dropped as if it were suddenly burning her.

"Professor, I know no one has ever believed you…but we do. This isn't a joke, I swear to you. We need your help."

"Please, sir," Guy chimed in. "We believe there will be some very serious repercussions for people on both sides of the portal if it's not closed soon. Outside of just nausea, disorientation, and seizures." Guy waved his hand between Talera and himself. Bex could see the toll this world was taking on their bodies, but could Huxby?

Bex's heart pounded.

He's got to believe us. He's got to help us.

"We wouldn't dream of wasting your time," Owen was saying.

"The portal is on the Golden Gate Bridge—remember that huge accident?" Bex couldn't stop the stream of words rushing from her mouth. "It was because of some other characters who came through. And contamination from the boundary between our worlds collapsing is causing the Fading—"

"And those black marks they say could be a new strain are actually from dark magic." Talera's calm began to unravel as she pleaded.

"We have a manuscript that explains the exact marks people are getting—" Guy said.

"What's going on over here, folks?" The security guard hooked a thumb into his belt, which his stomach spilled over.

Arthur's eyes flashed. "These people aren't supposed to be up here."

"Please, just listen," Bex said, panic brewing in her chest.

"We have manuscripts to prove what we're telling you!" Owen said.

The security guard stepped between them and Huxby, arms wide, and began to herd them back toward the stairs. "Come on, folks, let's not make this harder than it has to be."

"You don't understand!" Hot tears pricked behind Bex's eyes. *No, no, no—*

Owen gripped Talera's arm, holding her back as she drew herself up to her full height. "Talera," he hissed.

They were at the stairs now, and Huxby was turning into the lounge area, taking their hope with him. Talera cursed steadily under her breath. Guy ran a hand through his hair as they stumbled down the steps.

"What are we supposed to do now?" Bex looked between Guy and Talera, her throat tight.

"You shouldn't have held me back," Talera snarled at Owen.

"Yes, 'cause that would have turned out so well," Owen snapped.

Talera ignored him and turned to Guy. "We're wasting time here. We should just go back to the Realm and see if Branson and Adaira have made any headway with closing the portal. Everyone on this side is completely useless."

Bex looked at the ground, blinking back the angry tears threatening to fall. *Shit shit sh—*

"Adaira." Guy's eyes grew wide as he clapped his hands together. He barked out a laugh and spun on his heel. Cupping his hands to his mouth, he yelled up the stairs, "Adaira!"

"What are you—"

"Professor! We know Adaira! She's back where we came from with her Aldar, and she needs our help!"

Bex's heart fluttered like a caged bird trying to get free. She bottled her breath in her lungs as the four of them watched the upper level.

Huxby appeared, his brows drawn, holding a hand up

to the security guard. “Excuse me?”

Guy licked his lips. “I met Adaira just as she was about to inherit the crown of her people. She’s currently working tirelessly with the small amount of Aldar she still possesses to heal those affected by”—Guy’s eyes flicked to the security guard—“ what we were discussing with you.”

Professor Huxby worked his jaw a few times. After what felt like an eternity, he gave a curt nod. “Let them up.”

Bex sagged against Owen, Guy muttered some type of prayer, and Talera merely grunted as they all climbed the steps. They caught the security guard mumbling “bunch of nerds” as he stalked off.

Huxby led them away from the stairs, drawing them toward the railing a good distance from the lounge area. His hands twitched as he leveled them with a glare. “Speak,” he said to Guy.

“I’m a character from the Abandoned Realm. I read all the unfinished stories that come to the Library of Manuscripts. I knew your name was familiar. Adaira is a friend of mine. You wrote her.”

Huxby said nothing, and Guy wet his lips again. “Please help us. The Realm is suffering from the Fading, and its effects are rapidly expanding now that the portal is open. If there’s anything you know that could help us…”

Finally Huxby spoke, dropping his voice low. "When?" The word was gravelly and urgent. "The portal—where did it open? Tell me exactly."

"The middle of the Golden Gate Bridge."

Huxby's eyes glazed over, and his gaze drifted past them. He was silent for several moments, as if seeing another time when he had stood before a magical doorway.

"Of course," he whispered. "It's really happened again, then."

Bex and Owen exchanged a look.

"What do you mean, of course?" Guy voiced her thoughts.

Huxby shivered, or perhaps shook himself out of a daze. "The bridge—it's the culmination of creativity and human engineering. When magic and science intersect, it creates a powerful force, a kind of energetic vortex. The Tower of London, the Golden Gate Bridge…there must be dozens scattered across the globe." He trailed off, eyes shifting rapidly.

"Can you help us?" Bex hated the desperation in her voice. Her heart pounded at the implications of what he'd just said.

As if he hadn't heard the question, Arthur looked back to Owen and said, "You said you have the manuscripts that explain the marks?"

Owen gave a swift nod.

"May I see them?"

Owen dashed away as if Arthur might change his mind if he procured them too slowly, heading for the booth, where the manuscripts from the Library and the most relevant of Huxby's books were crammed in Talera's bag.

Bex's scalp prickled. She'd expected the tightness in her chest to release when Huxby got on board. Some piece of him believed them, so why wasn't there immediate clarity? Wasn't that what happened when the chosen one entered the story—some type of definitive shift or assurance? But Huxby offered no plans or promises to fix things, to take this burden from them, no reassurance that they'd done the right thing by finding him.

The only thought Bex could conjure was that this must have been how Frodo felt when he arrived in Rivendell and the Council offered no answers. But she wasn't a hero and couldn't be expected to continue this journey, and—

A piercing scream ripped the air. Bex's blood froze as they all whipped around to look out at the floor below. The screaming intensified. The crowd below swarmed like a kicked anthill. Great black wings caught her eye. A dark angel swooped through the air, snatching people up and dropping them from great heights, laughing as he did. More screams rose from the other end of the arena as a woman with wild hair leapt on someone and began pummeling them to the ground. Chaos erupted in pockets all across the floor like miniature fires being lit.

Talera wrapped her hand around Bex's arm in a viselike grip.

Blue light flared around a pale man in a dark cloak. He stood with his arms held out from his body. Something was spilled across the floor in front of him, and the people nearest him seemed to have slipped on it.

Talera squeezed Bex's arm to the point of pain. "That's him. That's Rehnir."

It took a moment for her mind to register that those dark patches on the floor were actually—

Blood.

The people hadn't slipped. They'd collapsed as lacerations appeared on their bodies like bloody ribbons.

People were futilely trying to distance themselves from the man, confusion and fear spreading through the crowd.

Bex couldn't move, couldn't tear her eyes away from the cloaked man.

Rehnir.

He was advancing across the convention center floor,

dark red stains blossoming from the bodies of his victims.

Bex's mind was sluggish and muddy. "Why aren't any of them getting up?" Her voice sounded far away.

Next to her, Talera pulled out an arrow and nocked it. She drew the string of her bow back and steadied her hand, taking aim. She released it, and Bex felt a whoosh on her face. The arrow cut through the air, streaking toward Rehnir.

Without so much as a glance, Rehnir threw his right hand up toward the incoming arrow. A flash of blue light engulfed his palm and then expanded outward. When the arrow came in contact with the light, it was as if it had hit a solid wall, and it dropped harmlessly to the floor.

Talera swore. Bex's heartbeat thrashed in her ears, her body rigid.

Why aren't they getting up? The question repeated in her mind as bile burned the back of her throat.

They're not moving because they're dead.

"Dad!" The volume of her voice jolted her, adrenaline flooding her.

Her body was unraveling, a dark wave suffocating her. Rigid against the railing, she wildly hunted for his familiar form. "Dad?!"

There. He was there by her booth.

The booth that was only one aisle over from Rehnir.

"Owen!" Guy's voice broke through her paralysis, and she jerked her head. Owen was pushing his way through the crowd, Talera's pack on his back. He was heading back to the booth, toward her dad. Toward Rehnir—

"RUN!" Bex screamed. "What is he doing? What is he doing?!"

"Talera, *do* something!"

Everything was happening too slowly and too quickly.

"What exactly do you suggest?!" Talera snarled as Bex continued to scream. "Nothing's working!"

"We have to get out of here!" Huxby was yelling.

"Talera, please!" Was that her pleading or Guy? Bex was outside her body.

"Get out of my way, Professor." Talera swung herself over the railing, gripped one of the long banners, and slid down, landing in a crouch twenty feet below. She sprang up and ran toward Owen and Grant.

Panic roared in Bex's ears. The air smelled burned and rancid. She watched, debilitated by anguish, as her dad was tossed around in the fleeing mob.

Someone gripped her shoulders, trying to haul her back from the railing.

No, no, no—

"NO! DAD—RUN!!" The words ripped at her throat.

"Talera! Hurry!" Guy was screaming in her ear.

The metallic smell of blood was overpowering.

Her dad was falling, disappearing into the mayhem—

Bex's heart restarted as he resurfaced. But his face was covered in something writhing and black. Rehnir was getting closer to him, electric-blue light crackling in his palms, chest heaving, a monstrous smile on his face, arms outreaching with flexed fingers.

CHAPTER THIRTY-ONE

BUYING TIME

TIME DISTORTED AS TALERA forced her way through the stampede, looking for Owen and Grant.

Get to them.

GET TO THEM.

Her ribs were too tight around her lungs, and nausea threatened to incapacitate her. She gritted her teeth, trying to get a better grasp on her Faelyn, but the usually strong current of power felt feeble, like a mountain stream drying up.

Where are they?

"Grant!"

Talera's head snapped in the direction of Owen's voice, and she spotted him in the frenzied mass. He was pale, sweat beading on his brow, and he looked like he was about to be sick. Talera jumped lithely up onto a rickety table in the nearest booth. Fighting for balance, she took a few bounding strides across two more shuddering tables and leapt into the air. Knees tucked up tight, she soared over several people's heads before landing a few feet in front of Owen. She grabbed him by the collar, hauling him back the other way.

"What are you doing? We have to—"

"You cannot fight him. You will die, do you understand?" Talera snarled, pushing him away from her. "Run."

"But Grant—"

"I said *run*. I'll do what I can." She gave Owen one more shove.

Talera spun on her heel, not waiting to see if Owen obeyed her. Her Faelyn was still smothered, and she was dizzy. Someone thudded into her shoulder as they fled past, but she hardly noticed, unable to tear her eyes away from Rehnir.

Distantly she remembered Guy explaining Rehnir's backstory, the way he'd fought his urges at the start. She could see nothing left of that little boy in the man who stood before her now. The whites of Rehnir's eyes had disappeared, leaving only gaping wells of darkness that sent a chill down her spine. It wasn't until she felt the hope of getting through to Rehnir extinguish that she realized she'd been holding on to it at all.

He was no more than forty paces away from Talera, but Grant was even closer to him. Her breath was sucked from her body as Grant crawled across the ground, all the veins in his neck tinged black, blood running from his nose and mouth freely as he pulled his weight along the floor. Talera cursed, seizing another arrow. Her aim was deadly, but once again her weapon was flung aside with a sharp slashing motion from Rehnir. Blue flames licked up his arms, and Talera let out a guttural cry, pushing down the panic that was rising in her. She strained her mind, frantically pounding on the damper constraining her Faelyn.

Silver caught her eye. The booth of weapons and armor was just ahead. Talera dashed forward and tore one of the javelins from a gauntlet just as a sweeping sensation cleaved through her like a dam breaking. Her magic suddenly unleashed, filling her muscles with strength and banishing the fog and dizziness from her mind.

There wasn't time to think about the strange effect Rehnir's power had on her magic. She cocked her arm back, and with a savage twist of her hips, she hurled the spear at him. Ignoring the scream of pain the movement caused in her shoulder, she sprinted toward Grant.

She heard the spear clatter to the ground, but deflecting the attack had cost Rehnir precious seconds. Talera skidded to her knees, grasping Grant firmly. He moaned as she pulled him to his feet.

"Get up!" she hissed. She threw a look back over her shoulder, her heart thundering in her ears.

Rehnir's black eyes locked on hers.

Invisible claws gripped her mind. She arched her back in agony, her mouth opening in a silent scream.

All she was and all she knew was terror. Her soul and body ceased to exist, ripped apart utterly and completely.

Her mother's mangled face, lifeless elven eyes staring back at her.

Someone was screaming.

She was screaming.

Cold snapped her back into her body. Her throat burned. Something heavy pressed into her, weighing her down.

The vision of her mother's face fractured, replaced by the chaos of the convention center.

She was holding Grant, his body leaden.

Run.

Her Faelyn was drained, and her body shook as those terrible claws continued to pierce her mind.

A low laugh reached her ears, and she looked up to see Rehnir slowly stalking toward them, his lip curled in a predatory snarl.

"You think you can stand against me?" His voice sent a shiver down Talera's spine.

Talera opened her mouth, but her throat was so tight that nothing came out. The pain in her head grew, and she tasted blood.

Rehnir raised his hand, a hungry lustful look in his feral black eyes.

BOOM.

Something exploded off to their right. Rehnir stumbled, and the invisible claws loosened. Talera gasped for breath, a ringing in her ears. Smoke and angry yelling filled the room as heavy boots hit the floor and armed men and women spilled in through the open doors. Talera didn't hesitate. Heaving Grant's limp body over her shoulder, she ran.

Don't stop. Don't stop.

Her breathing was ragged as she hauled Grant up the stairs. Owen and Guy fought against the current of those rushing to the upper level, meeting her halfway. They took Grant from her, each ducking beneath an arm to carry him. People pressed up against her, a mass organism moving up the steps. Everyone was trying to get as far as possible from the attack. A coppery taste filled her mouth and her lungs burned.

After what seemed like ages, she breached the top, rejoining the group. "We've got to get out of here." Her eyes flicked to Professor Huxby, who stood frozen against the railing, his mouth moving in silent horror. Bex pawed at Grant's face, pleading for him to open his eyes. "Now!"

Talera grabbed Bex by the upper arm and pulled her forcefully along. Now that she was farther from Rehnir, her mind was clearing, and her Faelyn now flickered like an ember in ashes. The fleeing crowd swept them up roughly. Down below, the armed forces were slowly closing in on Rehnir. Those nearest him held massive clear body shields, and the ranks behind fired their weapons. But their sheer number was the only thing in their favor; dozens had already fallen to Rehnir's dark power, forcing their companions to step over their fallen bodies as they advanced.

New shrill screams drew Talera's attention to the upper level doors, where she saw with horror that more villains from the Realm were cutting down people as they spilled into the building. "Shit." She reached behind her back, unsheathing the short sword she'd hidden under her cloak. She pushed Bex aside and called to Guy, "Find another way out. Keep as much distance as you can from Rehnir." She adjusted her grip on the hilt, eyes tracking the closest threat—a massive man with a hook for a hand and malice in his eyes. She drew small circles with the point of her sword, trying to ignore the fatigue in her limbs. "I'll buy us time. Run."

The brute came within striking distance, and Talera lunged, bringing the edge of her blade down in a sweeping arc. The brute threw out an arm, blocking the blade with the wooden stump his hook was attached to. The sword sank in an inch. Talera jerked the blade out, her free hand grabbing the dagger at her waist and plunging it up under the man's ribs. Hot blood gushed over her hand, and she tore a vicious slice across his abdomen. He sank to his knees as the life slipped out of him. Talera sensed an attack from behind, and with a tight pirouette, she brought up her sword to block the heavy rod that'd been aimed at the back of her skull.

"You're not playing fair, are you?" Talera sneered at the horned female, stepping in close to block her from swinging the rod, and sent an elbow crashing into her face. The she-devil's head snapped back, nose crunching. Black blood sprayed, flecking Talera's face. She retreated a step, slicing the blade across the she-devil's neck.

Talera spun, panting, head swiveling. The villains were attacking with bloodlust, each engaged in a skirmish. Sheathing her blades, she sprinted in the direction she'd sent the others. She drew her bow, twisting around every few steps to shoot arrows back into the fray.

She spied a smashed window that people were clambering through onto an outdoor terrace, broken glass slicing their palms and shins. Talera grabbed an older woman and hoisted her through before vaulting outside herself. Sunlight blinded her momentarily, and sirens wailed. The terrace was mayhem as people ran and shoved each other down the stairs that lead to the parking lot behind the convention center.

Talera scanned the crowd frantically for a moment before she saw her group on the stairs. Owen and Guy still carried Grant, Bex and Huxby just behind them. Talera made it to the balcony's edge, hesitating only a heartbeat before she swung over the rail, landing in a crouch on the pavement below. Her bones groaned in protest, proof of her depleted magic, but she ignored it, scrambling to her feet.

"Oh, thank god," Guy said when he saw her. Breathing hard, she just nodded, looking at Grant. He was barely breathing, and black marks covered his face, neck, and arms.

"What do we do?" Bex's eyes were wide. "He can't die, please, he has to be okay—"

"We need to keep moving," Talera said, urging them along, her mind racing.

"He needs a hospital!" Bex was crying.

A hospital wouldn't do any good against the dark magic. "We've got to get him to the Realm," Talera said, thinking of Adaira.

Bex choked out a sob. "Please, please, he can't die."

Guy grabbed Talera's forearm. "You're sure?"

"It's his only chance."

Guy's eyes were hollow and haunted. "Talera," he whispered. "The others there—"

"I know," Talera hissed.

She stopped and looked at them then. Bex's jeans were torn, her knees scraped and bloody, her dad hovering near death between Guy and Owen. The hem of Owen's shirt was soaked with blood, and Huxby's hands were cut up. Grant's only chance was Adaira's Aldar. Exhaustion threatened to drop Talera on the spot. If they didn't get out of here before more villains arrived…

She turned to Owen. "How far are we from the bridge?"

"It's about a ten-minute drive, but the streets are going to be clogged for sure." His voice was laced with pain.

"I have a car." Professor Huxby pointed a shaking finger at the row of cars parked on the street.

Talera squared her shoulders. "Let's go."

CHAPTER THIRTY-TWO

A Promise

REHNIR UNLEASHED A BOLT of power, blue light crackling and snapping along his limbs. The blow caught the three men nearest him, shattering their shields and sending them sprawling to the ground. His attackers wore helmets and thick uniforms that he guessed were lined with some type of armor. Rehnir whipped his head around, noting the circle they were trying to close in around him. He snarled, lashing out another mental tether, pulling on the Fear from the pair of soldiers now rushing him. Rehnir clenched his hand into a fist, watching as they staggered. Blood burst into the air like a red mist as they convulsed violently and collapsed.

A cacophony of sharp blasts assaulted his senses, and pain lanced through his leg. He faltered, knees buckling as blood bloomed on his trousers. A primal snarl tore from him, and he threw his hand out again, fingers flexed in anticipation of the rush of power. It came, taking down the first row of fools encircling him. Their replacements stepped forward quickly even as their companions died.

Something sliced into his arm, burning metal lodging deep, but Rehnir didn't flinch. The adrenaline that coursed through him, the Fear running rampant in his body, engulfed the pain.

A feathered arrow shot passed Rehnir, striking a soldier's neck. A second one impaled the shoulder of another who was advancing on him. Rehnir spun to see a barrel-chested man wielding a massive bow. His hood was pushed back to reveal a sadistic face with a jagged scar from his brow to jaw. He shot three arrows in quick succession, each finding its mark deep in the skull of one of Rehnir's attackers. He gave Rehnir a quick nod before turning to find more victims.

A pair of expansive black wings—the muscled fae he'd spoken to—was swooping through the horde, malice glinting in his eyes as he snapped necks. A flash of blinding purple light came from the other side of the convention center, and the screams intensified.

More and more characters were pouring in, lured by the tempting masses celebrating stories. The poetic irony pulled a sharp laugh from Rehnir. The inhabitants of the

Abandoned Realm slew their enemies, doling out the punishment for their exile.

Not useless, indeed.

Blood dripped from his arm and leg as he sharply inhaled the overwhelming Fear.

He was Fear's master, the only one able to control it, harness it. He'd never be weak again. He gave his mind over to the monster inside, letting the thrill intoxicate his senses.

Bodies fell before him. Howls filled his ears. Power surged in his veins. Black cobweb-like marks spread over corpses, and the dark magic pulsed with energy. He pulled in the Fear, and the Fear pulled on him. There was only the Fear and power, death and control.

He spun, spreading his arms wide, ready to release another bolt of energy. His rage was white-hot, this power exacting and all-consuming. Cleansing.

The darkness engulfed him.

Show them.

Monster.

Monster.

Monster, monster, monstermonstermonstermonster

Promise me, said his mother's broken and dying face. *You'll be better than him. Promise me, Rehnir—*

With a roar, he ripped himself from the choking, vicious darkness.

The agony of the hollowness dropped him to the floor.

Rehnir's vision tunneled as he watched thick boots storm toward him before hands grabbed him roughly.

PART TWO

The Abandoned Realm

CHAPTER THIRTY-THREE

Through the Portal

THE CAR VEERED TO the right, coming to a halt on the bridge as Huxby hit the hazard lights. The front of Bex's shirt was covered with her dad's blood. The neckline was soaked with tears, though only choked dry sobs came from her now. Talera and Guy pulled Grant, still unconscious, from the car. The bridge was nearly deserted, which seemed like a bad omen. Blood stained all of their clothes. The cold wind stung the cuts on Bex's knees from climbing through the broken window. Owen gripped her hand, but she could barely feel it.

"You're sure we shouldn't be taking him to the hospital?" Huxby asked for the third time.

Talera shook her head, keeping her voice low. "They won't be able to do anything. His only chance of survival is in the Realm. Adaira has treated wounds like this before."

"Well, how far is it?" Huxby asked.

"Professor." Talera whirled on him, causing Guy to pivot to keep Grant's limp form steady between them. "If you could please just…shut up and walk faster." She glared at them all, then turned back around.

Owen brushed his thumb over the back of her hand as they crossed to the center of the bridge. "It's going to be all right, Bex."

Bex nodded, but she couldn't find words. She took in the worry around his eyes, the tension bracketing his mouth. He winced, his free hand going to his hip. Her eyes dipped, tracking the movement. His shirt was stained red. Her heart hitched.

"Owen, is that Dad's blood or yours?" Bex pulled her hand from his, lifted the hem of his shirt, and drew in a sharp breath.

Just above his right hip was a long gash, but it wasn't the amount of blood that caused her stomach to turn. It was the black tendrils stretching out of the wound.

Owen yanked the shirt back down and grabbed her hand again. "Bex, it's fine." Owen quickened his gait, pulling her along behind the others.

Bex stumbled, pressing her hand to her chest. "Oh my god—"

"Bex—" But the word died on his lips, his face

twisting.

The crushing weight on her chest threatened to knock her over. This couldn't be happening. None of this should be happening. She pressed her hand over her mouth. Nausea rolled through her. The pressure was building in her ears, an unsettling wrongness heavy around them.

Owen's hand slipped from hers as he doubled over, clutching his side. "Owen?" She grabbed his shoulder, but he sank to his knees and began to convulse. *No, no, no—*

"What's happening?" Bex shrieked.

Guy swore, and she looked up, fear washing over her again as she saw her dad's eyelids flutter, the whites of his eyes showing as they rolled back before he began to shake as well. Owen slumped over on her. "What is happening?!" she yelled again.

Professor Huxby knelt swiftly, helping to brace Owen. "It's some type of seizure."

Talera swore violently. "We have to get them through *now*." She pushed Grant into Guy's arms, and he bent his knees under the increased weight. "Hurry, Guy, GO!"

Bex watched, mouth open, as Guy, hauling her dad along with him, walked straight into a metal beam. They blurred momentarily and then disappeared.

Talera's violet eyes swam before Bex's face. "Through

the portal." She grabbed hold of Owen, whose chin rolled onto his chest, and jerked her head at Professor Huxby. "Go."

Professor Huxby trembled as he stood but strode toward the beam, hesitating for only a moment before stepping through.

Bex's mind rioted against the implausibility of the situation.

"You can do this, Bex. You just have to trust me."

A heavy force pressed down on her, thrumming in her chest and ringing in her ears. The air tasted strange, and her vision distorted.

Bex breathed through her nose to keep from vomiting. She could sense it—a vague warping in the sky. A faint outline of a door, almost like there were several sheets of silk draped over the bridge, identical to its golden-orange color.

She cast one more desperate look at Talera before squeezing her eyes shut. She braced herself and took a step.

The world went dark.

The cold spread through her bones, into her brain, like she was being dunked into freezing water. Her breath was ripped from her, darkness pressing in tightly.

As suddenly as the sensation had started, it stopped.

Bex opened her eyes as she stumbled into the world beyond the portal.

The Abandoned Realm.

The sky was gray, swirling with ash. Professor Huxby was breathing heavily, staring at their surroundings. Guy had collapsed just a few steps from the portal after laying her dad on the ground. Bex dropped to his side, ignoring the smarting pain in her shins where the broken window glass had cut her during their escape. She ran her hands over his chest and throat. His pulse was faint, but it was there.

Talera stepped through the portal, supporting Owen. She ripped her pack from his back as she maneuvered his body to the ground, laying him beside Bex's dad.

"Adaira!" Talera yelled, her voice booming louder than Bex thought possible. Guy scrambled back to his feet, running toward a large building that looked similar to the pictures Bex had seen of the New York Public Library.

Talera ripped a cloth with her teeth, tearing a strip off, then pulled up Owen's shirt to reveal the gash. She shoved the remainder of the cloth into Bex's hands. "Hold this over his wound. Press hard; we have to stop the bleeding."

Talera didn't spare them a second glance as she turned toward Grant, tightly wrapping the bandage she held around a large cut on his arm to stanch the blood flow.

Bex's fingers shook as she pressed down on Owen's wound. His stomach muscles clenched spasmodically as she did, though the rest of his body had stopped seizing. Shouting came from across the square. Guy was trailing behind a woman running toward them, dreadlocks piled high on her head.

"What's happened?" Her serious tone underlined the severity of the scene before her.

"Both of them were hit with Rehnir's dark magic. I didn't know where else to bring them," Talera said.

The woman's expression darkened as she knelt next to Grant and Owen, letting out a hiss as she looked at their wounds.

"Please tell me you still have Aldar?" Talera's voice was tight, and Bex looked between the two women.

"Some, but…" The woman, Adaira, looked Talera in the eye and didn't finish her sentence.

"Please, you have to help them, please!" Bex's stomach was in knots, and she couldn't keep her body from shaking.

Adaira shared another look with Talera, but she finally nodded, tugging a chain from around her neck, a glass vial of shimmering liquid on the end. She pulled a dagger from her boot and Bex cried out in alarm, but Talera silenced her with another look.

Bex numbly watched as Adaira cut off her dad's shirt in a swift motion. He was covered in so much blood, she couldn't tell where it was coming from. His chest looked completely charred, and a molten writhing mass spread up his neck and disappeared down below his belt. Bex turned abruptly, dry heaving.

"Don't watch, Bex, just keep pressure on Owen." Talera's voice was flat. "You two, hold him steady," she said to Guy and Huxby.

But Bex couldn't look away. "What's wrong with him? What are you doing?" She pressed against Owen's wound, her hands trembling.

"We need to combat the dark with the light." Adaira held up the bottle, then dipped the knife into the iridescent liquid. Talera instructed everyone to hold Grant tightly.

Bex wasn't able to see what Adaira did after she positioned herself above Grant. A moan pierced the air, and her dad's legs twitched. Bex bit down on her cry, blinking away tears as she continued to put pressure on Owen's gash.

After what felt like an eternity, Adaira rocked back on her heels and swiveled toward Bex. Keeping her hands firmly where they were, Bex shifted to make room for her.

Adaira was already setting the shimmering vial on the ground, flicking her dagger deftly to remove Owen's shirt.

She instructed Bex to remove her hands, then tossed aside the bandage, stained red with blood. She repeated the same ritual with the liquid and the dagger. Hand steady, not taking her eyes from the blackened wound above Owen's hip, Adaira said, "Hold him down, please. He's not with us yet, but he'll feel this."

Talera held down one of Owen's arms, Guy the other, each of them also placing a hand on his chest. Professor Huxby looked like he was going to pass out, but he grabbed Owen by the calves while Bex scrambled to position herself at his head.

Slowly, Adaira pressed the edge of the knife to Owen's skin. Upon contact, the luminous liquid sizzled like water touching a hot pan. Owen's body jerked in response, but the woman pressed the tip down harder, breaking the skin parallel to the cut Rehnir's magic had made. Adaira ignored Owen's moaning and thrashing, carefully tracing the wound with her blade as everyone else held him down.

The shimmering liquid seeped into the wound, a faint glow beginning to spread under the damaged skin, reaching out toward the black mark. The ends of the mark slowly began to fade back to Owen's usual skin color, albeit flecked with blood, and the black tendrils snaking up his body began to disappear, leaving only the wound itself tinged with black.

Bex let out a quiet sob of relief, and the others expelled their held breaths as well. Adaira nodded to herself.

Bex bit her lip, looking between her dad and Owen. "Are they going to…" She couldn't finish the words. The marks on them were slowly fading, but their breathing was still labored.

Adaira turned her eyes to Bex, holding her gaze for a long moment before answering. "I don't know." She rose, speaking to Talera. "The effects of the boundary are strongest here; we need to move them."

A beat passed before Talera said, "They're not from our side."

Silence. The hair on Bex's neck rose.

Adaira stepped closer to Talera. "You mean you brought people from that world into ours? Do you know what—"

"We didn't have any other choice," Talera growled.

Adaira snorted, eyes flashing.

"What was I supposed to do?" Talera hissed. "Let them die?"

"Yes." Adaira shook her head, clicking her tongue. "It's what they've done to us." She turned her stony glare onto Bex. Bex's whole body felt hollowed out under that gaze.

"She's trying to fix it," Guy said softly.

Adaira studied her again before saying, "We'll see about that." Bex trembled at the unspoken threat in those words.

Adaira heaved a sigh, fists on her hips. "I would be careful who you tell about this. If other characters find out who they really are, I don't think they'll be as welcoming." She appraised Professor Huxby, who appeared catatonic, before striding away. She threw them another glare over her shoulder. "Come on, then."

Talera helped Bex lift Owen while Guy and Professor Huxby took hold of Grant. Even though she knew about Talera's powers, the ease with which she carried Owen's weight was jarring. Bex was sure that Talera was only acting like Bex was helping.

It was nearly impossible to comprehend the dissonance of the Realm. Everywhere she looked, a clash of fictional genres jumped out. There was a tavern straight out of the beginning of every fantasy adventure. Behind it loomed a large rocket ship, the metal dented and violently smashed in places. Bex could have sworn she glimpsed a ship that had run aground between two crumbling towers, the wood splintered and decayed. Her mouth went dry as her eyes roamed over the ground, littered with corpses. A fallen knight, a woman in a tattered ball gown, winged and horned beings, all with ghastly wounds tinged with blackness. Many of the corpses were translucent, an effect of the widespread contamination. Bex tried to quell the rolling in her stomach as she took in the gore.

A story graveyard. The words jolted her mind.

Bex felt Talera's gaze on her as they picked their way around the bodies.

"There won't be as many corpses in the Library," Talera said.

The words did nothing to ease the tightness in her chest.

This place…

This was where she had sent Talera, where she had banished every character she'd ever started writing and stopped. Every failure had doomed a soul to this hell.

CHAPTER THIRTY-FOUR

The Blue Man Group

THE STARK QUIET OF the Realm was disconcerting after the tumult of the Convention Center. Talera's blood roared with adrenaline after all the fighting, her senses alert and searching for a threat. The large number of villains who'd gone through the portal and the many characters who'd gone elsewhere to avoid the effects of the dwindling boundary had left the Library of Manuscripts void of voices. Adaira said nothing as she led them through the seemingly endless rows of half-finished books and manuscripts, toward the far back corner. The look on her face when Talera had informed her that Bex and the others were not from the Realm…

Talera bit her tongue to keep from lashing out with it. They just needed to get Owen and Grant situated, and then she could talk with the Council and figure out what to do next.

"Wait here." Adaira barely glanced at them as she left them in a small alcove carved directly into the wall, breaking up the otherwise solid wall of shelves. A single chair occupied the space.

Bex stood rigid, the muscles of her jaw flexing as she looked at Grant and Owen. She fiercely blinked back the tears threatening to fall.

"Shit," she swore. "Shitshitshit! This is all my fault!"

Talera was too tired to address the statement.

Tears ran down Bex's cheeks, her breathing becoming ragged. "If they…if…I'll never forgive myself."

Before long, Adaira returned, followed by a man and a woman. Talera assumed they were members of the Council, though she didn't recognize either of them. They each carried an armful of straw coated in a layer of grime. Adaira held two blankets that were equally filthy, but when she laid them over the bundles of straw to make two crude pallets on the floor, Bex and Talera gently laid Owen down on one without hesitation. Guy and Huxby lifted Grant onto the other.

A pang of guilt struck Talera as she looked down at them. What had happened to all the others at StoryCon? No one struck by Rehnir's magic could be cured. She knew it hadn't been possible to save everyone, but the taste in her mouth was still bitter. Was this how Mother had felt when faced with the inevitable truth that she couldn't save everyone and some people would die?

The truth felt too heavy.

And what of Rehnir? Surely the authorities were no match for his powers. Talera's magic hadn't been enough. She reached her mind out to touch her Faelyn. The reserve of magic answered her call, and Talera murmured a quick thank-you to the gods before bitterness jabbed her. There were no gods. They were all just part of the story Bex had been writing. Talera dug the heels of her palms into her eyes, forcing the thoughts away to be dealt with later. Adaira and the other Council members left without a word.

Minutes passed and Guy muttered something about finding some new clothes for Grant and Owen. Talera stretched her neck, realizing some of the aches and weakness she'd felt on the other side of the portal had significantly diminished. She rubbed a hand over her face.

"Guy," she said quietly, and indicated the direction Adaira had gone. Guy nodded, and Talera looked to Huxby, who was leaning against a bookshelf. His gaze hadn't left the spot where Adaira had stood. Bex didn't seem aware of their presence at all anymore.

They needed to speak to the Council.

Talera and Guy walked in silence through the Library. Voices in another language grew louder as they passed by the dais for arriving stories. A handful of characters were huddled together; the one who was speaking had blue skin with swirls of red marbling his face. Talera got the sense that they were badmouthing the new character arrivals to the Realm—hate was a universal tongue. Their clothes were tattered, and their expressions reminded her of the one Duke Decker had worn.

Footsteps tore her gaze from the group as Branson came into view, followed closely by Adaira and Sekzelt.

"Do you fools have any idea—" Branson cut off his tirade as he realized they had an audience. He dropped his voice to a low whisper. "You brought people from the other side back with you? Do they have a death wish?"

The blue man group shuffled away.

"They would've died if they'd stayed on the other side. I knew Adaira had the Aldar, and that was their best chance." Talera fixed them with a withering stare. "I didn't realize how closed-minded people would be."

Sekzelt leaned heavily on his wizard's staff, brows drawn together. Adaira looked away. But Branson held up his hands and continued. "You can't blame us for being upset—though it's not us you have to worry about." His eyes darted around, and he led them away from the dais. "The characters who went through the portal aren't the only ones who have a vendetta against those responsible for damning us. Not everyone wanted to cross through, but if they were to learn that there are people from the other side of the portal here…" Branson's voice was calm, but there was steel in his eyes.

"We didn't have much of a choice," Guy said. "Rehnir and the others are on a rampage. We can keep their true identities secret to protect them. No one has to know they aren't from here."

"One of them knows how to close the portal," Talera said. "At least we think he does. We sort of got interrupted before we could make sure."

Branson threw up his hands and scoffed.

"We can't trust them," Sekzelt said, his long white beard shaking.

"Listen," said Talera evenly, an edge to her tone. "None of them did this on purpose. They couldn't have known the results of their actions when they stopped writing their stories. It's not just our people who are in danger now. The contamination is spreading on their side as well, not to mention that we've unleashed murderous villains on them." Talera rubbed at her face again. "We're no better than they are if we don't help them now."

"Worse, really," Guy said.

Something shifted in Adaira's face, and Sekzelt glowered at the ground. Branson said nothing, working his jaw.

"I won't stand aside and watch innocent people die." Talera looked at Adaira. "How long until the Aldar fully reverses the dark magic?"

A shadow flashed over Adaira's face. No one spoke.

Cold caressed the back of Talera's neck. "What is it?"

"The Aldar has halted the spread of the dark magic for a time." Adaira hesitated before continuing. "But with the contamination growing stronger, their marks will start to spread again. Aldar's healing properties are temporary at best."

Guy swore so colorfully that Talera's cheeks flushed with heat.

"We simply can't afford to waste time trying to heal them. We need to focus our efforts on getting as many of the worthwhile inhabitants of the Realm as we can as far away from the portal as possible," Branson said. "We haven't found a way to close it, so we must try to outrun the contamination."

Before Talera could argue, a scream pierced their ears,

followed by a loud crash and shouting. Understanding and horror struck them simultaneously.

"Shit." Talera and Guy sped toward the back of the Library, Adaira close behind them.

Cursing in several languages, Talera tore around the corner and saw the skirmish in the alcove. Huxby was on the floor, wrestling with one of the men from the dais while two others jeered from the sidelines. Huxby threw a hand out, grabbed a heavy tome from the shelf as they rolled, and hit the man over the head with it.

One man held Bex from behind, but as another approached with a crude-looking knife, Bex leaned back, using one attacker's weight as leverage to kick both feet into the other's chest.

Talera raised an eyebrow. Bex's moves were clumsy, to be sure, but effective nevertheless. The dagger clattered to the ground as the kick sent the man sprawling.

Bex whipped her head back, slamming her skull into the blue man's face, and he immediately released her, spitting blood. The two who'd been watching the wrestling had turned their attention to the prone forms of Owen and Grant.

It was laughable that *this*—Bex's awkward approximation of her own fighting skills—was the most bizarre thing she'd witnessed in the last few days. It drove home the fact that she was literally the brainchild of this woman. Instinctively, Talera knew what Bex would do next—because it was what Talera would do.

Bex lunged for the wooden chair in the alcove and grabbed it, swinging it at the nearest man's head. The chair shattered against his skull. Bex brandished a broken chair leg, its tip now a splintered point, at the remaining attacker, feet planted wide as she stood over Grant and Owen. Her lip curled back, baring her teeth, as she snarled, "Don't you dare."

The whole thing was over before Talera and Adaira skidded to a halt in front of the alcove. The blue-skinned man was seething, blood pouring down his chin, but neither he nor his companions made to attack again. What kind of incompetent fools were they to have lost so easily to this professor and Bex?

Guy and Branson reached them.

"I told you," Branson hissed. "I told you it was dangerous for them to be here."

"Yes, you've made your position very clear, Branson," Talera snapped. How in the Seven Hells had news of them being from the other side traveled so quickly?

"You would dare to protect this filth?" The blue-skinned man spat on the floor. "You'd bring them through that damned portal and stand beside them?!"

"Oh, for hells' sake!" Talera burst out. "Being from one side or the other doesn't make someone inherently good or evil. Your actions do. Attacking people just because of which side they come from? I won't stand for that."

Sekzelt finally caught up, wheezing slightly, a few others trailing behind him with concern on their faces.

"All of our lives are in danger. *All of them*. It doesn't matter which bloody side you come from, if you wrote a character or you are a character. These petty vendettas aren't going to make a damn difference when the contamination kills us all." Talera looked at Adaira. "Get them out of here. Please," she added after a beat.

Adaira nodded, grabbing the collar of the blue-skinned man and roughly pulling him to his feet. As she rounded up the attackers, Talera and Guy approached Huxby and Bex. A bruise was forming on Bex's cheek, and her lip was bleeding a bit. Huxby's glasses were cracked and his shirt was torn.

"We shouldn't have come here. This was a mistake," Bex said.

"This was their best option," Talera said, gesturing to Owen and Grant. "Let's just get our heads on straight and figure out—"

"No." The word lanced between them, sharp as a blade.

Talera stilled. "Excuse me?"

"I should never have listened to you." Bex's chest was heaving, her eyes hard. "I knew nothing I did would help this situation, but I went along with it and tried anyway, and look where it got us." She gestured to Owen and her dad, her face twisted in anger and pain. "We don't belong here. Whatever your plan is, leave me out of it."

Talera let out a harsh laugh, her temper flaring. "You went along with it because gods forbid you make your own choices. How's that working out for you, Bex?" Talera stepped closer, her blood rushing in her ears. "Are you going to spend the rest of your life alone because you're too much of a coward to tell Owen how you feel?" They were nose to nose now. "You can't even manage a semi-decent relationship with your own mother. You had to make up a fictional mother who cared, and then you went and fucked that up, too."

"You're. Not. Real!" Bex screamed, shoving her backward.

Talera stumbled, caught off guard.

"You couldn't just leave well enough alone when I got

rid of you. You had to come and ruin everything!"

Talera bared her teeth. "Well, which is it, Bex? Because everything can't be your fault when it gets you out of having to try for once in your fucking life and my fault when you want to blame everyone else for your mistakes."

"Go to hell!"

Talera flung her hands wide. "Already here!"

Bex balled her hands into fists, visibly shaking now. "I don't care if you and everyone else in this godforsaken realm dies!"

"You made that pretty clear from the moment I met you." Talera sneered. "What a bloody disappointment you are."

Bex looked as if Talera had struck her in the face, her eyes rimmed with tears. Triumph and shame rose in Talera, but she shoved the emotions down. The air pulled taut between them.

"I should have killed you off when I had the chance!" Bex shrieked.

Talera's vision burned red.

She punched Bex square in the gut. Bex curled into herself, dropping to her knees with a broken gasp. Talera shoved her roughly.

"Well, it seems you can't do anything right." Talera

spun on her heel and shouldered past Guy.

"Talera," Guy called after her, trying to keep up. "Talera, wait—"

"Don't bother trying to defend her," Talera snapped over her shoulder.

"I wasn't going to, I just think…" Guy struggled to keep pace with her. "Can we all just take a breath? Emotions are running a little high—"

"A little high?" Talera snorted. "Could you drop the nice-guy act for once and be real?" She regretted the words as soon as she said them. "I didn't mean it like that. I just meant—"

"It's all right," Guy said quietly, though his shoulders sagged in the tense silence that followed. "I know it may seem put on, but…" He shrugged. "Looking on the bright side is how I've managed to survive this long. It is genuine."

Talera bit the inside of her cheek, mentally kicking herself. "I'm sorry, Guy. Really. I shouldn't take my anger out on you when she's the one—" She broke off, running a hand over her head.

They started walking again, this time at a slower pace. Guy said nothing, and in the quiet, her emotions seemed to untangle.

"I'm just so angry. She's the reason I exist and that

we're in this mess in the first place, and she dares to blame me? I don't know why I even bothered to help Owen and her dad."

Guy took his time before responding. "Do you remember the author at the panel who talked about crafting characters?" Talera didn't answer, but he continued, "she said anger is a secondary emotion. So what's the real emotion you're feeling right now?"

Talera scowled, the scuffs of their shoes echoing through the Library as they walked. Her pulse slowed as she rolled his words over in her mind.

"I thought that maybe…maybe if I could help fix some of this"—she gestured to the seemingly endless bookshelves of discarded stories—"if I could help save Grant and Owen… My mother always wanted me to be a healer like her. But I learned to fight instead. I thought that was the way I could fix things." The image of Grant's face twisted in agony as she tried to fight off Rehnir flashed through her mind. "If I can't help save people from the evils here or on the other side, what good am I? What's the point?" She didn't dare look at Guy as she finally uttered the truth aloud. "I'm ashamed. Ashamed of what my mother would think of the fact that I've utterly failed."

Guy stopped abruptly, grabbing her arm, his eyes fierce

as he looked at her. "Your mother would be proud to see you fighting for those who can't fight for themselves. She'd be proud that you haven't given up, haven't given in to despair and hatred and anger. Don't think for one second that you've failed her, Talera. Or anyone else."

Talera blinked at the sudden burning in her eyes, too surprised to say anything. She swallowed and inclined her head slightly.

Guy gave a curt nod and began walking back the way they'd come. "Right. So let's keep trying while we can, shall we?"

Something that felt dangerously like hope spread through Talera's chest as she grudgingly followed him.

"I didn't really want to hurt Bex. If I'd wanted to cause actual damage, I would've hit her in the face," Talera grumbled.

"Of course," Guy said, keeping his face suspiciously blank. "I'm sure that thoughtfulness will endear you to her even more."

CHAPTER THIRTY-FIVE

FAILURE DEFINED

STARS DANCED IN BEX'S vision from the piercing pain in her chest.

Huxby knelt beside her. "You just need to breathe."

She wanted to argue that she couldn't, but that would require her lungs and abdomen to stop spasming.

"Knees to chest. You have to relax."

Bex let Professor Huxby help her sit back against a bookshelf and draw her knees up. Slowly, so slowly, her body regained the ability to take shallow breaths. The muscles in her gut unclenched, and she greedily sucked in air.

She clenched her fists, jolting at a stinging sensation in her palm. A wooden splinter from the chair was lodged deep in her skin. Bex fumbled, trying to grasp the sliver of wood, cursing under her breath.

I should have killed you off when I had the chance.

Her horrible words played over and over in her mind. Her cheeks burned with shame. She avoided Huxby's gaze.

She could still hear the man's bones crunching under the force of the chair. Feel the vibration of it run up her arms and rattle her teeth. Feel the burst of pain in her stomach, the air driven out of her lungs when Talera had punched her.

When the splinter was finally out, Bex touched the cut on her lip with her tongue. She winced. Huxby cleared his throat. He proffered a relatively clean strip of material from his shirt, which had been torn in the scuffle.

"You're bleeding," was all he said.

Bex took it, gingerly dabbing at the blood on her chin. "Thank you." The top of her head throbbed where it had collided with her attacker's face.

"You've done that before?" Huxby gestured to the mess around them—the broken chair, the splatters of blood.

Bex shook her head. "I've never done anything like that in my life." Huxby nodded, his eyes trailing back to where Adaira had escorted their attackers. "So she…I mean…" She lost her nerve as Huxby looked at her sharply. "Is this where you came before?"

He studied her over his glasses, a crack in one of the lenses, and nodded. "Honestly, if it wasn't for this building"—he gestured to the Library around them—"I wouldn't have thought it was the same place. So much has changed."

Bex stayed silent, sensing that he was working through his thoughts, deciding what to share after keeping silent for so long.

"It didn't used to be this…bleak. This hopeless. It was full of life and promise and…" Huxby ran a hand over his close-cropped hair.

Something Guy had said back in San Francisco clicked into place. He'd said that Adaira had only recently arrived in the Realm. If this was indeed where the first portal had brought Huxby all those years ago, that meant he'd stopped Adaira's story even knowing what it would most likely mean for her.

Huxby's throat bobbed. "My father had just passed when I was working on her story." His eyes gleamed, and sympathy swelled in Bex.

"I guess I always just assumed that when someone's as talented and successful as you are, they don't…" She trailed off, cheeks burning.

Huxby gave a hollow laugh. "Fail? Quit?"

"I'm sorry, I didn't mean—"

"It's all right. I knew what it would mean for Adaira when I stopped. The shame of that alone was crippling for a while." He blew out a breath. "But life happens. Failure can't be avoided. That doesn't mean we should give up or that we aren't worthy. It simply means we were unable to meet an expectation. Failure doesn't dictate or define who we are. What we choose to do in the face of it does."

The words prodded at her mind. She had always thought success and failure were the litmus test of worth. Her mother had made sure to instill that belief in her with every offhand comment, every judgment, every impossible standard.

When other people were able to take failure in stride, it was simply more proof that something was irreversibly wrong with her. Bex was so far behind the starting line that every misstep counted against her. Others could afford to stumble, but she couldn't.

Her eyes flicked to her dad. He'd never been able to convince her otherwise, though not for lack of trying.

But…

Bex felt pulled between two warring beliefs. The dissonance left her feeling muddled and slightly sick—though she supposed that could be from Talera's sucker punch.

Owen let out a moan and shifted on his pallet. Bex scrambled across the floor, kneeling beside him, her heart trying to beat its way out of her ribs.

"Owen?"

His eyes fluttered open. A sob mixed with laughter escaped her, and she gripped his hand, her vision blurring with tears.

"What—" His voice was gravelly as he looked around, disoriented.

"Oh my god, Owen." She let out another relieved laugh, tears still flowing. "I thought…" She shook her head, trailing off. "Are you okay?"

"Bex…w-where are we?"

"We're in the Abandoned Realm. They took us through the portal after…the convention center." Her voice shook.

Owen groaned as he tried to sit up and almost immediately lay back down. "Shit!" he hissed through his teeth.

Bex looked over her shoulder.

"I'll find someone," Huxby said as he hurried off.

"Just stay still," Bex said. "Don't try to get up."

Owen closed his eyes, breathing deeply through his nose, his brow pinched. Bex gripped his hand, his skin clammy. He tried to even out his breathing. Several tense minutes passed before quick footsteps approached.

"You scared the piss out of me, Owen," Guy said from

behind Bex. Adaira knelt down, immediately peering under his bandages. Bex braved a glance up at Talera. The elf's lips were pressed together, and she stood with her arms crossed, attention fixed on Owen.

Owen cracked an eye open. "I don't…I don't remember anything after we got to the bridge."

"The contamination from the boundary seems to be interacting with Rehnir's magic," Adaira said as she took his pulse.

"The contamination," Owen echoed.

Adaira sat back on her heels and fixed him with a serious look. "The boundary between our worlds is weak. The contamination from that is affecting you more because of the dark magic in that wound."

Owen shook his head as if to clear mental fog. "This doesn't feel like any of the symptoms of the Fading." He looked at Bex. "I texted Benny about it when he first got sick. We messaged back and forth a bit about what he was feeling."

It was absurd to be talking about texting while in another realm with the fate of the world and those she loved most hanging in the balance. Laughter bubbled out of Bex before she clamped her mouth shut.

Owen continued. "What I felt on the bridge before I

passed out was the same as what happened when Rehnir was attacking." A shadow flickered in his eyes. "Horror and fear that feels like it will go on forever."

Talera nodded, a haunted look on her face.

Adaira furrowed her brow. "So you think that the seizures and the mark spreading, that's all from what Rehnir did?"

"Maybe the mark is some type of tether." They all turned to look at Huxby. He didn't take his eyes off Adaira as he said, "That would explain why the Aldar isn't working."

Bex's stomach lurched. "What do you mean, not working?"

Huxby continued, "If the magic is tied to Rehnir somehow, then until that connection is broken, the effects of the dark magic cannot be reversed."

"How can we break the connection?" asked Bex. He couldn't possibly mean they had to kill Rehnir. There was no way.

Everything seemed to warp as Huxby's words sank in.

Adaira went very still.

Huxby gave a nearly imperceptible nod. An answer. A condemnation. A confession.

When Adaira sprang to her feet, he didn't flinch, just

stood there with a solemn expression.

"You." The word lanced between them.

"I'm truly sorry." Huxby's voice broke.

Adaira's nostrils flared, and her hands shook as she stared tight-lipped at the man who'd made her—made her and then deemed her story unfit. Nimbly, Adaira pulled a blade from her hip and cocked her arm back to strike. Bex barely had time to cry out before Adaira hurled the dagger.

It landed several feet to the right of Huxby and sank deep into the bookshelf behind him. Huxby looked like he was about to soil himself. Guy let out a strangled noise.

Adaira glowered, chest rising and falling, then marched off without a word.

Guy carded a hand through his hair. He pulled two plain short-sleeved shirts from his back pocket, tossing them at Owen. "They're mostly clean." Owen raised an eyebrow and Guy continued, "trust me, you don't want to know where I got them. I'll go talk to her."

Huxby leaned against the shelves before sliding down to the ground as Guy left. Everything was happening so fast, it felt almost impossible to grasp onto an anchor. Bex's heart ached for Adaira, but Huxby's revelation rang in her ears.

They'd have to kill Rehnir in order to rid Owen and her dad of the dark magic, not to mention whoever else bore the mark. All she wanted to do was run and hide and wait for all of this to go away.

But it wasn't going to. They were running out of time and options.

Talera turned to follow Guy.

"Talera, wait." Bex's palms tingled as she moved toward her.

Talera finally faced her. The cords in her neck flexed.

Bex licked her lips. "Can we talk? Privately?"

Talera eyed her, then glanced away. "All right."

They walked, the air tense around them. They came to a stop at another small alcove cut into the wall. Talera folded her arms.

"I'm sorry, Talera. I shouldn't have said those things to you." Bex's voice wavered, and she swallowed the lump in her throat. "I said the most horrible thing I could think of because I didn't want to feel all that horribleness inside me."

Talera drummed her fingers against her biceps, but her gaze was open.

Bex lifted her chin slightly. "You were right. About me. I do quit everything. Ever since I was little, believing in myself has been—" Bex faltered, the words twisting in her stomach. Her mother's face leered in her mind.

Failure doesn't dictate or define who we are. What we

choose to do in the face of it does.

"I quit things because at least then it's on my terms. Or I don't try in the first place, because if I don't try, I can't fail. I've made so many mistakes since meeting you, and I know I'm gonna make a million more before we're through. But I'm not quitting. On you. On any of us. I'm in this with you." Her skin buzzed. Her feet were planted solidly; calm trickled through her bones. Bex pressed her arms close to her sides. "That is, if you'll still have me."

Talera tucked her chin, rubbing the back of her neck. "I'm sorry, too. I had no right to say those things to you." The corner of her mouth twitched up. "And no need to be dramatic. Of course I'll still have you."

Bex's chest swelled.

Talera grinned and inclined her head a bit. "I'll go get someone to guard the Library doors."

Bex glided back to the other alcove. Owen still lay on his pallet next to her dad. Huxby was slumped against the shelves. She sat down next to Owen. "As you can see, you've missed some things."

Owen chuckled, the sound warming her soul. "I can't leave you lot alone, can I?"

Without thinking, Bex reached out to brush the hair back from his forehead. Owen stilled under her touch; his eyes locked on her face. Seconds ticked by as they held each other's gaze.

Her chest tightened as she wet her lips. "I thought…" But she couldn't say the words. Saying them felt too real, and him being here—awake and alive—still felt too fragile. Too uncertain. She cleared her throat. "I'm sorry I yelled at you."

Owen's brows pinched together.

"The other night when…I know you were just trying to help, and I was a jerk. I'm realizing that I take my frustration and fear out on others when it feels like too much." She dropped her gaze, staring at his hand between hers. *I do need you.* The words washed through her body, but she pressed her lips together tighter, not ready to let them out yet. "I'm sorry."

Owen squeezed her hand. "I'm sorry, too. Just…let me be there for you when things get to be too much."

Bex let out a bitter laugh. "Well, if there was ever a time when things were too much…" Her gaze shifted to her dad.

Owen craned his neck. "Help me sit up."

"Owen…"

"Bex." He tugged on her hand, forcing her to look at him through her brimming tears. "Please," he said softly.

Bex nodded and leaned down, carefully sliding her

hand under his shoulders to help hoist him into a sitting position. Owen hissed sharply again at the pain the movement caused. Panting slightly from the effort, he looked at Grant, his eyes taking in the gruesome black marks inked along his veins. Owen reached down and gently peeled the bandage away from his skin. He swore, the color draining from his face as he took in the marks on his stomach and hip.

Bex grabbed his hand again tightly. "Hey."

Owen tore his eyes from the wound to look at her.

"It's going to be all right," she said. "Here, let me help." Gently she drew the new shirt over his head, trying to ignore the way his unbroken eye contact sent her heart beating faster. Taking care to not brush the bandaged area, she helped him get his arms through the sleeves. His breath was warm on her face. She pulled the shirt down his torso, her fingers suddenly warm at the contact of his bare skin. Bex cleared her throat and hooked a curl behind her ear.

"Thanks," Owen said, his voice a little more gruff than usual.

Bex nodded, forcing herself to sit back on her heels. The distance seemed to clear her brain. She needed to focus on the reality of their situation. The effects of being in a world not meant for her kept breaking over her in waves, trying to drag her under. If the portal could be closed and Rehnir was on the wrong side when it happened, would the connection still be severed? She had more questions than answers, but she knew one thing for sure: she was going to find a way.

"We're going to fix this."

A voice in her head purred with pride at the conviction in her words.

CHAPTER THIRTY-SIX

SEEING DOUBLE

TALERA STRONGLY DISLIKED BEING part of a group. Perhaps it was that she was, according to Guy, written as a "chosen one archetype," whatever that meant, or that Bex had made her this way by writing her as a lone wolf and only child. As she rubbed her temples to stave off an oncoming headache, she decided it was Branson's ability to spew endless words without saying anything at all that sealed the sentiment.

The Council had been arguing in circles for hours. Talera had had to witness the fallout of the reveal that Huxby was Adaira's author a second time. Branson seemed even more incensed about it than Adaira herself. *Yes, it's upsetting to meet someone who's partially responsible for all this, but by the gods, it's not your author! Aren't there bigger things to worry about right now?*

Branson had excused himself for several minutes to

calm down after Bex and the others had explained their connections to the Realm. After his tantrum, though, he'd returned with Rehnir's manuscript and begrudgingly agreed to play nice for the sake of the Realm.

Fear and fatigue held the reins of the discussion, cutting tempers short and rubbing salt into fresh wounds. Owen looked worse for wear, though he was still conscious, which was more than they could say for Grant. Bex was more vocal than Talera had expected her to be, the same determination burning in her eyes that had been there during their private conversation. Adaira and Huxby seemed to have reached a silent truce, and Guy kept getting distracted by Branson's talk of atoms and molecular cross contamination.

"For the love of all the gods!" Talera slammed her palm onto the table they all sat around, unable to take it anymore. "Can we please move on? We have beaten this horse to death. The portal must be closed. We have to find a power source equal to Rehnir's to close the portal." She turned to Huxby. "According to you, you came through a portal to this Realm thirty years ago. My questions are, Branson, how come we didn't know about this other portal, and Professor Huxby, can you help close this one?"

Branson cracked his knuckles, shrugging. "Perhaps time doesn't work the same way here as it does in the real world." He looked at Guy. "How long were you on the other side?"

"A few days." He looked to Talera and Bex. "Three, I think?"

Branson waved his hand. "Well, there you have it. Mere hours passed here. Probably no one is still around from when it happened before."

"That makes no sense," Owen said.

"I beg your pardon, young man?"

"If you're saying that time here passes much more slowly than it does out there, it has probably only been six months to a year since Professor Huxby came through the other portal."

Branson's nostrils flared as he glared at Owen. "Yes, well. It seems my thoughts are a bit addled, circumstances being what they are." He spread his fingers on the table. "With the constant influx of stories, genres, and timelines, time likely behaves erratically compared to the world out there."

Owen slumped a bit under Branson's glare.

Huxby licked the corner of his mouth. "There's a saying in our world: write what you know." He looked around at each of them. "My first book came out nearly a decade after the incident with the portal, but I'd written the story thousands of times over by then."

Bex leaned forward. "The way you wrote about portals is how it happened?" She laughed and blushed as everyone looked at her. "Sorry, that's just —" She covered her smile with her hand. "Never mind, it's not important right now."

A commotion broke out several aisles over. Talera tensed, whipping out a dagger. The shouting grew, and two figures skidded around a corner. One of the Council members whom they'd asked to guard the doors in case anyone came looking for trouble called out to them.

"You need to see this. I just found her, said she arrived a few hours ago," the man explained just as the person on his heels came into view.

Talera's mouth fell open. There was a collective gasp behind her.

"What the devil?" Branson took a step back.

Talera's palm was slick around the hilt of her dagger as she stared at the approaching woman.

At herself.

The her that was standing opposite them blinked rapidly. Then, with speed that only Talera could comprehend, she drew an arrow from the quiver slung across her back. The not-her nocked the arrow, aiming straight at Talera's heart, and loosed it. Talera pivoted and snatched the arrow midflight, the fletching burning her fingers, her heart racing.

"What the bloody hell?" she yelled, only to have it echo from the mouth of the woman in front of her.

"See?" The guard gestured between the two identical women.

"Well, I'll be." Guy appeared at Talera's shoulder, his eyes wide as he whispered, "Bex, where did you leave Talera off when you continued writing?"

Bex sputtered. "Uh, I think in a tavern just after the battle."

"Excuse me, er, New Talera," Guy said louder, gesturing to the new elf. "Did you just get pulled from your world while enjoying a drink after a battle? Were you were stuck in the leg with a throwing star?"

Talera's eyes dipped to the newcomer's leg. Dried blood covered the bandage wrapped around it. Talera's head spun as she noted how the bandage was tied off with a special knot her mother had once shown her.

New Talera's eyes flashed, darting back and forth between Guy, Talera, and Bex.

"Extraordinary," said Professor Huxby softly.

"How do you know that? What kind of witchcraft is this?" New Talera snapped.

Talera braced herself against a bookshelf. Her knees went weak.

Guy slapped his hands together, letting out a triumphant laugh. "Aha! I knew it, I knew it!" Everyone gaped at him. "Er—right, not the time. Damn, I wish I had written down my hypothesis about creating alternate timelines for this exact moment." Guy shook out his hands as he muttered to himself. "But I digress! Sorry about your luck, New Talera, but we're at a bit of a loss for time." Guy looked at Talera. "Care to do the honors? Might be easier, you know, hearing it from yourself and all."

Talera glared at him, then looked to New Talera. An ache pulsed in her chest. "Yes. Well, as he said, we don't have much time. Talera, you're me and I'm you. Bex here"—she clapped Bex on the back a bit harder than necessary—"was writing our story and then called it quits. So now we're here in the Abandoned Realm. Unfortunately, this new world of yours is currently being threatened with extinction unless we can find a way to close a magical portal before we all wither away from contamination. Once that's all taken care of, you'll have plenty of time to wallow, get drunk, and come to terms with the fact that you're not real." She looked at Guy. "That about covers it, yes?"

Talera knew that New Talera was no doubt trying to

figure out if the innkeeper back in her world had slipped a hallucinogenic elixir into her drink or if a spell had been cast on her. Guy looked annoyingly fascinated, his head swiveling between them. She gave him a discreet but distinctly crude hand gesture. Guy wouldn't recognize it, as it was from her homeland, but it seemed to transcend genres and worlds, as his face grew hot and he looked away.

"Um…" Bex pinched her lips. "Shouldn't that mean that there's another version of you wandering around here?"

Guy scrunched his face. "Oh, bollocks. You did start another draft of the story, didn't you."

"Bloody hell." Talera threw up her hands.

CHAPTER THIRTY-SEVEN

SHOW THEM

THERE WAS AN INTENSE throbbing behind Rehnir's eyes, heavy and cold. A foul taste filled his mouth. His stomach clenched violently. The room spun. Dry heaves racked his body.

After an agonizing minute, his muscles finally relaxed. He slumped back to the ground. The walls of the cell pressed in on him.

The chill of the floor seeped into his palms as he dragged himself toward the thick steel door to peer out the small window. The hallway outside was vacant. Rehnir reached out with his mind to find a wisp of Fear. But he was weak, so terribly weak, and the blasted hallway was as empty as he was inside.

He growled and slammed his fist against the glass. Need carved through his body, churning his insides. His skin crawled as if there were insects underneath it, searching for the darkness within him. He scraped his hands through his hair, gripping it tightly, his attention on the pain in his scalp. But the nagging, gnawing sensation in his gut, in his bones, in his brain rose, rose until it was a steady roar through his whole being. His nails tore into his arms, and he wished he could rip off his flesh.

Weak.

You are beyond redemption.

Revulsion threatened to drown him, to swallow him whole.

"Stop," he rasped.

I know what you really are.

He needed to feed. Needed to feed needed to feed needed to

Feedneededtofeedneededtofeedneeded—

I promised. Clarity raged against the chaos in his mind, but it was quickly losing its hold. The darkness thrummed and writhed.

Look at what seeking redemption has made of you.

His clothes were stiff with large patches of dried blood despite each of his wounds looking as if it had been healing for several months. If he hadn't had Fear coursing through him during the attack, his healing abilities would have remained that of a mortal.

Your promise keeps you weak.

The clang of a door opening echoed from down the hall. Rehnir clamped a trembling hand over his mouth.

Show them who you really are.

No.

No, no.

Promise me.

Monster.

Promise me!

Show them!

Monster.

Show them!

SHOW THEM!

His mind lashed out a tether, connecting to the source outside his cell. He could taste and feel him before he saw him—

Rehnir's whole body vibrated like a struck tuning fork. He pulled.

A throaty sigh pushed past his lips, the darkness inside swelling.

Rehnir pressed the connection harder.

The Fear was a cooling balm on the boiling hunger in his veins. His mind settled, his breathing becoming even as he straightened.

Someone thudded to the ground outside the cell.

Much better, he thought, chiding himself for the moment of panic he had felt before. The magic pulsed through him.

And now we wait.

Rehnir stood calmly by the locked door to his cell. Ten minutes passed, and then…

He heard someone shout from the far end of the hall. The buzzing of their Fear filled the air. Five people entered the hallway, the Fear seductively coiling into him.

He didn't care to wait this time. He latched on to their frequencies, yanking on the mental tethers, siphoning their Fear in one sharp inhale.

Blue light filled the small cell, momentarily blinding him as he sent his power toward the door—

An earsplitting crash followed, and then he was out in the hall, stepping over the bodies without a second glance. Lightning crackled and licked at his palms. Rehnir stalked down the hall, smiling at the Fear and screams that greeted him as he entered a large room.

The sickly sweet aroma slithered through him.

Show them who you are.

CHAPTER THIRTY-EIGHT

LOVE AND DREAMS

BEX RESTED HER FOREHEAD on her palm as she flipped through Rehnir's manuscript—again. The group had broken into several smaller ones. Owen sat next to her quietly, his face looking a little peaked. New Talera, Adaira, and Guy were huddled together, and Sekzelt and Huxby sat talking nearby while Talera stood behind them, listening in. Bex's dad was still unconscious in the back alcove of the Library.

Huxby had explained to everyone the complex hand formations and the phenomenon of clear intention behind opening or closing a portal. Branson had scoffed at their plan, saying that the Council had already scoured the stories in the Library and hadn't found any ritual that was sure to work. His stance was that they should gather all the "worthy" characters and flee deeper into the Realm to try and outrun the contamination.

Bex turned the page, eyes moving back and forth but no longer absorbing anything. Her mind replayed Talera's outrage at Branson's words. *Worthy characters? And you're the one to decide who is worthy?*

Branson hadn't even blinked at her scathing tone. *I don't expect you to understand the situation, Talera. You've been in the Realm only a few weeks. The divisions in this place are clear. Those who don't wish to live are nothing more than a drain on the magic keeping the rest of us safe. The only good thing about the portal is that it drew out a large group who were too focused on revenge to help with restoring the Realm.*

The veins at Bex's temples pulsed under her fingertips. Frustration pushed against her skull. She understood his resignation. But when the alternative was to just sit back and let everyone she loved die, it wasn't a choice she needed to think about.

They had to break the connection between Rehnir and those with his mark. The simplest way, in theory, was to kill him. If they could close the portal using Huxby's methods, he wouldn't be able to survive on the other side. But Bex was still trying to stomach the idea of their actions leading to someone's death, no matter how evil he was. These weren't just stories anymore.

She'd reached the end of the heavy tome and was about to close it when she noticed something.

Bex ran a finger along a few neatly cut edges close to the spine. Some pages were missing toward the back.

"That doesn't make any sense," she muttered, frowning.

"What doesn't?" Owen asked.

Bex tilted the manuscript for him to see.

"Huh. Guy, come over here for a second, would you?"

Guy came around to their side of the table.

"Some pages are missing from the back of this manuscript. Is that normal?" Bex asked.

Guy furrowed his brow as he inspected the book. "That's strange." He tilted his head. "Sometimes at the back there are notes from the author. You know, research or some plot points they want to include. Stuff like that."

Bex chewed on her bottom lip. "Do you think Rehnir took them out?"

Guy blew out a breath. "I supposed it's possible. Maybe there was something in there that he didn't want people to find. I do think it's strange that the pages are cut, though."

"How do you mean?" Bex said.

"Well, based on the behavior we've seen recently, he seems pretty volatile, doesn't he? Why not just tear the pages out? These were sliced very neatly." Guy flipped through the manuscript. "Of course, I have been reading an awful lot of mysteries lately—and I do mean *awful*."

"He's got to have some type of weakness, yes?" Bex tapped the manuscript. "Every character has a flaw."

Talera approached, listening keenly.

Bex rubbed her temples. Her head injury still smarted from the fight earlier. *Come on, Bex. Think. Some weakness...some flaw...anything!*

Her eyes flitted to Huxby and Sekzelt across from her, heads together as Huxby explained the hand shapes. She watched for several minutes.

Bex blinked, an idea seeping into her brain. "The boundary."

Guy cocked his head.

Bex put the words together slowly, letting the thought take shape. "When the boundary was stronger, it kept him contained and he couldn't get through. But when it weakened—"

"His power had the upper hand," Talera mused.

"Exactly." Bex studied Talera, tapping her fingers on her chin. Huxby was now staring at her, a trace of a smile on his lips. Emboldened, Bex continued, her mind churning.

"Branson's theory is that the boundary is fueled by

belief in magic, correct?" The members of the Council nodded; he'd only said it about ten times over the last hour. Bex snagged a loose paper from the ground. "I need something to write with."

Sekzelt pulled a thin pencil from inside his robes.

"Thanks. All right. Rehnir was only able to breach the boundary when he connected with you, Talera, and used your Faelyn." Bex sketched a quick T chart, writing rehnir and boundary on top. Under Rehnir's name, she wrote fear and faelyn; under boundary, she wrote belief in magic.

Talera narrowed her eyes but said nothing.

"Didn't Branson also say that magic, dreams, and love are all generated by the same type of brain waves as belief?" Bex's heart hammered against her ribs.

Guy was nodding. "Things of that nature all exist on the same frequency, just like fear, nightmares, and trauma do."

Bex added love and dreams under boundary.

"So we could reason, then, that love and dreams are foils to fear." She drew a line connecting them. "So…" Bex bit her lip again, ignoring the sting it brought. "So Faelyn is essentially the inverse of Rehnir's power."

"How?" Sekzelt asked.

"Faelyn is sourced from the dream world. The frequency of dreams borders the wavelength for fear—alpha and theta—and they overlap at times. We think that's why Rehnir was able to access so much of Talera's magic to open the portal. But if he was able to weaken the boundary that way, then maybe Faelyn could not only strengthen the boundary but—"

"—you could use the boundary's source against Rehnir," Huxby finished.

"Exactly," Bex said.

All eyes turned to Talera.

"Use my Faelyn to pull from the boundary's power and use it against Rehnir?" Talera's voice was flat.

Bex waved her hands. "Not the boundary, per se. But"—Bex tipped her head toward New Talera—"what about pulling from another source of Faelyn?"

"Could you do that?" Adaira asked in a hushed tone.

Talera snorted and shifted her feet. "Tap into someone else's Faelyn?" She laughed, but the sound came out strangled. "No. That's not how Faelyn works."

"According to who?" Bex asked.

"According to *you*," Talera snarled.

Bex shrugged. "Maybe."

"Not *maybe*." Talera's irritation rolled off her body. "That was the one very clear rule about Faelyn."

"But what if it wasn't?" Bex scrambled to her feet. "I

gave up on the story. I never really got a chance to figure it all out. But that doesn't mean *you* have to give up." Bex could feel everyone's attention on her now. She itched to walk away, but she held Talera's gaze.

"I gave up. I did. But don't let my screwup define you. I never figured out all that you were capable of, but there's still time." Bex pointed toward the Library doors. "You said only heroes get sent here, right?" A muscle twitched in Talera's cheek, and her eyes flicked to Guy before she nodded once. "If that's true, why are there villains running rampant through the portal? Because you can still choose who you are. You're not stuck with what I wrote."

Talera crossed her arms, glowering.

Guy cleared his throat. "It's worth a shot, isn't it?"

Talera pursed her lips as she continued to study Bex. Finally she let out a heavy sigh through her nose. "You're quite aggravating, you know that?"

Bex felt some tightness ease from her chest, and she smiled. "The worst." Owen was beaming at her. "What?"

"That's some impressive creative problem solving," he said.

Bex's cheeks flushed again, and she shrugged. "I've just read a lot of adventure stories." She cleared her throat, noticing the looks of surprise and awe etched on the others' faces.

Talera plucked the paper from the table, eyeing it critically.

This could work. This could work.

Dreams, belief, magic, love…all originated from the same place.

"If you can tap into another source of Faelyn," Bex said to Talera, "you could probably tap into that same frequency in every person in the Realm. They wouldn't need to possess Faelyn themselves. You could pull from the alpha frequency they all have."

The group seemed to be collectively holding its breath.

Talera was silent for several moments before she looked up.

"We're going to need a lot more people who believe in magic to pull this off."

CHAPTER THIRTY-NINE

An Ember

TALERA'S PALMS WERE SWEATING as she stalked to the edge of the city with not one but two versions of herself following after her. She squeezed her shoulder blades together, trying not to think too hard about it.

She even found herself wishing Bex had come along, if only to have her incessant chatter as a distraction. But they'd all decided it would be best if Bex, Owen, and Huxby stayed in the Library and out of sight for now. Talera had sensed the growing angst in the characters of the Realm as she had exited the crumbling city. She was grateful Adaira had volunteered to stay back with them, since she didn't trust Bex's combat skills and Guy had insisted on joining Talera for 'moral support'.

They'd run into the final version of Talera on their way out of the city. Talera had ground her teeth, and Guy had quickly assumed the responsibility of explaining to the third

Talera what in the Seven Hells was going on.

Guy's voice interrupted her thoughts. "I think, for the sake of simplicity, that we should come up with distinct names to call you all by."

He cleared his throat as all three Taleras turned to him with icy glares. He chuckled nervously.

"Talera"—he motioned to her—"I think it's only fair that since you were here first, you should continue to be called Talera. And…uh, you." He looked to the Talera who'd arrived second. "How about Tal? And for you"—he gestured to the third and, thank the gods, final Talera—"how about Lera?"

The three women looked at each other, a silent agreement passing between them. Talera tried not to shudder at the strangeness and instead said, "Now that that's settled, let's get this over with, shall we?"

They reached the empty land that stretched on and on just outside the canyon wall. Talera rolled her shoulders and stretched her neck, wishing some of the tension would leave her body.

"Do you, uh, think this will work?" Guy asked. He tried to look casual as he brushed invisible lint from his clothes, but the strain in his voice was evident.

Talera shrugged. "Bex seems to think so." She began

stretching her arms to limber up. "I don't mind that second-guessing, self-deprecating Bex is gone. I just wish that didn't mean that everyone's fate now rests in *my* hands."

Guy flashed a crooked smile and leaned against a large boulder. "It is rather exciting, isn't it?" Talera shot him a look, and he spread his hands. "Though I can understand the pressure this puts on you. Please proceed."

Talera sighed. Tal stood poised, ready to spring into action if needed. Lera, on the other hand, slouched slightly, her gaze wandering toward the horizon. Talera furrowed her brow. Lera had been oddly silent since they'd found her, allowing them to do all the talking. *Interesting*, Talera thought, tucking away the discrepancies between the three women to think on later. One thing they didn't have was the luxury of time. Every minute that passed here in the Realm meant much more time was passing on the other side, where Rehnir was destroying the city. She'd seen signs that the Fading was taking hold of Bex and the others before they'd split up to put both pieces of the plan in motion.

Talera gave her hands a shake, bringing her attention to Lera and Tal. "Right. So. We are technically the same person…so connecting to each other's Faelyn should be possible."

The three of them faced each other in a triangular

formation while Guy leaned against a large boulder. The sand crunched beneath the soles of Talera's boots. The wind lifted a few strands of hair that had come loose from her intricate braids.

Right. I can do this. Just reach out and find Tal or Lera.

She envisioned the pull she'd felt from Rehnir, how he'd reached out and stolen her powers. Perhaps proximity would help.

"Step closer," she said to Tal, who took up a position by her shoulder. She stretched her mind out, trying to find Tal's source. But as time passed and nothing happened, she felt increasingly foolish. How was she to know if she was even attempting this correctly? It made no sense. Trying to find someone else's unique magical essence felt like trying to start fire underwater. Where did one even begin?

The mental effort was exhausting. Guy suggested they switch up and try different combinations—Talera reaching out to Lera, Lera reaching out to Tal, alternating who went first. But no matter how hard Talera tried, she couldn't pull anyone else's power into her. Frustration prickled along her skin, and she stopped counting how many times she stormed off, kicking up dust and letting loose strings of curses. Tal was equally frustrated and constantly griped, "Just do it already!" More than once, that led to shouting matches between the two elves that left Talera feeling unhinged and irritable.

"This is pointless." Talera whirled on Guy, throwing her hands in the air.

"Just keep trying," Guy said. "I know this must be hard, but you're doing great—"

"Don't patronize me," Talera and Tal growled in unison.

Guy snapped his mouth shut as he looked between them. "That is…very off-putting," he said finally. "Look, if you don't think you can do it, let's just go back to the Library and tell them we have to come up with a different plan."

Talera looked at Tal and Lera in turn, their stubborn looks surely a mirror of her own expression. She ran a hand over her eyes. "No," she moaned. "Just…I need a moment to think." She turned and walked a few paces away toward the nothingness before her.

A desire to see her mother hit her square in the chest, making her ache. Talera kept walking, as if she could simply leave the pain, Rehnir, and her inadequacies behind her.

You're not stuck with what I wrote, Bex's voice said inside her head.

Sand crunched beneath her feet.

You can still choose who you are.

Talera thought of the steely look in Bex's eyes as she had held a chair-turned-weapon in front of her.

You're not stuck with what I wrote.

Talera stopped walking, her eyes searching the gray sky above her. Empty and never-ending. What was she stuck with? The same inadequacies that haunted Bex? The fear of not reaching her potential?

You already have all the magic you need inside of you. Her mother's voice whispered the words she'd said to Talera on their last night together, just before the battle. Before—

Talera lifted her chin, looking into the sky and releasing her thoughts.

Emptiness. Emptiness in the land around her and in the sky.

But…

Perhaps the emptiness called to be filled. Perhaps it wasn't condemned to remain that way forever.

Breath filled her lungs, stretching her rib cage, expanding—

Talera blinked.

The power was already inside her. Those words repeated again and again in her mind as she turned and raced back to the others.

"All the magic we need is already inside us." Lera and

Guy cocked their heads, but Tal held her gaze as understanding seeped into her eyes.

"We don't need to pull any more in. We have what we need, we just need to—"

"—reach out," Tal said.

Talera nodded. "Let it expand like a breath or—"

"—coax it like a flame," Tal finished.

Talera knew the grin spreading across her face looked identical to the one on Tal's.

ᛞᚨᚦ

Knowing and executing were two very different things.

Talera and Tal had repeated their mother's mantra over and over as they tried to connect their powers while Guy and Lera watched, offering encouraging smiles. Several hours passed, but if the trick was to coax their magic like a flame, they were apparently working with damp tinder.

A headache began to throb behind Talera's left temple as she and Tal faced each other. They'd opted to sit cross-legged instead of wasting their energy standing. Their knees were touching as they both rolled their shoulders, expelling heavy sighs.

"Let's try again," Tal said, and this time, she held out

her hand, palm up.

Talera slid her hand into Tal's, trying not to think about the fact that she was holding hands with herself, and closed her eyes, concentrating on her breath.

Talera took a long inhale and let it out slowly as she closed her eyes, spiraling down to the quiet part of her mind, the bridge to her Faelyn, the moonlit waters deep within herself.

The familiar swell of her magic rose to meet her. Touching that wave with her mind, she felt her power rush into her palms, pulsing, ready to be released. She let the power roll and coalesce for a moment before imagining her Faelyn expanding with her ribs as her lungs opened. Heat emanated from Tal's palm like there was a spark clasped between them. Talera sent her breath toward it, imagining the flame catching, their united breath stoking its power.

Her Faelyn expanded a fraction, hovering just past the edges of her body.

Talera's eyes snapped open as her breath caught. The power diminished back to the confines of her own body.

"Did you feel that?" Talera asked.

Tal barely moved her head as she nodded, as if she was afraid a sudden movement would undo what they'd done.

Talera closed her eyes again. It wasn't easier this time,

even knowing it was possible. Several minutes passed as they both focused inward. Then her Faelyn unfurled, the magic hovering outside her body again. Talera held it there, sweat beading on her forehead as she tried to get used to the feeling of working a muscle she'd never used before. The air around her crackled with power, and Guy let out an excited whoop.

Spirits renewed, Talera and Tal practiced expanding their Faelyn until they were able to easily hold the magic outside of themselves. Talera was able to expand hers by about a foot, the magic sending out a vibrant glow as she did. During a hilarious attempt from Guy to land a blow on her, they discovered that the glow functioned as a shield. Guy was thrown backward about ten paces and landed sprawled on the ground. He declined to participate in any more tests after that.

"All right, enough showing off," Guy said, as Tal snickered as he rubbed his behind. "Let's see if you can combine forces."

Talera took a steady breath, the light from her Faelyn glowing around her, and let her focus shift back to the task. She imagined separating her mind in two. With one part of her focus holding the space for the Faelyn, she used the other to reach out slowly, and carefully. At first there was no change. But as she waited patiently, directing her power outward, she sensed another source of energy. It felt…familiar. Her Faelyn responded to the mirroring essence like a cascading waterfall. Force erupted between them, knocking them both to the ground. Talera's concentration shattered and the connection abruptly ended, but the air still sizzled with the kiss of magic.

"Well, I'd say Bex was right—we aren't stuck with what she wrote," Tal said.

CHAPTER FORTY

Out of Thin Air

Bex, Owen, Huxby, and Adaira had gone back to the corner of the Library to be near Grant while Guy and the Taleras went to practice wielding magic at a safe distance. Grant's condition hadn't improved, but it also hadn't worsened, which Bex kept reminding herself was no small thing. Her stomach rumbled loudly, and Adaira looked at her with a raised eyebrow. Bex silently cursed her elven hearing.

"Is there…food anywhere?" What had Talera and Guy told them regarding food in the Realm?

Adaira pursed her full lips and eyed their group. Bex willed herself not to shrink under her perceptive gaze. Huxby stood a good distance from the elf as if trying to make her forget he was there. Which was, of course, impossible now that the truth of him being Adaira's author was out in the open.

"Food is very hard to come by here since most of us arrive with only the clothes on our backs," she said.

Huxby hunched his shoulders a bit more, trying to make his large frame small and unremarkable.

"But I'll see what I can do." Adaira said no more as she turned and left them.

Huxby let out a long, slow breath and wiped his brow with a handkerchief from his pocket.

A wave of dizziness washed over Bex, and she swayed where she sat, bracing her hands on the ground to stop the room from tilting. Owen touched her arm. "Are you all right?"

Bex tried to blink the blurriness from her vision. "I—I got light-headed is all. I think I just need some food." She smiled weakly at Owen, who didn't look convinced.

"That's how it started the last time for me. Dizziness, nausea, feeling weak and achy," Huxby said. "I told you back at the convention center that we can't survive in this world for long. Proximity to the portal isn't the only thing we need to worry about. It'll get worse the longer we are here."

"How long were you here?"

Huxby was thoughtful for a moment. "I can't be sure.

It felt like only a few hours, but a few days had passed when I returned home." A shadow crossed his face. "My parents thought something terrible had happened to me, that my insistence that I'd gone through a portal was some type of trauma response."

"Before…you mentioned the Tower of London?" Bex shifted, a particularly large manuscript poking into her back.

Huxby expelled a breath. "We were visiting London, my parents and I. I'd wandered off for a bit during the tour of the Tower of London. It was like something was…pulling me along. I was just walking along one of the outer walls, and then suddenly there was this shift in the air." He waved his hand in front of his face. "In the wall itself."

They sat in silence for a moment before Huxby cleared his throat. "Food isn't necessary for you here. I know it feels like it is, but that's because our brains are wired for hunger. It's just our atoms adjusting."

"How can you be sure?" Owen asked, glancing at Bex.

"When I returned home, my parents insisted on taking me to see a doctor to rule out any physical harm. All the test results showed normal values for hydration and caloric intake, though by our world's time, I hadn't eaten for several days. You'll be hungry, but as long as we're back home before too long, your bodies will manage. Food is the least of our worries."

"Do you remember anyone you met last time?" Bex asked.

Huxby's face was drawn, his gaze hooded. "No. No, I can't say that I do. If you'll excuse me."

Bex and Owen exchanged a look as Huxby slowly walked off into the stacks, his hands shoved deep in his pockets.

Bex leaned against the bookshelves, tipping her head back. "What a mess," she said softly.

Owen nodded slowly and tapped her knee gently with his fist. Bex didn't think the way it sent her stomach rolling had anything to do with hunger.

"How do you think Talera's doing?" Owen left his fist perched on her knee, eyes fixed on the floor in front of them.

"If anyone is stubborn enough to figure this out, Talera is." Bex let out a huff. "Not to mention there's three of her." She looked over at her dad, watching the movement of his chest with each breath. A lump formed in her throat. Owen's hand spread out to cover her knee, and he gave it a small squeeze. "Even if they do figure out how to pull power from each other, what if that's all the magic allows?" She'd not let herself admit her worries before when explaining the plan to the group. But now… "What if there isn't enough belief to make a difference?" She didn't dare look at Owen as she whispered her fears. "He has so much power."

Owen didn't say anything. He knew better than she did the type of power Rehnir had.

She tore her gaze from her dad and looked at Owen. His eyes searched hers intently, his brows furrowing and forming a small crease. The pain on his face sent an ache through her chest, and she suddenly realized this was the first time they'd been alone since their fight in her apartment.

As if he could read her mind, Owen said quietly, "When he was attacking, I kept hearing you say you don't need me." His fingers pressed harder against her knee as if he needed to reassure himself that she was real. "You kept saying it, and then all I could see was you dying, and—" His voice became thick, and Bex's heart pounded so hard she was sure he could hear it. His eyes ran over her face, and she gripped his hand tightly. He licked his lips. "Bex—"

"Owen, before," she blurted out, her voice husky. "Before, when I thought you were…" She leaned forward slightly. She needed to tell him. To explain what he meant to her. Because when he'd collapsed on the bridge and she had thought she may never get to tell him the truth…never get to tell herself the truth…

"Owen, you're my best friend in the world, and I—"

But then she broke off, gripped by that old familiar fear of losing him if he didn't feel the same. The air was taut between them, but she couldn't make the words come out. Owen's expression flickered—

Adaira rounded the corner.

"It's the best I could do," she said, tossing a very stale loaf of bread at them.

Owen caught it, looking away from Bex. The moment was over.

Bex shut her eyes, pushing down her agitation—at herself, at Adaira's terrible timing, at her inability to ever do anything right—

Stop. The voice in her head interrupted the derailing effect that thought usually had on her. This was not how this moment was supposed to go.

She grabbed Owen's wrist, taking the bread from him. She didn't let go as she gave him a look that she hoped said this conversation wasn't over. Then she inspected the bread, wrinkled her nose, and turned to Adaira. "If this is the best the Realm can do, I'd be better off writing another character and sending them here with something a little fresher."

Realization crashed over her, the words lighting up her brain. "Oh my god."

She leapt up, anticipation blooming in her chest.

"We're going to need paper. A lot of paper."

ᛞᚨᚦ

Bex cleared her throat and looked expectantly at Professor Huxby. "Any ideas on where to begin?"

They sat at one of the tables near the center of the Library, which was now covered with loose paper. They had gathered as many pages they could find with only a few words on them, which was—sadly for the Realm, luckily for them—quite a lot.

"Well," Professor Huxby said, "if we can give our characters knowledge of the existence of this place, we'll be able to streamline things."

Bex nodded, bouncing her foot under the table. She wasn't sure why none of them had thought of this earlier, though she guessed it was somewhat reflexive to vow never to start and stop a story again, knowing what they now knew. This plan blurred the moral lines a bit.

"So each main character needs to believe not only that magic exists but that it matters. That will help reinforce the boundary and hopefully buy us some time."

"Not to mention that it'll give Talera more great sources to pull from," Owen added.

Please let her be able to do it. Bex chewed her lip. "Then I guess we just…start?"

The pen hovered above the page. Her stomach tightened a fraction as she realized what she was about to do. What she'd said she'd never do again.

Failure doesn't define who we are. What we choose to do in the face of it does.

"Society represses creativity as we get older," Huxby said. "So if you're fighting to have creativity in your life, you have to reject perfectionism."

"Am I that obvious?" Bex slouched in her chair.

Huxby chuckled. "I just recognize myself in you. Creativity is a process, and it's unique to each individual. Everyone feels uncomfortable. But that doesn't mean we should stop doing it."

Bex turned the words over in her mind, staring at the empty paper. Then she began to write.

Quin sat quietly, patiently waiting. Relaxed. Today was the day. It was finally time for their mission to the Abandoned Realm. Their sword lay across their knees, hands resting gently on the flat of the blade. The people of their homeland had been sending soldiers to the Abandoned Realm for millennia. They'd had grown up knowing the stories of those who had been sentenced there. These were people who had given up hope, given up their will to live. They knew that the land was under attack, threatened with contamination by an outside evil. Their mission was to enter the Abandoned Realm and help instill in its people the will to live. To help inspire in them a hunger to remain alive, to fight for what they had left and for the promise of what they could create. They needed to stay until they could help the people establish a thriving community.

The walls around Quin flashed with different-colored lights as monitors buzzed and pulsed. They checked their watch. Any minute now. The floor began to rumble slightly. Their heartbeat quickened, but they slowed it back down by taking a long inhale through their nose. They were ready.

Smoke seeped in between the floorboards and the walls. This was it. The walls began to rip apart, dazzling light bursting in. Quin threw a hand up to shield their eyes. Then—

Bex stopped and ripped the paper up quickly, dropping it to the floor. She flashed a smile. "Trash."

ᛞᚨᚦ

The hours passed in a blur of ink, hand cramps, and racing thoughts. Adaira hovered near them, throwing out ideas when they got stuck. She had initially tried to write as well, but since she was from the Realm, none of the stories she wrote appeared in the pile on the dais at the heart of the Library. The soft sound of papers landing on the desk was pleasant background noise as they worked. Between Owen, Huxby, and Bex, they'd written and torn up more than three hundred beginnings of stories.

Bex shook out her right hand, exhilarated. She'd never written so much or so freely. The floor around them was littered with discarded pages. There was a soft thump as the last story Owen had started fell from the air and onto the large dais. He stretched, wincing a bit as the movement pulled at his bandages. Adaira, who'd been checking his wounds frequently, strode over to do so again.

A door slammed open, making them all jump. Guy, Talera and the two other Taleras came rushing toward them.

Bex stood up quickly when she saw the look on Talera's face, her chest tightening. "Did it work?"

Talera grinned, and Bex thought she'd never seen anything quite so beautiful. "It worked."

"You should have seen it, Bex!" Guy gushed, bouncing on the balls of his feet.

Talera's eyes took in the flurry of ripped pages on the floor and jerked her head toward the entrance. "Are you lot responsible for that, then?"

"*That* being…?"

"The small army that's amassed out of thin air." Talera smirked, and Bex grinned back.

"Why, yes, that would be our doing."

CHAPTER FORTY-ONE

RAEBOURN

TALERA COILED THE TENDRILS of their combined Faelyn, weaving and twisting it into an energetic shield once more. It illuminated the bookshelves around them with moonlight. Bex squinted against the magic's glow, her smile threatening to crack her face in two. Huxby looked like a proud father, and Owen let out a low whistle.

"Bloody brilliant!" Guy repeated what he'd said over and over the whole way back to the Library.

Talera released her hold on the Faelyn, and the shield evaporated, a pleasant hum echoing in its wake.

"Did you try to connect with anyone else?" Huxby asked, his eyes curious.

Talera's grin stiffened.

"Uh—yes, but…" Guy answered slowly.

"So far all we can do is connect to each other," Tal said.

"Well, that's to be expected. You're not going to get it

all in one go," Bex said, her excitement unwavering. Talera had a strange desire to hug the woman. "Just keep practicing. What else did you find out?"

Talera straightened, glad for the new question. "The shield grows stronger as more Faelyn is pooled together. We tried out some hand-to-hand combat, and the increased source amplifies the powers I already possess." She ticked them off on her fingers matter-of-factly. "Strength and speed—both of which are extended to whatever weapon I use—and my cognitive abilities are razor sharp. The downside is that the source runs out considerably faster than usual. The more potent the magic is, the quicker it burns off."

Bex sucked her teeth. "Okay. Well, hopefully we can work around that when the time comes."

Talera nodded, trying not to think about how incredibly drained and empty she'd felt after connecting to Tal and Lera. It went beyond the normal exertion of using her Faelyn; it felt like a piece of her soul had been used up, an offering of her own blood that the magic had demanded as payment.

She brought her attention back to what Bex was saying about the army of characters they'd conjured outside the Library.

"We wrote an understanding of this place into each one's backstory to make it an easier…transition. And each has a strong belief in magic and a desire to continue living in order to fortify the boundary and be a source for you to pull from," Bex explained.

An idea shot through Talera, and she blurted out, "Why not just write a new character who could defeat Rehnir?"

A look passed between Huxby and Bex.

Talera cocked her head. "Well?"

"We did consider it," Bex said.

"We simply don't have the time to fully flesh out a character," Huxby said. "We were only able to instill the most basic character traits and beliefs. We'll only get one chance against Rehnir, and we thought numbers were more important." His eyes darted to Lera, who was staring blankly at them, then back to her. "You are our best shot, Talera. All of this is to give you as much support as we can."

Anxiety trickled down her spine, chilling her. She glanced at Tal, who shrugged one shoulder. Talera swallowed, her mouth suddenly very dry.

All the magic you need is already inside you.

She repeated her mantra and blew out a breath. When she had first connected to Tal, their combined Faelyn had felt like a waterfall: powerful, rushing, and unstoppable. But her confidence in her ability was more like trying to grasp water and hold it in her fist. It kept slipping through her fingers, or it dried up completely. Shouldn't belief be more solid? Something substantial she could rely on, not something she had to replenish continuously?

A commotion at the front of the Library pulled everyone's attention away from her. Everyone save herself, Bex, and Lera moved toward the shouting. Bex halted in front of her and gripped her arm.

Talera met her eyes, her words barely more than a whisper. "What if it's not enough?"

"It will be."

Talera eyed her skeptically. "*Now* you don't have any doubts?"

Bex barked out a laugh. "What about me makes you think I don't have doubts?"

A smile tugged at Talera's mouth.

"I don't think that part—the fear and doubt—ever goes away." Bex shrugged. "We just get more resilient." Her brow furrowed, a realization hitting her. "Actually, I think maybe that's how our demons win—we spend our time trying to get rid of the fear when that's impossible and just keeps us from doing anything that matters."

Talera arched a brow, fondness swelling behind her

ribs.

"*You* are magic, Talera. The same thing that powers the boundary—the same thing that was strong enough to contain Rehnir for so long. That is the magic that you are. And what you did today? I didn't write that power. *You* did that."

A lightness spread over Talera's shoulders, and she lifted her chin. "You know, I think I might actually like you."

Bex laughed, but sincerity sparkled in her eyes as she said, "High praise."

They turned as Guy jogged toward them, Owen close behind with a hand pressed over his hip.

"We've got a problem," he said.

ᛞᚨᚦ

Talera scowled out at the square teeming with characters. There was a clear divide between the two factions. Closest to them, spilling over the steps, were the new characters. Across from them, their anger and hate palpable, was a growing mob of old characters. Atop one of the crumbling buildings perched the red-and-gold dragon, its intelligent eyes taking everything in.

"The plot thickens," Huxby said in a hushed tone as he peered over her shoulder. Talera cast him a withering stare, and his shoulders crouched closer to his ears. “Sorry,” he muttered.

Talera heard Owen whisper to Bex, “How upset is your dad going to be when he wakes up and realizes all the pun opportunities he’s missed out on?”

Despite the tension in her face, Bex laughed softly.

“How did they find out what’s happening?” Talera asked no one in particular, though she had a good idea how. She scanned the crowd and found the blue-skinned man with swirls of red marking his face. *Zia is his name*, she thought, recalling what Branson had told them shortly after the attack.

“Does it matter?” Adaira answered, waving a hand at the opposing forces. “They know, and they’re obviously not pleased.”

Guy clicked his tongue. “I find it rather disappointing that this is what they’ve finally decided to care about.”

This being the fact that the Realm was harboring fugitives from across the portal. From the other side.

Zia pushed his way to the front of the crowd. He locked eyes with Talera, then spat on the ground. “I told you they were traitors. You thought you could hide that filth and we wouldn’t find out?”

Talera’s eyes shot to Branson, her irritation growing. He’d been foolish enough to allow Zia to overhear him talking about said fugitives, and he hadn't dealt with him when he'd had the chance.

Zia kept speaking, shouting so everyone could hear. "You brought those monsters here, and then you helped them bring *more* people here?" He gestured to the new characters. "Have we not suffered enough without our own kind striking out against us?"

The dragon snorted, a plume of smoke escaping its nostrils, and Talera sensed the solidarity in the sentiment.

"And isn't that exactly what you are doing?" Talera replied coolly, amplifying her voice with her Faelyn so everyone could hear the deadly calm in her words. She ran her eyes over the inhabitants of the Realm. They were dirty and downtrodden, but anger had awoken in them. Anger could be channeled and used…

The portal pulsed in the background, the incessant buzz and vibration blending in with the voices of the crowd.

Anger is a secondary emotion.

These people felt something. Enough to act. Finally.

"I know you're angry," Talera began, her voice carrying. "Our lives were ripped from us. We were cast aside. Forgotten. Banished to this terrible place and told our lives were never real. Honestly, it seems like a self-fulfilling prophecy, calling this place the Abandoned Realm." She could see a handful of people who bore the mark of Rehnir's magic—the onyx tendrils and veins under their skin.

"I'm glad you're angry," she said, "because anger is better than the terrible empty apathy this place is so good at creating. You're right, we've suffered enough without striking out at each other."

Talera angled her body so she could see Bex, Huxby, and Owen behind her. "What happened to us was not done out of malice. These people aren't the enemy. The real threat is our own minds."

The crowd shifted on their feet, a few people muttering to those around them, confusion clear on their faces. Talera's heart dropped as a large number of characters simply turned and walked away. She pressed on, trying to explain.

"The boundary that has protected us and given us a home here is deteriorating quickly. It's weak, and both worlds are responsible for that. Our thoughts have physical impacts, real consequences—our very existence is proof enough of that. Those thoughts have the power to strengthen the boundary or weaken it.

"We don't have much time." Adaira took a step forward, projecting her voice as she surveyed their audience. "We need anyone who is willing to help." She pointed to the portal. "There's a battle about to begin to protect the lives of innocents and the chance to build life anew. We will fight to take back our power. Our voices. Our stories."

Talera involuntarily shivered. Adaira's words sounded silly…but damn if they didn't stir something in her.

"There is a well-known elven rune back home," Adaira continued. "The word for it in the old tongue was Raebourn."

Huxby went still as stone behind them, his breathing stopped.

"It means rebirth or awakening." She looked Talera in the eye. "We're not here to be forgotten and abandoned. We're here to be awakened."

The red-and-gold dragon tossed its magnificent head, stretching its wings.

"We're not asking you to fight for the Abandoned Realm. We're asking you to fight for Raebourn."

"What would you have us do?" The dragon's voice reverberated in Talera's bones.

"We're running out of time. We must close the portal and strengthen the boundary or we'll all die," Adaira said. "We brought these others here to help us." She gestured to the new characters. "They're here to fight all those who are killing on the other side, specifically Rehnir, who made the portal. They'll also provide a source for Talera to pull from to try to seal the boundary."

"We know not everyone can fight," Talera said, "but every person here can help strengthen the boundary. Our thoughts matter."

Branson stood off to the side, his face unreadable.

"We don't stand a chance if we fight amongst ourselves." Adaira glared at Zia.

The ground trembled as the portal sparked and crackled. Groans and whimpers rose from the crowd. Owen sucked in a sharp breath, sweat breaking out on his brow.

"The boundary isn't going to hold much longer," Huxby warned.

Adaira drew her blade, eyes burning bright. "Who will fight?" she boomed.

The crowd came alive, moving and shifting as more divisions became clear. A surge of characters came toward the steps of the Library, eyes trained on Adaira. The dragon flew closer, landing atop another building. Zia turned his back, leading a large number of characters toward the portal.

Talera didn't spare them another glance, turning to address those gathering around her. Time seemed to speed up, rushing forward as she spouted battle tactics, designating Quin and a few other newly written characters as commanders. One of the automatons rolled out of the

Library, and Guy instructed it to hand out the extra weapons that had been written in with the new characters.

Talera's palms were hot. She could sense time slipping through her fingers, rushing them toward this finale she'd not expected or wanted. Bex was pale, her fingers tightly twined with Owen's. A ringing filled Talera's ears as she watched everyone around her spring into motion. She surveyed the growing army of characters. Branson's face had been swallowed up somewhere in it.

Bex touched her elbow, jarring her. "Are you okay?"

Talera swallowed. "I just need a minute."

She needed so much more than a minute before she had to cross through the portal. To face Rehnir. To try to save the Realm and the world before the contamination wiped them all out of existence. She gave out instructions on autopilot, making sure everyone knew the tasks they needed to perform before making an excuse to peel away.

And then she was running. She needed to be alone, needed to let her thoughts settle from their constant swirl, needed stillness, needed to let her Faelyn replenish, needed to breathe, breathe, breathe…

Breathe in…

Breathe out…

Raebourn.

She was at the outskirts of the city.

Her knees hit the dirt, and she sat on her heels, eyelids heavy.

Breathe in….

How many of them would fight?

Breathe out…

So many had turned away, some in defeat, others in hate.

Breathe in…

More characters had crossed through the portal, spurred into action, but not the intended action.

Breathe out…

Let it be enough. It has *to be enough.*

All the magic you need is already inside you.

Talera slipped into a half-awake, half-dreamlike state. Her muscles relaxed and loosened. Her mind stilled. Her breath expanded her ribs gently. A soothing coolness washed over her slowly, gradually filling every corner and crease of her body. A soft vibration hummed in her core as the Faelyn seeped back into her bones.

And then she was nothing and everything, limitless and finite, light and dark, stardust and moonlight…

Whole.

Talera opened her eyes, coming back into her body.

The ground around her was full of scuff marks and boot tracks in complicated patterns, the product of their earlier training session. She ran her hand lightly over the sand and dirt, which flaked and bit gently into her skin. She made to stand, but something caught her eye.

Talera reached out, her fingers brushing a tiny mushroom cap.

Impossible.

Her eyes followed the small ring they formed, a circle of life that shouldn't be here, couldn't be here.

And yet…

Talera was on her feet, careful not to step on the growing caps. As distracted by her thoughts as she had been, she hadn't noticed them before. They were so small it was easy to miss them. But there was not one, not two, but three separate rings of tiny mushrooms pushing through the unforgiving terrain.

Talera looked around quickly, noting the boulder off to the side where Guy had sat and watched her and Tal practice right where she was now standing, right where the mushrooms were growing.

She didn't know what to make of it. Nothing could grow here—that was what everyone said. But these hadn't been here before. How was it possible for something to grow not only in an impossible location but with such speed?

A roar split her ears, sending adrenaline through her veins, arresting her thoughts.

The dragon…

Talera took one last look, trying to sear the image into her mind, then turned from the hope and promise that was springing up from the land and sprinted toward whatever fate lay ahead.

CHAPTER FORTY-TWO

INTERLUDE IN THE LIBRARY

BEX'S BLOOD RAN COLD as the dragon's roar pierced the air. Even deep in the Library the bellowing cry rattled them. They'd been on their way to check on her dad, but froze where they were winding through the stacks.

"That's not a great sign," Owen said.

"No," Bex agreed as they looked at each other. They held each other's gaze until the air between them shifted. The urgency of what was happening outside faded now that it was just the two of them. The section of the Library where they stood was lit low. Intimate. The shelves, looking like they'd been honed from solid trees, stretched high. Each ledge, crammed with weathered scrolls and damaged spines, had large gaps between them. A small table was shoved up against the books, covered in a pile of fading parchment.

Owen hissed through his teeth, pressing a hand to the

wound on his hip.

"Are you all right?" Bex asked.

Owen grimaced as he leaned against the shelves, but he waved her off. "I'm fine, it's just—"

Bex ignored him, reaching for the hem of his shirt, but Owen was too quick. A hand closed around her wrist, gently halting hers. She glared at him, reaching out with her free one. Owen let go of his side and laced his fingers through hers, stopping her again.

Was it actually possible to hear another person's heartbeat if you weren't supernaturally inclined or pressed against them? The thought of being pressed against Owen sent heat to her face, and she suddenly had trouble remembering what they were supposed to be doing.

"Bex," Owen said softly.

Her eyes dipped to his lips as he said her name.

"I'm fine," he said.

She tore her gaze from the crooked smile playing at the corners of his mouth.

And before she realized her lips were about to betray her, the words were out. "I do need you."

Owen's eyebrows rose slightly. The air around her seemed to vibrate in anticipation.

She swallowed. *Now, before you lose your nerve.*

"Before, when I said you're my best friend…what I meant to say is that even though you're my best friend, I want more." She wet her bottom lip. His eyes dipped to track the movement. "You're the best part of my day every day, and you have been since we were sixteen and skipping class to go to Dairy Queen and talk about books."

The heat of his fingers still holding her hands was unsettling in the most wonderful way. "I know you just broke up with Heidi and we're both covered in blood and god, there's a freaking dragon out there." Owen chuckled, and the sound made her head spin. She was losing the thread but couldn't seem to reel herself in; every piece of her heart that she'd kept so tightly wound was unspooling.

She took a shaky breath. "I just—if I go another second without telling you, I think I might explode. I…I want *you*, Owen. I always have."

The smile that had been playing on his face faded as he stared at her.

Her heart seized.

"Please say something."

Owen tugged her to him, one arm circling her waist…

And kissed her.

The world stopped and started.

His lips were hot against hers as he pulled her closer,

fingers spread wide across her low back and between her shoulders. His touch was adoring, like magic caressing her skin. Owen captured her bottom lip gently between his teeth, lingering before breaking their connection. Bex blinked, trying to clear her head, but all she could focus on were the freckles under his eyes and his ridiculous cocky grin and the smell of the books and the taste of him—

Owen dipped his head again.

"I—" Bex's throat closed.

Owen didn't pull away, but he stilled. His eyes searched her face.

She took a steadying breath. "Are you sure?"

Owen let out a husky laugh that made something curl low in her stomach. One hand slid up to the nape of her neck, his thumb brushing her jaw, sending shivers down her spine.

"Bex." He tipped his forehead to rest against hers. "You are quite possibly the only thing in life I'm sure about."

Tears stung her eyes, and her chest swelled. She almost didn't recognize her own voice as she said, "Then kiss me again."

A grin broke across his face before his lips met hers.

Oh god.

Owen's kisses were thorough and unhurried. As if he'd imagined it so many times, he was determined to do it right.

Her head swam like she'd had several glasses of wine. Owen took hold of her hips, pivoting them until she was pressed against the bookshelf, stripping her of any second-guessing or pretense of self-preservation.

Bex tilted her head, arms twining around his neck, her mouth growing more insistent as his hands roved over her back. How had she ever convinced herself that this would be a mistake? Kissing Owen felt like falling into her favorite story, like every part of her soul was sighing, making her think they should have always been doing this. Warmth and light like sunshine, like Aldar, spread through her body. The kiss turned urgent as their tongues danced, claiming each other; pouring out years of unspoken longing and want and *need* for each other. She ran her thumbs along his jaw, holding his face tenderly, the faint stubble rough under her fingers.

Nothing else mattered, not the portal, not Rehnir, not the impending battle, as he dropped his lips to kiss along her jaw, breath ghosting across the shell of her ear. Bex arched, pressing her chest closer to his, clinging to his shoulders as his mouth traveled down her neck to her collarbone.

She must have canted her hips against him because Owen sucked in a breath through his teeth in pain. Before she could form a coherent thought, Owen spun them, sweeping a hand across the table to their left. Pages fluttered to the ground. He bent down and slid a hand behind her knee, keeping eye contact as he did. The intense heat in his gaze and mischief curling his mouth was enough to make her feel lightheaded. She bit her lip.

"Up," he said, voice gruff and low as he helped lift her onto the table, his mouth on hers again as if he couldn't bear any more space between them. Her breath hitched as he angled himself between her legs, leaving just enough room to protect his injured side. One hand skated up her ribs, the other tangled into the hair at the nape of her neck, slanting his mouth over hers.

A soft moan escaped from the back of her throat.

"Sorry to interrupt." Guy's voice was like a foghorn.

Owen and Bex abruptly pulled apart, though Owen didn't step back from where he was tangled with her. His lips looked deliciously kiss stung and hers felt slightly swollen. Bex brought a hand to her face, not sure if she was trying to hide her smile or her damning blush. Owen tried to school his grin and failed fantastically.

Guy crossed his arms, smirking.

Bex slid off where she was perched on the table, straightened her shirt, and lifted her chin an inch. "Yes?"

"Just thought you might want to know what's going on

with the plans to defeat the growing army of villains and stop the portal from poisoning both our worlds." Guy flashed a cheeky smile.

Owen, maddeningly, was doing a much better job than Bex of exuding a casual air. He rested his hand against the small of her back, sending another wave of shivers through her as he said, "Very considerate."

"Good news first," Guy said. "The boundary appears to be strengthening. Barely, but we'll take it. Second, Huxby and Sekzelt have been totally nerding out about portal magic and hand gestures, and we may actually have a shot at sealing the damned thing."

Bex squeezed her hands together tightly. "And the bad news?"

Guy's face tightened. "Bad news is, some of the characters who were mad before got right pissed after our little speech. They shot down the dragon—"

"What?!" Bex and Owen cried in unison.

"—presumably because they knew that a dragon would significantly improve our chances—"

Owen swore.

"—and Branson fled with quite a sizable group of characters who couldn't decide which side to support. So the minimal progress we were making with strengthening the boundary has halted, and we have significantly fewer people for Talera to pull from."

"He did what?!" Bex leapt into motion. "What is he thinking?!" she yelled over her shoulder to Owen and Guy, who trailed after her.

"I'm not sure; Adaira just informed me before running to find Talera. We've got to get a move on if we're to have any shot against Rehnir."

Bex ground her teeth, seething as she realized the position Branson had put them in. He knew they needed all the characters they could gather to boost the boundary and help fuel Talera's power. If Talera didn't have enough—

Bex didn't let herself finish the thought as she exited the Library and sprinted down the stairs two at a time. A wave of nausea hit her, the world tilted, and she fell hard on the stone steps. She threw out her hand to catch herself, swearing under her breath when she heard Owen groan in pain. Her head was still swimming as she turned to him.

Owen hadn't even made it down the steps. He was sprawled on his hands and knees, his face sickly pale, tremors wracking his body. Guy, his mouth open in horror, knelt beside him, trying to steady him.

"Owen!" Bex scrambled up the stairs, banging her shin painfully as she did. Owen moaned through his teeth. Bex grasped his shirt, tugged it up, and swore again, much more loudly. Black tendrils from the mark were spreading past his bandages, crawling up to his chest.

Owen followed her gaze and groaned again.

Bex's hands were shaking so violently his shirt shuddered in her grip. "Adaira," she said. "Guy, where is Adaira? We need the Aldar."

"There." Guy sprinted down the steps and across the square to where Adaira had just appeared from an alleyway with Talera.

Owen curled into himself. Bex helped lower him to the ground. "Hold on, Owen," she sobbed, not sure when the tears had started, as she watched Adaira start running toward them. "Hurry!" she screamed. If Rehnir's poison was spreading again…

Dad—

The world threatened to fall out from under her.

Adaira reached them, the vial of Aldar already uncorked, and knelt swiftly beside Owen.

"Bex, you've got to go now," Adaira said as she smeared the shimmering liquid directly into Owen's wound, not bothering with the dagger.

"No." Bex shook her head. This was happening too fast; they needed more time.

"Bex." Adaira's voice was laced with steel.

"My dad—Owen—I can't leave them."

"You can and you must." Adaira fisted Bex's shirt, shaking her roughly. "Talera's already gone through. Rehnir is close. That's why this is happening." She waved an impatient hand toward Owen. His breathing was still ragged.

Adaira gripped her shoulder, urging her away. "Go. I'll help your father next."

Heart cracking in two, Bex obeyed.

CHAPTER FORTY-THREE

BETRAYAL

THE GROUND BENEATH BEX'S feet shook, and she stumbled, trying to stay upright as she raced through the Abandoned Realm—Raebourn—the name didn't matter now, not if they all died. She sprinted through the square, shoving her way past characters who were running in all directions; chaos had taken over, derailing sense and plans and letting panic take the reins. Bex threw a single glance toward the portal in time to see Tal and Lera vanishing through it. The characters she'd written with Owen and Huxby were gathering together to go through next; an army ready to stand against Rehnir and all the other villains on the other side.

Bex barely spared the corpse of the dragon a second look before sprinting into the winding streets. Her lungs burned with effort. She skittered around a bend, hand scraping against a broken building—what used to be a turret, by the looks of it.

"Branson!" she screamed, hot anger sluicing through her when she finally caught up to the retreating characters. He pulled up short, eyeing her warily as she approached. Those with him didn't stop walking.

Bex threw up her hands. "What are you doing?"

Branson drew himself up to his full height. "I'm doing what needs to be done."

"You realize that by taking so many people away, you are dooming everyone on both sides of the portal, yes?"

Branson laughed, a grating sound. "You're so naive, child. Did you honestly think this story would have a happy ending? Hmm? I've read enough stories to know how this one ends."

"But we've figured out how to close the portal! This is what you wanted—"

Branson's face contorted into an ugly snarl. He stepped toward her so quickly that she flinched. "You think this is what *I* wanted? I never wanted any of this!"

Bex faltered, taken aback by his anger. "Y-you said you wanted to save the people here."

His eyes bulged. "You still think these people should be redeemed? This contamination is a gift."

Cold encased her whole body.

"Our only chance of survival is to cull the wretched fools who're a constant drain on the boundary's magic."

Bex's struggled to wade through his worlds. "You want…to purge the Realm?"

Branson continued as if she hadn't spoken. "Rehnir never could grasp that with his twisted brain. He was so eager to redeem himself." The word dripped with disgust. "As if a monster like him could ever make amends. As if I could allow him to threaten the Realm's return to glory!"

The words rang out like gunfire. Blood rushed in Bex's ears, and her hands shook as she brushed sweat from her forehead. "You knew Rehnir?"

"He would have destroyed this whole Realm with his attempts to compensate for his murderous past. He refused to see that the contamination was taking those who didn't deserve to be here. He thought he could play the hero, that he could encourage disreputable characters to see the error of their ways. He would've taken us all down with him!"

"But Guy said only heroes are sent here." Strength seeped from her bones; dread dripped down the base of her skull. "It's our choices and actions that determine whether we become villains."

"The moment he could, he ripped into the boundary and proved himself to be the exact sort of monster I knew he was!" Branson's cackle was vicious; his words were coming in a rush, a sick confessional Bex couldn't walk away from.

"You never intended to help close the portal." Her throat ached. Guy's explanation of Branson's obsession with the "glory days" flashed in her mind. She pictured Branson's face in the crowd, near the angry man who'd attacked them; it had struck her as odd when he hadn't joined them on the steps during their speeches. Now it was glaringly obvious that he'd stood exactly where he'd intended, throwing his lot in with those out for blood. The realization crashed like a boulder into the pit of her stomach.

"Close it? Ha! The portal has accelerated the purge. Even a monster has its uses."

"But *everyone* will die if the portal isn't closed." None of it made sense.

Branson was speaking quickly about something that sounded like a bomb shelter, saying too many scientific words for her to comprehend. There was a place he'd intended to go this whole time? Her head pounded.

"After the first portal was opened, I knew it was only a matter of time before the boundary was weak enough for another. I've been making plans ever since. I only wish I'd cut ties with him sooner."

Him. Rehnir.

"You were here last time, when Huxby came through." Her lungs squeezed as yet another lie was revealed. "You…you knew this whole time."

"I am the only one who truly cares about this godforsaken place and is willing to do what's necessary to save it. The villains of this Realm are the ones responsible for this whole mess."

"Even if you don't pull the trigger, if you supply the loaded gun, you're just as culpable—"

"IT. IS. DESERVED." Branson shoved her hard.

Bex hit the ground, gravel biting into her elbows.

"You deserve what's coming. All of you. You did this to Talera, just like your father did it to me!"

A roaring, keening noise filled her brain.

No.

"Ah, yes. Finally putting it together, are you? I must say, I'm a bit disappointed none of you figured it out sooner, that you all just accepted my weak explanation about time warping to explain why I didn't know about the portal Huxby came through. Guy never pulled his head out of books long enough to realize I had to have known Rehnir personally.

"Unfortunately for you, it's too late to stop what's coming. I made sure of that when I took those pages from

Rehnir's manuscript." Branson bared his teeth in a sinister smile, crouching down to look her directly in the eyes. "You can't save them, Bex—your dad or that lovesick friend of yours. Rehnir's mark cannot be undone. Its source is tethered to Rehnir's very life. So you see, either Talera will manage to kill Rehnir and everyone with his mark will die with him, or Rehnir will kill you all first."

Anguish tore through Bex. Her heart thrashed against her ribs. *No, no, no.*

Branson shrugged. "My bet's on the latter. Either way, justice will be served."

Bex scrambled across the ground, hyperventilating. Heat burned through her, ripping out of her throat in a scream. Jumping to her feet, she ran.

Ran as her soul shredded, praying she would get there in time.

PART THREE

The Bridge

CHAPTER FORTY-FOUR

A Different Sort of Monster

MEMORIES SANK THEIR CLAWS into Rehnir's mind, demanding that he watch, wrenching his consciousness from where he stood on the streets of San Francisco and dropping him in another time and place.

The darkness inside him was in control, forcing him to remember his choices. To see that he'd willingly taken every step on this path down to hell.

The pavement he'd been standing on shifted to dirt and broken cobblestones, the sky bled from blue to a sunless gray, and the noise of the city was replaced with a deathlike quiet.

He was in the Abandoned Realm.

"I know what you are."

Rehnir spun. Branson was approaching from the steps of the Library. Rehnir eyed the man warily, noting how Branson's hands trembled as he held up a tattered manuscript.

Rehnir's breath caught in his lungs. He knew the abandoned story in Branson's hands. Rehnir had held it so often when he'd first arrived, not daring to believe in his new reality. This place—the Abandoned Realm, as they called it—wasn't a punishment. It wasn't a type of death or something to bemoan.

It was a chance at redemption.

To write his story anew.

To take control back from the monster inside him.

To finally make good on his promise to his ma to not be like his father.

Rehnir nodded toward the manuscript, trying to force ease in his voice, and said, "I thought you viewed other people's manuscripts as private, Branson."

Or so you said when you found me reading your story...

Rehnir had been looking through the pages more out of curiosity than anything; except for that scientist character, no one else in the Realm seemed inclined to pass eternity reading. Rehnir found it rather ironic. He'd loved to read when he was little, especially when his ma read to him. But that was so long ago, before—

"Yes, well, an eye for an eye and all that," Branson said,

cutting into his reverie. "And a good thing I looked, too, because now I know what a monster you really are." He tossed the manuscript into the dirt between them, and it skidded toward Rehnir.

Rehnir spread his hands. "A monster? I thought we were all heroes here." His lip curled into a snarl, but his heart pounded and his blood ran cold. He gestured to the listless characters milling about the square, devoid of life, purpose, or meaning.

"I was wrong. You are beyond redemption." Branson shook his head. "You're even more of a monster than your father was."

A muscle in Rehnir's face twitched.

He flicked his gaze back to the Library doors. Several figures watching intently from just inside. He scoffed. "Don't insult my intelligence by pretending to have suddenly found an ethical dilemma regarding my past. I threaten your position here. You want to stand by and let everyone you don't see value in rot away. You can't have someone going around proposing that we all have a place in the Realm."

"You're a vile creature, Rehnir. You taint everyone you come into contact with."

Rehnir cocked his head. "Do you think you're better than me, Branson, because you weren't forced down a terrible path? Because your story was wonderful and clean before it was thrown out? You forget that I've tasted the hate and contempt that roils beneath your skin. I know what you're building underneath the ground out there. Do you think there won't be blood on your hands? That you'll simply be able to rid yourself of everyone who doesn't agree with you?"

"Enough!" The veins in Branson's neck bulged.

Rehnir laughed softly. "You're a different sort of monster, Branson. You're too cowardly to deal the killing blow, but you don't hesitate to pick the mark."

"You went down your path because you are weak."

A ringing filled Rehnir's head.

Weak.

Monster.

Fear was coming off Branson in powerful waves, stinging his nostrils, begging to be claimed.

But Rehnir didn't move. He barely breathed.

The promise of power was a siren call.

Revulsion and self-loathing threatened to consume him.

I will not be a monster.

His spine was rigid as he reached into his cloak and pulled out one of the last remaining cigars he'd had on him when he'd arrived. Rehnir knelt and struck a match on the ground, not taking his eyes off Branson. Wordlessly, he lit the cigar. He took a long, heavy inhale, drawing himself up as he held the smoke in his mouth.

Weak.

Monster.

Rehnir blew a plume of thick smoke toward Branson as enmity scorched through him. He turned and strode away through the throngs of characters, past the elven woman breaking someone's arm, toward the edge of the city. The smell of Fear and Branson's words chased after him.

Weak.

Monster.

ᛞᚨᚦ

Reality snapped back into place, and Rehnir's breath sawed in and out as he fought to orient himself. The citizens of San Francisco were fleeing in a frenzy. Screams and clangs of battle rang out as fellow characters attacked them aggressively. There were far more now than there had been at the convention center.

The vibrating in Rehnir's head was incessant, drowning out all other sounds. He ignored the freshly killed bodies littering the street in front of him and lurched forward. He needed to feed. How long had it been since he had escaped that cell? Minutes? Days? Weeks?

The Fear around him called to him. The monster lurking beneath his skin was in control now.

He needed to make up for lost time. Make up for every moment he had been weak. He would never be weak again—the Fear was too powerful.

Blood was rushing in his ears, and the muscles along his jaw twitched. He lashed out a mental tether, connecting to a couple ahead of him. *They deserve this*, he thought as he felt the life seep out of them. He'd been forced into a life of fear and pain, and now it was their turn to feel fear and pain. He roared, nostrils flaring; he felt as if his skull were on fire. The smell of Fear nearly choked him.

In the distance, the enormous bridge where he'd made the portal stretched over white-capped waves. The Fear called to him like a heady dark mist. He inhaled sharply, relishing the scent, and exhaled.

The sky above him erupted, and other characters howled with rage as the air whipped around them, sirens blaring. Several large flying crafts were circling them, the metal barrels of guns pointed down at them.

"We have you surrounded! Put your weapons down and

put your hands in the air!" a voice boomed from above.

He realized the sinister laughter he heard was coming from his own mouth. Rehnir drew himself up, arms tensed, and kept laughing uncontrollably as he reached his power into the sky. He found the connection to the pilots' Fear easily, the vibration strong and ready to be tapped.

He *pulled.*

Dark magic exploded from him, slamming outward in a seismic wave of cold blue light. The ground rolled, glass shattered, and metal crunched under the force. He swung his hands upward, eyes wide. The power was swallowing him, a torrent building inside him.

For a heartbeat, Rehnir stood still, poised, letting the power build to a new height like the quiet before a thunderclap, and then—

BOOM.

The next surge of power ripped through him.

One of the aircrafts exploded. Burning, twisted metal tore apart, and shrapnel crashed into buildings, littering the cracked earth.

Rehnir *was* Fear. Arms outstretched, he greedily tapped into the Fear of people he couldn't see, feeling their lives draining from them as he let the power barrel through his system.

Bullets whizzed past him, and he spun around, sending out a flash of blue light to deflect them. The force redirected their trajectory, sending the shots toward new targets.

The darkness inside him turned toxic. The world spun. Torment radiated through his bones, and his grasp on the power slipped. Spittle gathered at the corners of his mouth. He gripped his head, ripping at his hair, his chest heaving. He wanted to crawl out of his skin.

Rehnir swore violently. When the pain loosened its grip, he stumbled blindly toward the bridge. All he wanted was to get to the portal, to cross back into the Realm and regain control of the Fear. It was growing too feral, like a wave slamming over his head, denying him breath. He needed to rein in the insatiable hunger—

Someone was caught under the rubble of a building. The man was coughing up blood and convulsing, his body burned and broken. Dark tendrils spread across his skin.

Rehnir was next to him in an instant. He gripped the man's face between his hands, and the man struggled in vain to pull himself free. Rehnir's eyes rolled back as he lost himself in the thrumming pull of the power that begged to be in his veins.

The man screamed, dying in Rehnir's grasp.

CHAPTER FORTY-FIVE

THE BRIDGE

THE GROUND SHOOK BENEATH Talera's feet, and she grabbed hold of the railing as the Golden Gate Bridge trembled. The water in the bay thrashed and roiled as another quake shot through the earth. Flames and smoke rose from the city. Pandemonium erupted on the bridge as cars tried in vain to get around one another, everyone desperately trying to get to safety.

Talera threw a glance over her shoulder. Tal and Lera both had tight expressions on their faces. Lera's bow was drawn, and Tal adjusted her grip on the hilt of a sword. All three of them had several quivers strapped to their backs. They moved away from the portal entrance to allow the full battalion of characters to come through, but as Talera ran her eyes over the group, her stomach clenched. Less than a quarter of their forces were present.

"What's holding up the others?"

Tal shook her head, her eyes fixed on the end of the bridge. "I don't think we have time to worry about that."

Talera whipped her head around and sucked in a breath.

Making their way through the mess of cars and running people, spreading like the dark tendrils marking so many of their victims, the villains of the Realm stalked toward them. Their weapons glinted in the fading light. Behind the wall of mercenaries, blue light snapping and crackling around him, was Rehnir.

"Talera." A deep voice rippled over her, and she tore her gaze from the oncoming assault. The soldier who had addressed her, Quin, whom Bex had written, was looking at her intently. "We're ready. We'll lead the strike against the characters, giving you the chance to handle Rehnir."

She knew the plan—how could she forget the bloody plan?—but the way they said it seemed like a kindness, like they meant to give her a moment to gather her flagging courage. A lump formed in her throat, and she steeled her heart. She nodded and nocked an arrow in reply. The bowstring dug into her fingertips, steadying her as she hovered the weapon at an angle. There were no more than fifty members of Bex's army with her on the bridge. It wasn't enough, but they had no alternative but to act.

Talera leapt over the barrier that separated the walkway

from the cars, the others following her lead, and jumped up onto a deserted car. She planted her feet firmly, pulling back her bowstring.

Breathe in.

Breathe out.

Her Faelyn rose to meet her, the now well-practiced shield forming around her body, extending to the arrow and the bow as if there was no distinction between herself and the weapon.

Her magic glowed all around her as she took aim. The arrow flew across the bridge like a bolt of lightning and sank into the skull of a large ogre. Green blood splattered those around him as he dropped dead. Talera drew another arrow before the first found its target, hitting a white-haired witch with elongated fingers squarely in the stomach.

Talera had a line of sight to Rehnir, and she set another arrow against the bow. The Faelyn-enhanced arrow didn't pierce the shield around him, but it wasn't redirected, as her arrows had been at StoryCon. If she could get closer…

Talera leapt off the car, dropping to kneel behind another as she picked off several more enemies. "We need to get closer," she called over her shoulder to Tal and Lera. Tal flipped a dagger to grasp it by the blade, then cocked her arm back, throwing it directly into the face of the blue-skinned man whose sword was shoved deep into the belly of one of their own.

Talera arched an eyebrow in approval as Tal lifted a shoulder and said, "Lead the way."

Tal and Lera kept close to Talera, the three of them focusing to keep their shields up. They wouldn't combine their magic just yet; they had decided to wait until they reached Rehnir. Otherwise they risked burning up the source before they needed it most.

Gunfire, arrows, and blasts of magic hailed down onto the bridge from every direction. Ahead of them, Quin swung their blade in an upward arc, severing a head from its body before launching themself at a horned male with a wicked barbed tail. The demon raked its talons through the air, and Quin dropped to a crouch to avoid the blow, then popped up behind their attacker. Using their momentum, they sliced their sword through the demon's spiked tail. The beast's blood-curdling scream cut off as Talera's arrow pierced its neck, severing its vocal cords.

The assault raged on. Talera was used to smaller battles, and those had been inadequate to prepare her for the harsh reality of combat on this scale. She was outside her body. Time seemed to slow as she advanced down the bridge, slaying as many enemies as possible. She shot another arrow and hit her mark: the eye socket of a large brute wielding a club. She looked away and quickly aimed again. The arrows in her first quiver were running low. The hiss of the arrows and the stinging kiss of the bowstring as it dug into her fingertips were all she knew. If she lost her focus for a moment—

The thrum of the magic running through her whispered a warning. The dagger at her hip was in her grasp in an instant, the blade parallel to the ground. Talera threw her arm out to the side, catching her would-be assailant in the throat. The woman dropped the large axe she held, her blood spurting into Talera's face.

"Keep your bloody shield up!" Tal screamed from her left as her sword met another. The weapons clashed, and Tal's light pulsed brighter, sending her attacker stumbling backward. The killing blow she delivered was quick, and then Tal rushed ahead to the next enemy.

Talera climbed up one of the thick cables, the metal cold beneath her fingers as she scanned the bridge. The smell of blood and sulfur filled the air. She took down three more enemies from her perch, all the time searching for Rehnir.

The pulsing darkness of his aura seemed to swallow the natural light around him. The distance between them was shrinking, and she watched as those within reach of his power fell to the ground, thrashing uncontrollably as darkness spread like poison through their veins.

Carnage covered the bridge, and Talera fought down the bile rising in her throat. It was hard to distinguish hero from villain once their lifeless forms were sprawled in the rubble. She nocked another arrow numbly, her body instinctually continuing to move even as her thoughts raced.

Something grazed her left hip, and she ground her teeth against the stinging pain. Her eyes snagged on Quin as they wielded a sinister-looking mace against three men. The broad sweeps of the mace forced them to dodge and rendered them unable to land an attack. But a fourth man crept up behind them, sword raised—

Lera shot an arrow into the back of the man's skull. Quin spun in a tight pirouette, the mace an extension of their arm, and knocked out two of the remaining assailants. The fourth shrank back, having just witnessed three of his companions die in the space of a breath. The hesitation cost him, and when the mace connected with the side of his skull, he crumpled without a sound.

Smothering darkness clutched at Talera's chest, gripping her mind. Cold shot through her, but she couldn't move, couldn't breathe—

She needed to get down from the bloody railing and

find more cover, needed to reach Tal and Lera. But she stood frozen, paralyzed with fear as she watched Rehnir stalk closer.

CHAPTER FORTY-SIX

HOW DEMONS WIN

BEX SKIDDED INTO THE square, frantic. She had to reach Talera, had to warn them—

If Talera killed Rehnir, Owen and her dad would die, along with everyone else bearing his mark.

Characters clashed throughout the square. Blood ran over the cobblestones. The stench was suffocating. Bex gagged, burying her mouth and nose in the crook of her elbow to block out the sickly sweet smell of death. She caught sight of the dragon again, now impaled by dozens of crude and evil spikes, large bolts piercing its membranous wings. Black ichor dripped from vicious wounds, and something broke in Bex's chest as she looked at it, a sob ripping from her. Her knees shook as she took in the scene, the fighting that blocked the portal.

The characters from the angry mob had wedged themselves between the portal and the soldiers who were meant to be on the other side of it right now, helping Talera, fighting off Rehnir—

Oh god, no—

Her ribs clenched like a fist around her lungs as she searched the fighting figures. At the front she saw Adaira, a long sword arcing and slicing through enemies as she tried in vain to press nearer to the portal. A few paces behind her was Guy, swinging a club.

A loud bellow was Bex's only warning before something hard collided with her hips. She went sprawling and was pinned to the ground. She spat dirt and squinted against the intense burning in her eyes, throwing her arms up. She gripped fistfuls of long coarse hair, grunting as a knee landed a blow between her legs. Tears streamed from her eyes, both from the dirt and the pain. She yanked on the hair, earning a slew of slander in a Scottish-sounding accent. As she blinked furiously, her assailant came into focus.

The bearded mountain dwarf had dark war paint on her face, giving her a menacing and dangerous look. Her fur shoulder belt was matted and muddy. An elbow came rushing toward Bex's face, but it only landed a glancing blow as Bex tucked her chin to her shoulder. She gritted her teeth, muscles groaning in protest as she fought to shift the dwarf's weight. She dug her heels into the ground, scrambling for purchase. She clawed up the beard, searching for the eyes, the mouth, anything. Another blow landed sharply across her cheek, and her whole face throbbed. A sob tore from her lips, but she dug her nails into the dwarf's skin.

Then the oppressive weight lifted off her torso, and she sucked in air. Coughing and cradling her stomach, Bex scrambled to her feet. An eight-foot-tall vampire wearing a barista's apron had his fangs in the mountain dwarf's neck, and she recognized one of Owen's come-to-life characters. The vampire met her eyes urgently over his thrashing victim. Mouth opening in horror, Bex bolted.

She sprinted up the Library steps and through the large doors. The sight of Owen and her dad on their pallets sent a tremor through her body. Their skin was waxy, sweat shone on their faces, and the hideous black marks were writhing through their veins. That meant Rehnir was close on the other side, either killing her friends or about to be killed himself, which meant…

Bex's breathing was ragged as she pressed her hands against her stomach.

"I can't—I don't—please—" she pleaded to the crypt-like silence, to the stories never finished or given a chance.

They were all going to die. She couldn't save them. They were all going die in this godforsaken place.

Tears stung her eyes, splashing down her face. She was gasping for breath, on her knees, though she didn't remember falling. Papers crinkled beneath her.

I can't do anything...I can't save them...I can't save myself...we're all gonna die here, useless and powerless and—

"I'm sorry," she sobbed, rocking back and forth, brushing back Owen's hair. "I'm so sorry."

She ran her fingers over her dad's face, pain crushing her chest. Neither of them reacted to her touch. Bex braced her hands on the floor, trying to push down her rising panic, clutching the scattered pages, her knuckles white.

There won't even be a body for Mom to bury.

She was going to die here in this world of forgotten characters, people deemed unworthy and pointless—just like she was. Powerless. She'd given away her power at every turn in life. Let her mother strip her of it, let her insecurities rob her of it, let her circumstances trample it. And now everyone she loved and cared about would die because she was powerless to do anything about it. Her dad, Owen, Talera, Guy…

People always think they're the good guys in their stories.

That was what Guy had said. But Bex had never

thought she was the hero of her own story.

Our choices and actions are what determine who we become.

Bex's brows pinched, and she stared at the pages clutched in her hands.

That's how our demons win. When we let our fear and doubt keep us from doing what matters.

Her heart beat faster, her pulse slamming against her skin. She threw one more glance at Owen and her dad before she snatched up a pen from the ground. Smoothing out the paper in her hand, Bex furiously began to write.

ᛞᛁᚨᚦ

The Library shook as Bex jumped to her feet. A roar made the bookshelves shudder, the vibration rolling through her bones as she ran for the exit. She burst through the doors, spilling out onto the steps, and looked up just as a huge winged creature flew overhead, darkening the sky. The air crackled with the energy radiating off the golden scales of the massive dragon. Another ear-piercing cry ripped from its lungs as it drove for the portal and the battle in front of it.

A pillar of fire erupted from the dragon's mouth, shooting down onto the soldiers barricading the portal. The air suddenly smelled like burning rubber and scorched hair, and Bex had to breathe through her mouth as she pressed through the crowd. The dragon swooped, soaring around again to lay siege to the now-fleeing enemy. A sword flashed, reflecting the flames and catching Bex's eye. She reached down, grasping the hilt and pulling it free of the body it was lodged in, ignoring the chill that slithered over her skin as she did.

She had no clue how to use it, but the weight of it was reassuring in her hands as she clambered over charred bodies, nearing the portal.

Guy staggered into her line of sight. He was winded and sweat was pouring from his skin, but his eyes were sharp. Adaira danced behind him with her sword, a bringer of death.

"Guy!" Bex's throat hurt. "Guy, my dad wrote Branson. He wants us all to die, and I have to warn Talera—we can't kill Rehnir!"

"That filthy piece of—" Guy swiped his club, fending off a few angry nuns.

Someone bellowed off to her right, and Bex whipped around, struggling to lift the sword as a man rushed at her, his weapon held high—

Hot blood spewed in her face as the tip of Adaira's

sword emerged from between the man's ribs. Bex staggered back as Adaira yanked the weapon free. The body hit the ground with a fleshy smack. Adaira spun away on her knees, thrusting her sword up into another man.

"Go!" Adaira shouted, drawing the sword upward, innards spilling over her hands.

Bile burned Bex's throat as she closed the distance to the portal in several quick strides and sprinted headlong through it.

For a split second, the world fell away and all that was left was the plunging cold sensation and nothingness—and then Bex was through the portal, hurtling onto the Golden Gate Bridge.

CHAPTER FORTY-SEVEN

ANOTHER WAY

ANOTHER BLAST OF MAGIC hurtled toward Talera, the impact making her shield tremble. Talera ground her teeth and took another step, her bow held before her, Tal and Lera flanking her on either side. Her shield could do nothing to block Rehnir's magic, which gripped her mind. The same invisible claws she'd felt before clutched at her. His face was all sharp angles, gaunt and hollow, surrounded by dark limp hair, his eyes completely black.

They had to reach him.

His horde of villains had slaughtered most of their forces. One after another, characters sacrificed their lives to give Talera an opportunity to get close enough to land a killing blow.

The others weren't coming. They were on their own.

Talera shot another arrow, her final quiver running dangerously low. The arrow glanced off his shield again.

Her heart splintered.

"We can't get through!" Tal called over the din.

No one was coming.

Rehnir was only twenty paces away now. Lera moved away from her side, stalking toward him, twin daggers held at the ready. The wind whipped her hair back like a tattered flag.

Terror seized Talera. "Too close—Lera, you're too close!"

Black poison began to spread across Lera's skin, but she didn't falter.

Rehnir greedily locked eyes with her. Talera's hands shook as she drew an arrow, but it glanced uselessly off the Rehnir's shield. Tal was calling out, but Lera walked closer still. Only five paces away now.

Lera hurled the daggers, penetrating the shield.

Rehnir let out a howl as one of the daggers sank deep into his shoulder. It was not a fatal blow, but Lera had hit him.

Gravel crunched beneath Talera as she moved, smoothly drawing another arrow, aiming for the spot the dagger had pierced. She pushed her Faelyn into the arrow, her whole focus on that weak spot—

The arrow tore through the shield, but Rehnir dodged,

the arrow narrowly missing him. Enraged, he clenched his fists, screaming–

And then Lera slumped to the ground.

A cry tore from Tal as they felt Lera's Faelyn being ripped from them.

No.

Talera gazed in horror at Lera's lifeless body.

"NO!" The word tore out of her as a wailing, keening scream filled her mind.

Rehnir's shield pulsed with power, the weakness now gone. He focused his cold black eyes on her. Talera's insides turned to ice, and her blood screamed in protest at the confines of her body. Agony wracked her bones.

Darkness overtook her mind. All she could see were broken and bloody faces. Lera. Her mother. Bex. Owen. Tal. Guy. Adaira. Their limbs torn apart, bodies broken, motionless. Blood soaked her clothes—her own and that of those she'd failed to protect.

You are worthless.

The pain threatened to incapacitate her.

The sounds around her distorted. She felt like she was underwater. She couldn't breathe.

Then the battle on the bridge slammed down around her again with an eruption of noise. Everything was moving at a frightening speed.

Talera staggered.

Rehnir was bellowing in pain; one of Tal's daggers had sunk deep into his thigh. His focus was broken. They had to attack him now, before his power overtook them again, before that empty terror engulfed her mind once more—

"We have to do it now!" Talera screamed, reaching out her power to connect to Tal, trying to ignore the hollow ache where Lera's source had been.

"Talera!" Someone shouted for her in the distance, but she didn't break her focus.

Her Faelyn crashed through her and her power surged, combining with Tal's. She sent the force out, creating a large shield, holding it steady, readying her bow—

"TALERA! NO!" The terror lacing the voice made her snap her head around.

Bex was making a mad dash toward them, awkwardly holding a sword, the fire in her eyes burning fiercely. "Don't kill him!"

"WHAT?!" Rage roiled off of Talera, and the shield shuddered.

"If you kill him, everyone with the mark dies with him!"

All the blood drained from Talera's face. "He's going

to kill us all—"

"You have to find another way—"

"THERE IS NO OTHER WAY!"

Before Bex could reply, a wave of power slammed into the shield. Tal flinched, crying out as she was thrown back, blood blooming from her shoulder, her wound tinged with black. Hate and pleasure twisted Rehnir's features as he advanced. The Faelyn left Talera's body in a whoosh as Tal faltered, their connection broken. Pressure built in her as she struggled to keep steady. A twisted, sinister touch raked over her mind again. Slick blood poured from her nose and into her mouth.

They were all going to die.

The Faelyn was bleeding from her, slipping quickly from her grasp as Talera frantically tried to regain control. Bex cried out in pain, clutching her gut as she keeled over.

Talera couldn't protect them.

Worthless.

Worthless.

The pain threatened to choke her. Her skull was going to split in two. Talera grunted, trying to keep her balance. The shock of the pain sucked her breath from her lungs, but she didn't release her hold on the Faelyn.

But her power was draining quickly, and when it was

gone, Rehnir would slaughter everyone. The wind picked up on the bridge as several large flying aircrafts came near—more people for Rehnir to kill. Everyone here was going to die, and she could do nothing to stop it—

Bex moaned as she dragged herself toward Talera, her words clipped with pain as she yelled over the din of the battle. "You—have—it—in you!"

Rehnir took another step, his power overwhelming, and Talera's knees gave out. His power was heavy, like a thick blot of ink spreading across a page, covering the words in its path. Terror and revulsion rose in her, and she knew this churning darkness would consume them both.

What am I doing?

Her body felt hollowed out, and her mouth was dry. "I can't do this." Her lips were cracked, and blood oozed down her chin. "It's too much. I can't…" Her throat ached.

Bile rose in her throat, but hands pressed against her from behind, steadying her.

Another hand grabbed hold of her. "Talera, dammit, don't you dare give in!"

Her Faelyn was still there. It was a small flame compared to the raging fire before her. But it was there.

What you must discover, dear one—her mother's face swam before her—*is that you already have all the magic you need inside of you.*

Heat burned behind her eyes, and salty tears mingled with the taste of blood in her mouth.

She was dying. She must have been dying, because the hallucination of her mother was so real she could feel her. If she could just reach out and touch her one last time—

I'm sorry, Mother, I've failed. I can't heal this wound. I can't fight this evil.

Her vision darkened. The smell of burning flesh and the sounds of screams were fading. Talera fumbled her hand out, searching for Bex. She should tell her…tell her she didn't hate her…tell her…

Talera's mind snagged on the last ember of her Faelyn, and she took a sharp breath in, savoring it.

But the magic wasn't her own.

Talera shook her head, trying to understand, watching as Rehnir came closer still.

The essence wasn't her own Faelyn. Her eyes went wide as she realized—

Bex.

Talera threw all her mental energy at the spark of power between them.

A trickle of strength returned to her body. Tal stirred next to her.

It wasn't the same as when she'd connected to Tal or Lera. The bridge between them was more subtle, like trying to see something out of the corner of her eye.

A thunderous noise crashed around them, sending soldiers on both sides tumbling and causing Rehnir to falter. With effort, Talera looked over her shoulder.

A golden dragon tore through the portal, and riding atop it, bellowing a battle cry, her face and sword painted with blood, was Adaira. The dragon breathed fire, flames licking down the bridge, burning their enemies. A battalion of characters spilled through the portal and into the fray. Guy led the charge, eyes wild as he brandished a club.

Adaira leapt down from the dragon's neck, hurtling toward a vampire. She sliced him open navel to neck before knocking his head clean off his body, sending a geyser of blood into the air. From across the bridge, she locked eyes with Talera. Flames reflected off the vial of Aldar around her neck.

We must combat the dark with the light.

The words hit Talera like lightning.

The answer snapped into place in her mind.

She didn't have to kill Rehnir. She didn't have to destroy his power.

Talera reached out her mind, pulling in Bex's essence.

Her mind expanded, light radiating from her limbs, and she breathed into the source, siphoning Tal now.

Her mother was still standing there in front of her, impossibly, and Talera let the warmth of her mother's essence flow into her.

And then she felt another connection—Adaira. Then Guy.

She didn't dare look behind her, didn't question what she was doing. The magic swelled in her, more and more rushing into her from the characters fighting alongside them now. Quin. Sekzelt. Huxby.

The power swirling in her pressed outward, extending past her body, and she channeled the Faelyn pouring through her straight at Rehnir.

Darkness met light, the two locking together. Talera pictured how Aldar seeped into wounds, her mind straining to do the same.

The darkness resisted, pushed back.

Talera left her body, her consciousness spread across time and space.

She saw a small cabin covered in blood, and the smell of a body decaying clawed at her nose.

Her hold on the Faelyn weakened, the darkness heavy.

Then she saw him.

Rehnir was no more than a boy, chained to the wall, his ankle bloody and the smell of infected flesh punctuating the air. His gaunt face was listless, empty.

Something abhorrent clawed at her, demanding that she to turn and look, the inky talons sinking deep into her mind—

Talera's soul was breaking, being ripped from her through the connection to Rehnir, a black hole pulling everything into extinction.

Terror tore at her throat. The light dimmed around her.

She was going to shatter into oblivion. The roiling mass of darkness was too much, and she couldn't hold on much longer.

CHAPTER FORTY-EIGHT

FISSURE

REHNIR TRIED TO WRENCH free as the Fear rioted inside his body, rearing back from the connection with the elven woman. The mental tether burned, lightning dancing across it.

A guttural snarl erupted from his throat.

Nothing was more powerful than Fear. He and only he could wield its power.

The nefarious monster roared inside him, choking him. Darkness seeped from his soul, dampening the light that shot down the mental bridge between them.

Anguish whipped him; he was falling into the dark emptiness of his mind, falling, his control over the Fear ripping away—

Ma was dying.

She was dying all over again, and he stood there, unable to move, unable to stop it.

Worthless.

Powerless.

His father's body was deteriorating in front of him, his eyes bulging, his limbs bloated and distended.

Horror shredded his soul.

Monster.

"NO." The voice that snarled the word wasn't his own, but he felt it pass his lips.

His body strained as the Fear held its ground against the attack.

A fissure appeared in the wall of Fear, and something whispered against his mind.

CHAPTER FORTY-NINE

LIGHT

THE DARK MAGIC RESISTED, pushing back. Oblivion threatened to swallow Talera whole.

She grunted as every muscle screamed in exertion, squeezed her eyes shut as she willed herself not to fall into the impenetrable darkness of the Fear raging through Rehnir.

She wouldn't yield.

She would not.

The struggle lasted an eternity.

And then, like a dam breaking, Rehnir's power cracked, and her Faelyn crashed into him, overtaking and filling every inch.

The darkness fled, and light erupted from her body, from her soul, from her essence, a piece of her lost forever as an offering to the magic.

All the warmth leached from Talera's body as she hemorrhaged Faelyn, and she retched violently. Emptiness cleaved through her, tunneling her vision, and her body hollowed out. The last thing she saw before unconsciousness claimed her was Rehnir crumpling to the ground.

CHAPTER FIFTY

VOID

REHNIR WAS A VOID.

The gravel beneath him bit into his skin, but he couldn't move.

The desire to feed—that constant, soul-sucking, life-crushing desire to have Fear in his veins—was gone.

He was hollowed out, every nerve raw.

He opened his eyes. The battle was still raging around him, heroes and villains clashing together.

No more than a few dozen paces away, the elven warrior lay in a heap on the ground next to several other figures. Another elf who looked identical to her was dead before him.

Wreckage surrounded him. With effort, he raised himself up on his elbows. Bile rose in his throat, and he heaved violently. His body was wracked with tremors, but his mind, though sluggish, was finally clear. He could no longer smell Fear.

Realization crashed down on him, and an anguished moan tore out of him.

Monster.

He pressed a hand to his mouth, fingers digging into his cheek and jaw, nails drawing blood. He heaved again, but nothing came up.

Bodies. The bridge was littered with bodies, and smoke and ash covered the sky. He looked behind him. Flames licked several buildings, thick columns of smoke rising into the air. The earth was cracked, and he could see them all—the bodies of the victims. His victims.

The pain robbed him of his breath, a choked scream pouring from his throat as he clawed at his chest. He clutched at his clothes, cutting his knees as he crawled toward that cursed portal, that tear he had ripped open between the worlds.

He didn't know where to look, for nowhere was free of the carnage he'd caused, the slaughter and the ruins, the rubble, the pain, the fear—*the fear.*

It was no longer there. His power had been stripped from him, ripped out. In its place was a buzzing sensation, swirling thin ribbons of magic that didn't roar but purred softly.

Without the urge to feed running rampant in his veins, the shame and horror crushed him.

I'm a monster.

An elf appeared and kicked him to the ground, pressing her boot into his chest, holding the edge of a sword to his neck. Blood splattered her rich brown cheeks. He gripped her boot with his bleeding hands.

He opened his mouth to speak, but nothing came out.

CHAPTER FIFTY-ONE

OUT OF TIME

A RINGING FILLED BEX'S EARS, her body bruised and battered as she pushed herself up. Blood matted her hair, and she tasted its metallic tang in her mouth.

Helicopters swarmed above, cutting through the sky along with the golden dragon.

Rehnir…

He was still alive, screaming and wailing as he tried to tear off his skin. Bex stumbled to her feet, nausea rolling through her, her legs unsteady. An oppressive headache split her skull, and she pressed her hands to her ears, trying to muffle the sirens and the screams, and the clash of weapons.

Talera was now slumped on the ground, but the image of her still burned in Bex's mind: kneeling with blood streaming freely from her nose, soot and dirt covering her face and coating her outstretched hands. The blinding light of Faelyn had rolled off her in undulating waves as she'd let out a roar so primal Bex knew it would haunt her forever. The power behind it had been unyielding.

"Please…"

The word coming from Rehnir snapped her out of her daze.

Adaira stood over him, her sword at his throat, and a strangled cry came from Bex even as hate boiled in her blood.

"Wait—" She had to be sure, had to know if whatever Talera had done had gotten rid of the mark before—

"You must listen to me—time is running out." Rehnir's eyes were wide with desperation as he pawed at Adaira's boots. "The portal—"

A screeching, grating noise filled the air and Bex spun toward the portal, heart in her throat. The magical doorway was flickering unstably.

"No, no, no." The air left Bex's lungs.

"Please, I can fix it—I can hold it open long enough for you to get through safely." Rehnir was writhing on the ground. "When the portal closes, anyone on the wrong side will die."

Adaira swore as Guy knelt next to Talera, shaking her roughly.

Bex didn't pause to listen to another word. She was

running with no thought in her mind except getting to her dad and Owen *now*.

The characters near enough to hear Rehnir had started to scatter in panic, rushing toward the portal, while the ones farther away continued to fight one another. The throng jostled Bex, and she pushed her way through the crowd, shoving down the terror that was building in her chest, clawing at her throat.

She reached the portal, not slowing as she crossed from one world to the next. She raced through the burned rubble that covered the square, evidence of the battle on this side assaulting her senses. She fought down revulsion at the sight of the mangled bodies and the putrid smell, at the sound her feet made as she stepped on unidentifiable debris. Wails of agony raised goose bumps on her arms, and the sight of the gore brought a vile taste to her mouth.

But there were no marks on anyone.

She had just reached the bottom of the Library stairs when the large double doors were thrown open.

Owen emerged, tight-lipped and pale.

And standing with an arm wrapped around his shoulder, leaning heavily on him but alert and walking—

"Dad."

A sob escaped Bex's lips, and she ran up the stairs. Her

hands shook as she lifted her dad's shirt. Her whole body sagged as she took in his healed torso and heard Owen confirm that the marks from Rehnir's poisonous magic were gone.

They'd done it.

She clutched her dad, ducking under his other arm to help Owen support his weight. "We have to get out of here now."

With effort, the three of them made their way down the stairs. Grant's breathing was labored and shallow, and Bex could see the panic and confusion on his face, but he said nothing, concentrating on staying upright.

"What happened?" Owen asked, and Bex nearly wept at the sound of his voice.

"Branson was written by my dad." Bex's brain spun. Her dad swiveled his head toward her, blinking slowly as he tried to piece together her words. "He never wanted to help. He wanted Rehnir to kill us all."

Owen swore as they maneuvered Grant around a fresh corpse. He was so heavy, even though he was supporting some of his own weight.

"And the marks?" Owen said.

Tears pricked Bex's eyes. She was shaking with relief, fear, and exhaustion.

They were nearly there. She could see the portal fading now that Talera had somehow severed Rehnir's connection to it.

"I don't know what Talera did, exactly, but we have to hurry. The portal is about to close," she rasped. "Faster!"

CHAPTER FIFTY-TWO

Show Them

A HARROWING SCREAM YANKED TALERA back to consciousness.

Someone was shaking her.

The world tilted as she opened her eyes. With enormous effort, Talera pushed herself off the ground, a moan escaping her lips. Every inch of her was thrashed, her exhaustion bone-deep.

Lera's broken and lifeless body was heaped on the ground next to Adaira, who had the tip of her sword pressed to Rehnir's throat.

Rehnir's gaunt face was devoid of the rage and ferocity she'd witnessed in him moments before. The dark circles under his eyes accentuated the devastation in them.

Talera pulled herself upright with help from Guy, trepidation shooting through her as she watched Rehnir raise his hands. She reached for her power, though she knew it was utterly spent.

But then Talera recognized the way he was positioning his hand. It wasn't the exact same motion Bex had shown them in her living room, nor was it one of the myriad of complex gestures she'd watched Huxby and Sekzelt practice, but it conveyed the same intent.

Rehnir locked eyes with her, his irises normal now. Talera repressed a shudder at the memory of the sinister power that had pooled beneath his skin, the monstrous command it had held.

His voice was broken and almost impossible to hear over the sirens wailing in the distance. "I can hold it open long enough for you get through safely."

A murmur of his power reached her. Her mind opened instinctually to feel it, and she blinked rapidly. There was no whisper of the malevolence that had been there before; rather, it was a twin to her Faelyn.

She shifted on her feet, resisting the urge to look over her shoulder at the portal, which was emitting a concerning whirring sound.

Rehnir gaze drifting past her, his focus on the shapes his hands were slowly tracing in the air. As if in response, the whirring sound diminished. "You can't." The answer was honest, his voice resigned, his body still shaking with tremors. "I gave in to the Fear. It overcame me, and I cannot…I cannot undo…" His voice caught. "I cannot reverse the destruction I've caused."

Talera's gaze swept from the bridge, which was still pandemonium, to the portal surrounded by debris, smoke, and death.

"Talera," Guy said, an edge to his tone as he gestured to himself and the remaining characters. She looked at them, and for a moment it felt like she was looking through a windowpane after a rainstorm. Her heart faltered as she realized they were all taking on an ethereal glow. "We're out of time."

A collective fading washed over the characters on the bridge, the large wings of the dragon turning translucent and blurred. Those still locked in combat—admittedly few, as most had retreated through the portal or died—stumbled.

Pain etched Rehnir's face. "Go, now."

Adaira placed her fingers between her lips, letting out a piercing whistle signaling the remaining warriors to fall back. Guy grabbed Talera's arm, pulling her along, limping slightly. Huxby grasped Sekzelt's robe, helping to haul the sorcerer toward the portal. Tal gently picked up Lera's body, tears streaming down her face as she rushed for the portal.

There was a shimmering ripple, and Bex and Owen

stepped through the portal, holding Grant between them, breathing heavily.

Talera and Bex locked eyes, so many unspoken words flashing in each.

“I thought—I thought we’d have more time.” The words tumbled out of Talera’s mouth, and she wasn’t sure if she meant before the portal closed or before they’d have to say goodbye. Her heart was suddenly thumping hard against her ribs.

She could see the fear grip Bex as she looked at Rehnir.

“It’s all right,” Talera said, unable to put into words how she knew what Rehnir would do. How she knew that the darkness was gone, driven out by the light, and that he’d give the last of his power to do penance.

Bex pressed her lips together and nodded. No doubt. No hesitance. Just trust.

Guy and Owen gripped each other’s forearms, brief and fierce, before Guy looked Bex in the eyes. “Thank you.” Her chin quivered, and she gave him a quick hug, trying to be gentle as he winced. Guy nodded toward Grant. “Take care of that one, you hear?”

And then Guy slipped through the portal. Adaira dipped her head, pressing a hand to her heart in a salute as she followed.

Talera looked over her shoulder. A few steps away, Rehnir was still making fluid motions in the air, his jaw clenched, his fingers rigid. Talera could sense the magic he was weaving as it sizzled, straining to hold the portal open a little longer.

She looked back at Bex.

Bex was blinking back tears, her voice thick as she said, "It's been an honor. I'm…I'm so sorry for—"

"No," Talera said, surprising herself as she reached out to grab Bex's hand. "No. The honor has been mine." She was light-headed, her legs threatening to buckle at any moment, but she pulled Bex into a tight embrace. "Thank you," she whispered. "Thank you."

Bex was weeping openly when she pulled back, rubbing the snot from her nose with the back of her hand. "You have to go."

Talera looked down at herself—her body was blurred and hazy. She looked back up sharply, eyes jumping back and forth between Owen and Bex.

"*Go*," they both said firmly.

Talera obeyed and stepped through the portal.

Coldness gripped her as a thrumming vibration filled her ears, and then she emerged into Raebourn. The people who had fought for this realm, for a second chance, watched her. Talera slowly turned to face the portal's iridescent glow, the world beyond it shimmering faintly. An ache throbbed in her chest as she sensed Bex through the boundary. The oppressive fog that had settled over her mind lifted as she breathed in deeply, her Faelyn easing back into her body now that she'd crossed over the threshold.

Sekzelt was beside her, muttering to himself as he read a sheet of paper covered in furious notes.

Talera glanced at them, then back to where she could faintly make out Rehnir on the other side. "We won't need those."

Sekzelt's head snapped up. "What? What do you mean? The portal—the boundary—"

Talera was too tired to explain.

Tal stood at her elbow. Making a connection between them was easy now. She breathed in deeply, the power and light swirling inside her, crashing into her senses, and a sigh of relief escaped her lips at the infusion of strength and energy. Guy stepped up behind her, resting a hand on her shoulder.

Talera closed her eyes, expanded her Faelyn outside of herself, and pulled his energy into hers, electric and warm. Beside her, Tal added Adaira's essence to the growing power before pulling Sekzelt's tentative source to theirs.

Talera let the magic expand. It cascaded all around them, undulating and swelling as more and more inhabitants of Raebourn offered up to the collective their essences, their vibrations, the magic from their very souls. It radiated from Talera like a million dazzling stars, the unapologetic glow of a full moon, and she felt another piece of her soul splinter at the sheer beauty of it, a spark of her essence offering itself to the magic as it flooded the boundary.

The image of Bex showing them the intricate hand motions from Professor Huxby's novels flashed into her mind, and a laugh escaped her lips as her Faelyn responded to her intention before she even understood it herself. A pale blue flame shot from her palm. Her fingers bent into the delicate position the magic demanded, and she felt a tether connect to Rehnir through the portal. Bound to him, she mimicked his complex pattern of movements, her fingers moving as if guided by an unseen hand. The buzzing grew to a crescendo as the portal sealed and the boundary between the two worlds was restored.

CHAPTER FIFTY-THREE

REDEMPTION

REHNIR DIDN'T LET HIMSELF think about how different the magic felt.

He didn't dwell on the fact that he'd been able to siphon power from the humans around him not by ripping it from them but merely by tuning in to their collective energy.

He didn't let himself think about what might have been if he'd only known how to do that sooner.

He didn't replay any of the horrors that haunted him or the ones he'd inflicted on others.

As the tear between the worlds closed and the boundary was infused with strength and belief and hope, as tears splashed down his cheeks…

The only thought he let fill his mind was how lovely the air was.

His breathing became labored, an unseen weight crushing him. His mind was slipping away, fading…

He took one last inhale and held it. He wanted to experience it just one last time—one final breath that was free of the smell of Fear.

CHAPTER FIFTY-FOUR

SHOCK

IF SHE HADN'T BEEN helping to hold her dad up, Bex would've collapsed onto the bridge. Her body was begging to shut down, to turn off her brain. She didn't want to deal with watching Talera disappear through the portal; seeing Rehnir deteriorate before her eyes; hearing the deep echo as the portal sealed shut or the moaning of the wounded around her on the bridge. She didn't want to look at the death she knew surrounded them.

"Bex."

Her name cut through her stupor, and she blinked at Huxby, who was speaking to her urgently, his eyes wide.

"What?"

"Do you understand?"

Bex didn't understand anything anymore.

"Bex," he said again, looking anxiously over her shoulder, "just keep telling them you're in shock and you don't know what happened."

She let out a hollow laugh at the irony.

"The authorities will have a hard time with the fantastical elements." His words took on a distorted quality. "They'll let us all go home without any trouble if we don't explain anything right now." Then Huxby moved away from them.

Her dad was so heavy, and her head was pounding; pain radiated from the cut on her scalp, and she could smell the blood in her hair.

"Bex?" Her dad's voice was thin. "What…what's going on?"

Tears burned her eyes again, and she cupped his face. "It's okay, Dad. Everything's going to be okay."

Suddenly firefighters and police officers were rushing toward them, guns at the ready. A paramedic was easing her dad away from her, putting him on a stretcher as someone else wrapped a wool blanket around her shoulders. It was coarse and itchy. Someone asked her name.

Asked where she was hurt.

What had happened here?

Did she know what day it was?

Did she have any allergies?

Was she experiencing any pain?

Bex's lips were dry and cracked, her throat coated with dust as she tried to speak. "I…I think I'm in shock…"

CHAPTER FIFTY-FIVE

FAIRY RINGS

TAL HAD WANTED TO stay a bit longer at the grave they'd dug for Lera, so it was only Guy and Adaira standing with Talera on the outskirts of the city, staring down at the perfectly shaped rings of mushrooms growing out of the ground. Adaira murmured a prayer to the old gods as Guy knelt, pure joy on his face as he inspected the fungi.

Talera folded her arms. "So? You said nothing could grow here. How is this possible?"

Guy narrowed his eyes, muttering to himself as he crawled along the ground. "Amazing…" He finally lifted his gaze to them after several minutes.

"Well?" Talera shifted on her feet.

Guy stood, brushing dirt from his knees. "It's a fairy ring."

Adaira snorted, and Talera cocked her head. "Excuse me?"

Guy waved his hands, rushing to explain. “That’s what this type of pattern is called, when mushrooms grow in these circular formations. People used to believe that elves, fairies, witches, or other magical beings dwelled inside them.”

Talera blinked. “But how in the bloody hells did they get here?”

Guy began walking around the area, eyes darting back and forth as he said, “Well, the only explanation I can think of is that when we came back through the portal, we unknowingly carried some spores along with us.” He stopped pacing and looked up at them. The memory of the night before the convention dropped into Talera’s mind. When she and Bex had finally begun to find common ground and understanding of each other as she’d picked all the mushroom caps.

Guy continued. “Mushrooms break down dead organic matter and then make the nutrients available to other plants. The entire web of life is connected through fungi; it’s literally how everything is reborn. They make up an entire network underground.”

Adaira frowned. “How could all that have happened so fast?” She looked to Talera, who was equally intrigued.

“You said yourself that this was where the three of you practiced using your Faelyn,” Guy said.

"Yes, but what does that—"

"It stands to reason that just as the Faelyn enhances your abilities, it could similarly enhance things around you when you expand it outside your body."

Talera's mind spun as she remembered the feeling that the magic was demanding an offering, a piece of herself in exchange for its power.

"You could've infused the very land with a spark of your Faelyn, speeding up the development cycle of the mycelium." Guy's laughed, and it was a hearty, victorious sound.

"How in the seven hells do you know all this?" Talera gaped at him as Adaira began to snicker.

Guy gave a flourish of his hand, and his eye twinkled as he said, "Because while my author didn't take the time to give me a proper name, he did extensive research for my backstory as a botanist. My specialty?" he said with a grin. "Mushrooms."

Adaira's snickering soon grew to a howl. Guy burst out laughing again too, and after a moment, Talera was unable to stop herself from dissolving into peals of laughter along with them.

CHAPTER FIFTY-SIX

Brave Enough

Meredith Andrews

I just had a very interesting phone call. What's this I hear about you turning down the Lynx job??

Bex

I've been doing a lot of thinking, and I've decided that I am going to stay at Between the Lines. I love it there, and even though it's not great money, it makes me happy. And it gives me time to keep pursuing writing. I spoke to the tuition office, and I have a plan in place to pay off my loans. I know this probably isn't what you want to hear. I really do appreciate you helping out with Lynx.

Meredith Andrews

> I realize it was too much to hope that you'd grown out of your irresponsible and childish attitude.
> Those payment plans charge a ridiculous amount of interest. I hope you did your due diligence before agreeing to anything.
> I won't be putting my reputation on the line for you again.

ᛞᚨᚦ

Bex eyed the display for the upcoming book club at Between the Lines, a satisfied smile on her face. Soft music played over the speakers in the café. On the other side of the shelves, Benny chatted with a customer while he rang up their purchase. He'd been released from the hospital about a week ago now—he and nearly everyone else who'd had the Fading. Every news anchor in the city was scrambling for a satisfactory explanation for the widespread cure that had rippled through the infected soon after the large earthquake, for the sudden decrease in the deadly disease that'd plagued the population for decades.

Despite the hundreds of witnesses who'd said otherwise, the news outlets had declared that there had been domestic terrorist attacks at StoryCon and on the Golden Gate Bridge. They also speculated over Arthur Huxby's mental state as a red herring to keep the general public from paying attention to what those who had been there were talking about: magic; a golden dragon; a portal to another world.

Bex's skin prickled with awareness a moment before Owen's arms wrapped around her. He pulled her back against his chest, and her heart fluttered as she tried to spin toward him. He pressed a kiss to the column of her neck, sending a thrill down her spine. "Owen," she whispered, looking around quickly.

"No one's over here, I checked." Owen chuckled, resting his chin on her shoulder.

"Hmmm," was all she could manage as heat flooded her face.

Owen retreated a step. "*Tsk, tsk, tsk*. Still such a stickler for rules." He swept an errant hair from her face. His fingers lightly brushed the scab that ran from under her hairline to her right temple. "You're going to have the coolest scar," he said, and his words skittered over her skin.

"Can't let you be the only one who gets a cool battle scar." Bex nudged him playfully.

Owen smirked, then jutted his chin at the display behind her. "Looks great. You almost ready to go?"

"Yeah, just about."

He followed her up to the checkout counter. "Hey, Benny. Good to see you, man. How are you feeling?"

"Much better. Still get a little light-headed randomly, but I'm almost back to one hundred percent," Benny said.

"Well, we're all glad to have you back." Bex smiled at him as she stepped up to the computer, closing out the tabs she'd left open earlier.

"Glad to be back." Benny's attention shifted to a customer at a nearby display who was waving him over. "I'll see you guys later," he said, and went to offer his assistance.

"Ready?" Owen held out his hand.

She intertwined her fingers with his. "Ready."

Her phone buzzed as they exited Between the Lines.

THE Arthurt Huxby (OMG!?!?!?!)

"I'm assuming you're responsible for changing his contact info." Her heart rate picked up.

Owen squeezed her shoulders as he stared at the phone, giving her a gentle shake. "Well, answer it!"

She stood rooted to the pavement. Pedestrians wove

around them.

"Bex," Owen said, startling her out of her daze.

She answered. "Hello?" Why was she so nervous? A phone call shouldn't make her so nervous, should it?

"Bex! How are you?" Huxby's voice reverberated through the phone and into her bones.

"Uh—" Bex sputtered for a moment. "Good, I guess. You?"

Owen leaned forward, trying to hear Huxby's voice on the other end.

"As well as can be expected, given the circumstances."

"Yeah, I saw those news articles…I'm really sorry about that."

"Oh, I didn't mean that—don't worry," Arthur said easily. "I've handled far worse. I just meant under the circumstances of trying to pick up the pieces of regular life after all we went through."

"Ah." Bex switched to speaker phone as she looked at Owen and mouthed, "Why is he calling?"

"The reason I'm calling," Huxby continued, "is because, as you can imagine, I've been thinking a lot about what happened over there. And my mind keeps circling back to what you did in the Library of Manuscripts."

"Well, it wasn't just me—"

"You're a talented writer, Bex. Unpolished, yes, but that's where we all start."

Owen silently fist pumped. Bex curled her fingers into the front of his shirt, her heart beating fast.

"For what it's worth," Huxby said, "I believe that every author doubts their ability at times. Every artist, everyone who creates something, experiences fear of not being good enough. But now I think you know the power that comes from taking action regardless, the importance of not letting fear win out. You have stories in you, Bex, stories that no one else could tell." He paused. "The question isn't whether or not you are good enough, it is whether you are brave enough to tell them."

Excitement and apprehension surged through her. "I—yes."

"I am glad to hear it. Because the world needs storytellers to inspire people to believe in magic and the power of words. You know as well as I do what that lack of belief can lead to."

Bex shuddered, trying to push away the memories of the battle, the contamination slowly sucking the life from her, the touch of Rehnir's power…

"When you have a complete first draft, reach out to me. I would like to introduce you to my agent."

Bex's hand went to her throat. She felt dizzy, and she had a strange urge to laugh as Owen jumped up and down.

"I—" Heat spread through her chest. "Professor—"

He barked out a laugh. "I think we've officially surpassed the need for formalities, Bex. Call me Arthur."

"Arthur. Thank you."

She could hardly comprehend anything else he said as he ended the call or what she said back. She blinked rapidly, the world around her more vibrant than it had been a moment before. People moved around them on the sidewalk as something shifted inside her. Owen let out an excited whoop, then swooped down, kissing her fiercely and pulling her into a tight embrace.

Bex burst out laughing.

"You've got to call your dad," Owen said, eyes wide with excitement.

Smiling so wide her cheeks ached, Bex did just that.

Epilogue :

Between the Lines

Between the Lines Bookshop was packed, the crowd tittering with excitement, much like her nerves were. Bex couldn't make out what song was playing over the hum of the guests. She inhaled, refraining from biting her lip. Her eyes flicked to the clock again. There were several familiar faces in the crowd, and she returned their smiles. Her dad beamed, his chest puffed out as he stood off to the side.

The bell over the door rang, and Owen finally entered. He wove around people, making apologies and ignoring a few dirty looks as he pushed his way toward Bex. Her chest warmed, and she began to relax as his gaze found hers.

"Holy hell." He finally reached her and bent to give her a quick kiss on the mouth. "Sorry I'm late. I should've known parking would be a nightmare." He scanned the crowd. "This is incredible, Bex."

She smiled. "I can't believe this is happening."

Owen snorted and lowered his voice. "Sure, you can conjure fire-breathing dragons from thin air, but *this* you find hard to believe."

Bex rolled her eyes, grinning.

"Let me ask, though." Own rubbed his chin, a playful twinkle in his eyes. "As the fiancé, do I have to stand in line to get my copy signed, or can I get mine first?" He produced a thick hardback book.

Bex smirked, her chest tightening at the word *fiancé*, absently rubbing the cold metal band on her finger. "Cut the line at your own risk. I can't promise you safety." She took the book.

"Excellent." He rubbed his hands together excitedly, giving an apologetic smile to the people nearest him. He mouthed *fiancé*, pointing at Bex.

Bex traced the words on the cover: *The Raebourn Manuscripts* by Bex Harmon. Below the title were the runes for the awakening, alpha, and theta.

She flipped the book open to the dedication page.

For Dad, for teaching me to believe in magic and

myself.

I love you to Raebourn and back.

She smiled, pausing for a moment to take it all in before grabbing her pen and bending over the signing table to hold the book. She wrote:

To Owen, for loving me and seeing me. Love, Bex

Owen grinned, reaching for the book. Before taking it, though, he dipped his head, kissing her again, a little longer this time. Her cheeks burned.

Owen pulled back and whispered, "Go get 'em, B." He slid the book from the table and pushed through the crowd toward her dad.

Flushing, Bex cleared her throat and gave Peter a small nod, then turned to look at the gathered crowd.

"All right, everyone. Thank you for your patience. We are so thrilled to have you here to celebrate Between the Lines' own Bex Harmon! In a few minutes, you'll be able to come forward and get your copy of *The Raebourn Manuscripts* signed. Please, let's keep things moving along so everyone gets a chance to meet her. You're not the only one here." He eyed a few teens who were bouncing on their toes. "But first, Bex is going to do a reading."

There was eager applause. Bex rolled her shoulders back and crossed to the front, allowing herself a true smile.

Turning to the first page, she began to read about the elven warrior Talera.

EPILOGUE :

RECTIFICATION

RAEBOURN WAS BARELY RECOGNIZABLE as the place Talera had first been dropped into. The underground network of the fairy ring outside the city had indeed been infused with her Faelyn. Green plants now spread across the ground, their leaves stretching toward the sky, saplings stood tall, and the air felt alive.

A group of children rushed by, making Talera pause in her tracks as she strode toward the Library. She smiled, waiting for them to pass before continuing her morning ritual. Each day, she went to the Library to collect the new manuscripts that arrived and then set out to find the newcomers. Though there was still always sorrow and grief when people initially arrived, the lively colors, the healthy flora and fauna, and the cheer of those living there helped to lessen the blow. Since they had sealed the boundary, the contamination plaguing Raebourn had all but disappeared.

Branson and those he'd convinced to flee to the shelter he'd made deeper in the Realm had yet to return, but Talera had decided her energy was better spent on the city they were building than on tracking them down. And though Adaira's expression still darkened anytime someone brought them up and Guy had taken to calling Branson a rather nasty nickname, she knew her friends felt the same. They'd already wasted enough of their lives being angry.

In the last several months, there'd been fewer unfinished manuscripts coming through; even though she knew it was foolish, Talera liked to think that Bex had something to do with the dwindling numbers.

A familiar twinge of sadness struck her, as it always did when her thoughts turned to Bex.

Talera hoped she was well.

Well and happy and writing.

Talera strode through the Library, approached the large desk at the heart, scooped up the newest manuscripts, and checked the main characters' names. As she turned to leave and search for them, a ruffle of paper and a soft thud stopped her.

Talera looked at the latest manuscript. It was small, only a handful of pages. Talera picked it up, flipped to the author's stamp, and swore.

"Bloody gods, Bex, did you learn nothing?" Talera scanned the inscription again.

The author's name was Bex Walker-Harmon, and the reason for stopping was…

"Rectification?"

Talera flipped back to the first page. Her heart pounded and her eyes began to burn as she read:

Gaelira was tall and lean, her red hair like a flame, cascading down to her waist. She wore the usual leather vest, trousers, and tunic of the elven people, favoring the fae style. A thin leather band circled her forehead, keeping her hair out of her face. Her green eyes were fierce and wise—

The pages tumbled from her grasp, scattering on the floor. Blood roared in her ears, her breath caught in her lungs, and then she was running out the library doors and down the steps, warmth radiating through her body.

There—she was standing at the edge of the square, taking in her new surroundings.

Talera watched her slowly pivot until their eyes locked. A sob erupted from Talera as her mother dashed toward her with open arms.

THE END

Acknowledgments:

It feels very surreal to be sitting down to type these acknowledgments. There are so many people involved in turning this book a reality, and it's been four years in the making.

I had amazing editors helping me polish this to get it to the condition it's in. Thank you to Jenny Proctor, Emily Martin, Alison Cherry, and Emeric Davis for carefully combing through my drafts. For your suggestions, expertise, and hard work. Thank you, Jeff Brown, for the cover of my dreams. Thank you to Natalie (@Elivrayn) and Sosnovska Anastasiia (@Lazy_dragon_art) for the incredible inside artwork.

Jolene Perry, you are a wizard with words and you gave me the invaluable gift of genuine excitement for this story when I needed it most. Thank you. Thank you for your contributions to me and other writers, for being our biggest cheerleader and sounding board.

Maggie Stiefvater, it was a highlight of my life to get to work with you on a different project as this one came to an end. You made me a stronger writer and elevated my craft. I was able to come back and make this final version of *The Abandoned Realm* what it is.

Mackenzi Lee, thank you for forging a path in our shared dream of becoming authors. Your encouragement, friendship, and insight have been so appreciated. Caitlin Jacobs, you were a constant source of inspiration and direction whenever I felt lost in this process. I'm forever grateful for your generous soul.

To my writing group: Scribbles & Snatches (see, it's forever here in ink.) You came into my life at the exact right time. Brooke Emery, Rachael Stoll, and Jess Coleman, you've helped me grow, listened to endless Marco Polos, read through so many versions of this story, and fangirled your hearts out and it will forever mean so much to me. Thank you for helping me see the forest through the trees when I get lost in my head. I love you.

Thank you to all my beta readers on all my various drafts for the feedback, excitement, and ideas you offered: Ben Wagner, Derek Williamson, Nicole Maddy, Tyson Maddy, Sally Goodger, Jillian Hicken, Melissa Goodger, Kelly Wilson, Annie Butterfield, Allison Steinman, Makenna Matheson, Sarah Tyler, Justin Bishop, and Brooke Bishop. I am forever grateful for the support you gave in crafting this story: the time out of your schedules, the discussions over wine, and the tedious notes taken.

Thank you to Gillian Eliza for the Ho Notes™ ; Farrah

Abernathy for the ARC tour genius; Christy Bishop for the ARC box witchcraft; Stephanie Hamel (@Stephysbindery) for this gorgeous typeset; Sharon Halpin, Brandy O'Bagy, and Nicole Maddy for helping cross the T's, dot the I's, and pack ARC boxes; Olivia Winn for helping with the ARC swag; Desiree and Erick Rangel for the awesome Between the Lines logo; Brooke Lockie, for framing the positive feedback I got from my first editor; Josh Tyler for offering to (and refraining from) punching me in the face so I could know what it felt like, and answering my very specific questions about grappling; Sean Steinman, for telling me all about mushrooms.

Kristen Reuter, thank you for all drop ins after work to entertain the kids while I edit or to help me with the pronunciation guide.

Thank you Amanda Auler for being so generous and answering all my questions on self publishing.

Ghada Jmail Bishop: you were my first reader, getting daily updates of the story as I pieced it together. Your love of this story has been a rock for me over the last four years. Merci beaucoup, ma belle-soeur. For always believing in me and all the behind-the-scenes pep talks when I'm doubting myself.

Thank you to all my friends, siblings, and family.

Gourmet Gals, my Gryffindor babes, the Dramione fanfiction community, Hot Mess Express, Meme Squad, and my D&D group. I adore you all. You've asked about, encouraged, and been supportive of this endeavor and it means so much to me. Thank you to Annika who works at Alpha Coffee for dropping everything as you took my order to pull out a pen and paper just to jot down the title of my book (that wasn't even close to done,) so you could buy it when it comes out.

To Lindsi Stevens, Jessie Peck, and my Wyld community: thank you for providing the space for me to rediscover my creativity. Thank you, Lacey Peterson. For all of it. This book is a result.

None of this would've been possible without my in-laws, Scott and Nancy Hansen. Thank you for so happily looking after my babies on Wednesdays so I could carve out writing time. Your love and support mean more than you'll ever know.

To my two little wildings: Lexy and Nolan. You both inspired me. You reminded me of what's important in life. You've both grown from newborns to toddlers as this story has grown. I love you forever.

My darling husband, Brad. I love you. You're my person, my safe place, my Aldar. Thank you for being with me as I find my way out of the darkness to the light. Thank you for all the dinners brought to my desk, coffee refills, the listening ear as we split a bottle of wine while I vent about all the trouble my characters are giving me, and the unwavering support. Thank you for instilling in me the belief that I can do this. You and our children feed my soul. I love you, unendingly.

And lastly to you, dear reader. I hope you can see yourself in this story. That a piece of you released a sigh and felt seen. You matter. Your story matters. Keep using light to combat the dark.

B

Ingram Content Group UK Ltd.
Milton Keynes UK
UKHW010811060623
422954UK00004B/401

9 798218 142063